TAINTED LOVE

LAURA CARTER

Boldwood

First published in 2016 as *Vengeful Love: Black Diamonds*. This edition published in Great Britain in 2025 by Boldwood Books Ltd.

A CIP catalogue record for this book is available from the British Library.

Paperback ISBN 978-1-80600-096-8

Large Print ISBN 978-1-80600-097-5

Hardback ISBN 978-1-80600-095-1

Trade Paperback ISBN 978-1-80656-118-6

Ebook ISBN 978-1-80600-098-2

Kindle ISBN 978-1-80600-099-9

Audio CD ISBN978-1-80600-090-6

MP3 CD ISBN 978-1-80600-091-3

Digital audio download ISBN 978-1-80600-092-0

This book is printed on certified sustainable paper. Boldwood Books is dedicated to putting sustainability at the heart of our business. For more information please visit https://www.boldwoodbooks.com/about-us/sustainability/

Boldwood Books Ltd, 23 Bowerdean Street, London, SW6 3TN

www.boldwoodbooks.com

1

GREGORY

Heavy rain blasts my face as my feet pound the path through St James's Park. It mixes with sweat and saturates the light-grey hoody pulled over my head. I run across Blue Bridge, the impressive sight of Buckingham Palace to the left, Big Ben and the London Eye to the right. But even if I could see through my wet eyelashes and the January morning darkness, I wouldn't care for the view of the buildings, just like I don't care for the dead trees or the lifeless lake beneath the bridge. I stopped caring a long time ago. For more than twenty years, I've concentrated on justifying my existence, finding a purpose, the reason I'm alive. The only building that's carried any semblance of meaning is my office block because until three and a half months ago, all I had was power and money.

Three and a half months ago, I found my reason to live. I found the reason blood runs through my veins, the reason my heart beats. Now she's gone.

Each day, I extend my running route and lengthen the time I spend in the gym when I get back to my apartment. I stay in there, beating the shit out of the punch bag, until Jackson forces me to stop. I keep running and punching until my mind is crushed by a lack of oxygen and my body is physically drained.

For those final ten minutes, before I either stop or pass out, I have nothing left to give, my mind and body are numb, but my heart pounds in my chest and it's the only way I know I'm still alive.

I used to have nightmares when I was a kid. Sometimes, I still do. Countless nights, I've come close to dying in my subconscious. That's the thing about your consciousness; it always takes over just before you fall from the cliff, get hit by a train or get beaten to death by your father. But it wakes you up. No matter how much you want that train to smash straight through you, your consciousness wakes you up like it's doing you a fucking favour. It's not. It returns you up into a living hell. Three and a half months ago, I started to believe in dreams. That dreams could exist where you don't come close to dying every night. Where you don't *want* to die. Then that dream turned to a nightmare, slowly, surely, the way it was destined to do. Five weeks ago, that's when I saw the train coming at me down the tracks. When I realised she couldn't take any more. That I'd mounted enough of my shit on her. That I'd broken her.

When Scarlett took that call and when she got on that plane, I willed my subconscious to let the train hit me. But it didn't. After thirty years of nightmares, I woke to the worst version of hell yet. And I only have myself to blame. I shouldn't have dared to dream. When she walked into my boardroom, I should've let her be.

I didn't, and this is my penance. This is what I deserve. I let myself taste goodness and now the black I see every day is a darker shade.

I don't encounter another soul as I run the loop of St James's Park then along the tree-lined path between the grass verges of Green Park and into Hyde Park. I turn right, passing the finery of The Dorchester hotel and the murmurings of morning traffic, then further into the park's centre, lapping the lake, taking the webbed path on routes to nowhere until I give in.

Then I work my way back across Westminster Bridge and along South Bank – dead because the tourists are still sleeping – back to the Shard.

Amy is already in the apartment, preparing to make breakfast. I nod in response to her smile but I keep my music drumming and move straight to the gym room off the lounge. Jackson halts his reps on the leg press and stands behind the punch bag. He holds the bag ready whilst I peel my soaked jumper from my torso and let it pool on the floor. Then I start nailing the bag, blow after blow, not missing a beat of the track playing into my ears.

'Greg, enough.'

'Hold it still,' I growl.

My fists land again, a hook with my right, an uppercut with my left, then Jackson lets go and steps away. I pummel every bit of temper and frustration into the blow as my shin impacts with the bag and sends it swinging hard left.

As my back slides down the gym wall and my legs give out in front of me, Jackson hands me a bottle of water and I finally take the buds from my ears.

'This's gotta stop,' he tells me.

My teeth clamp down on the rim of the bottle, jaw clenching, as I glare at Jackson in an attempt to deflect the speech I've received at least once in each of the last five weeks.

'What's done is done. You made the choice.' He hovers over me.

'It was the right thing to do.'

'If that's true, why do you feel like shit?'

I take another swig of water and wish it was an acceptable hour to replace it with Scotch. 'It's what she would've done. She would've done the right thing. Maybe I learned something from someone for a change.'

Jackson shakes his head and flicks a towel over his shoulder. 'So quit beating yourself up over it.'

With that, he leaves the gym. This is what he's started doing. Dropping a statement like that then pissing off, leaving me to dwell on it. What's more fucking annoying is that he's ruined those only ten minutes in my day when my body is too drained to think.

* * *

'Pop your bottom down on that stool. I've made scrambled eggs and smoked salmon.'

It's hard to be a dick with Amy, no matter how foul

my temper is. I mumble thanks and try to crack something close to a smile. Try but fail.

Christ, I need to get a grip. It's the group's Annual General Meeting today and I need to put on a show. The group is doing well; I've seen the results. Something concrete I can rely on.

I'm arrogant about business because I'm good at it. Corporations, investments, innovations, markets. I just get it. I'm always ten steps ahead so even if I get set back two paces, I'm still better than the next guy. Regardless, my board and my shareholders expect to hear from their CEO today, the other Gregory, the version of myself I rely on to mask everything else.

'These are good, Amy.'

She blushes at the compliment. I envy her. She cooks and cleans for me, looks after her children – I'd stake money on the fact she's a good mother – takes care of a husband. She doesn't want anything more than she needs and she's *happy*.

After placing my cutlery at six o'clock and scrolling the three emails that have landed on my phone in the time it took me to eat scrambled eggs and drain my coffee, I nudge my plate towards Amy and lift a foot to the rim of my breakfast stool. Laces tied, grey trousers adjusted, white shirt cuffs tweaked to lie just lower than the cuff of my blazer, I'm ready to perform.

'Hold the phone, mister. What would you like for dinner?' Amy calls.

Hold the phone. For the first time in days, I genuinely smile. It was the night of the hunt, Opening Meet of the season: another thing I got wrong. Scarlett was pissed at me for ignoring her all night, for buttering up Adriana to get to her husband, a private equity investor. Then Williams's sister, Charlotte, nearly went to bed with some arsehole and I swear I could've killed him, would have, if Scarlett hadn't put those damn beautiful eyes in front of me. She was reeling from everything that happened when I found her sitting on the four-post bed in our room. It killed me seeing her like that again, a mess because of me. But just like every time I screwed up a saying, she couldn't resist giggling when I said, 'Hold the fort.'

'You mean hold the phone,' she said. I knew it was but after the first time I got one of her English sayings wrong and she laughed like an angel, I just kept doing it. And she laughed every time, the sweetest sound. Even when she was angry, I could break her by being goofy. It became a sort of addiction. As much as it wasn't like me, that sound could melt me, so I guess she found a side to me I hadn't known myself before her.

'Whatever you like,' I tell Amy. 'Surprise me.' I really couldn't care less.

'Oh. Err, I'll go for one of your favourites in that case.'

* * *

Lawrence, as chairman of the AGM, declares the meeting quorate. Leaning over his tan leather document folder – designed for him by my mother – he wiggles those goddamn varifocals that he really ought to have given up on by now and draws a tick next to item number one on his agenda. He has a slightly larger information pack than the other twelve directors around the table, including me. Christ knows what extra stuff he has in there, it's probably packed out with blank pages, but the AGM is his big event. Batman has a cape, Spiderman shoots webbing, Lawrence has stacks of wasted trees. God help any man who stands in the way of Lawrence and his agenda – or who asks him to go paperless.

'Agenda item number one, previous year's performance and financials, one January 2025 to thirty-one December 2025. Gregory?' He lifts his specs to rest on top of his head and looks up at me. I'll never understand why people do that, like they're standing on the deck of a yacht, Monaco sun blazing down, and the varifocals are a shaded pair of Tom Fords. Lawrence is in the boardroom of GJR Enterprises in the middle of London City and it's raining outside.

Sipping coffee is a good tool. It creates a pause, short enough and legitimate enough to not appear rude but long enough to let every other man – and one woman – at the table know that this is *my* show, agenda or no agenda. Coffee cup slowly and purposefully back in its place, I sit taller in my leather chair and undo the middle button of my suit jacket.

'Morning all. It's good to be around one table. I want to begin by expressing my gratitude for what's been another strong year, in a market that's still volatile. Turnover and EBIT have increased across the group year on year. Gross profit is up in all but one company but net profit is down in two subsidiaries.'

I nod once to Williams, who sits to the right of me, looking sharp in a navy pinstripe but for that mass of intentionally messed-up dirty-blond which is going to have to go. A daddy-to-be can't look like a student. Having said that, nor should a man of thirty-two years. One glance and a nod is all it takes; Williams and I work like a well-oiled machine – most of the time. He clicks through the next slide on his laptop that's being projected onto a large screen. There's no need to close the black blinds across the floor-to-ceiling windows because London's ominous sky is providing us with all the darkness we need, but he does turn out the ghastly fluorescent lights.

A graph depicting the gross profit of all companies in GJR Holdings Limited is displayed. I dip my head once more and Williams moves to the next slide: a close-up of the two companies with falling net profit from last year.

'GJR Communication Solutions seems as good a place to start as any. As you know, this is primarily a vehicle for research and development.' I gesture to Mark Flemming, a stereotypical Scotsman with red hair and freckles. A stocky chap. Looks untidy in a suit. Much happier behind a desk in a pair of jeans and a thick check shirt developing new software, or lying on his back fixing up a new machine. 'Mark, you can fill in the detail when we work round the table but suffice to say, last year was one of generation. Profit won't be realised on our latest project before quarter four this coming year, at best.'

'Aye, all right, Gregory.'

'Moving on to Constant Sources. This is an English incorporated company with offices in England

and France. Nick Henshaw, as you all know, retired his directorship two months ago. Since then, Tim and Jean-Paul have been taking care of operations. Which of you will be picking up the presentation?'

'I will, Gregory.' Jean-Paul is still brown-nosing after the episode with Nick. He knows the only reason I kept him and Tim is because they do a good job with that company. He also knows one wrong move and he's gone.

'The floor's yours.'

Williams clicks over the slide presentation to a graph I've already seen and Jean-Paul starts talking through figures, justifying the drop in net profit with various R and D investments.

To everyone else, I'm focused on the screen but her face comes into my mind. The look in her eye when she asked me, *Why?* I told her she needed space to think, away from me, to decide if she wanted to be with me. On some level, I think I wanted that to be the case. In truth, I knew as I was typing an email to her boss, telling him Scarlett wanted to take the Dubai secondment, that her stubbornness, her pride, her insecurities about me, would make her end it. She was right when she called me a coward.

I took the easy way out because I couldn't bring myself to say it. I couldn't tell her I don't love her.

It's never been a problem before. When women have swooned and fallen in love with me in the five minutes I've kept them around, I've told them straight. The thing is, I can't fall in love. I *won't* fall in love. I've loved people. I've loved two people and that turned to shit. My mother nearly died being beaten to a pulp by my father, all because of me, because I hid. And the other...

Focus. It's the AGM. Jean-Paul. Constant Sources.

'...it's called *Black Diamonds*. It's extremely similar to our game, *Jail Run*. It's a very similar concept but *Black Diamonds* is cheaper to download. It's burst onto the scene in a big way in just a matter of weeks and it continues to grow. It would be fair to say it's going viral and it could really put a dent in our *Jail Run* profit margin.' Jean-Paul has moved onto his SWOT analysis for 2026: strengths, weaknesses, opportunities and threats on the horizon.

Nick Henshaw is still fishing around, trying to get his claws on more money for the shares he sold back to the company when I forced him to resign; there's a threat I'm still fending off.

'Who's the owner of the *Black Diamonds* software, Jean-Paul?' The question comes from Zara Vanderbilt-Delores, the only female director. Sometimes, I wish there were ten of her. She's shit hot. Really knows her stuff, gets markets and business. Her knowledge tears strips off some of the men and God is she vicious when she wants to be. She's in camp *You've Got to be a Bitch to Get Things Done*. I would've said that was true of all successful women before Scarlett. As a lawyer, Scarlett knows her stuff, she's quick and her advice is pragmatic, she's rightfully a high-flyer. But she's not arrogant or nasty. She's territorial. She'll fight for the people she loves. But she won't hurt someone until she's pushed to the edge; she won't shit on someone just to get what she wants.

Stick with it, Ryans – eye on the ball.

'That's the crazy thing,' Jean-Paul responds. 'It seems to be a young man, a boy. Nineteen. Zimbabwean.'

'Let's buy it,' I bite, taking my frustration out on Jean-Paul.

'We've explored the potential, Gregory. The boy's lawyers aren't interested.'

'How much did you offer?'

'Five hundred thousand. They wouldn't even speak to us.'

If you want a job done properly... 'Set me up a meeting. I'll close it.'

'We'll need a lawyer,' Williams says. His voice is wary. As it should be. I know what he's thinking.

'Then find one.' I glare at him, daring him to challenge me.

'What about—'

'No.'

Lawrence breaks the stand-off by announcing the next company on the agenda. I watch the slides flick over to another financial graph that I've already seen. I know all eyes are trained on me as I push out my chair and move to the window. The room gets back to business as I stare at the first drops of rain dusting the glass pane in front of me. She *thinks* she loves me. She doesn't know me. She knows the man who gets impossible tickets to the Dame Judi Dench play she's desperate to see, the man who whisks her away to a vineyard because she used to enjoy fine wines with her father, the man who flies her to the opera. *I* don't even know where that man came from.

She doesn't know *me*. Maybe I should go to Dubai and tell her. Tell her everything. Tell her who I really am. Then she'll see that I'm not a man to be loved and I'm a man who can't love. I should've told her. She wanted to know. She kept pushing and I was too... what... afraid? If I'd told her, it would've ended us. I wanted to. God, I wanted to. Just like I wished I'd left her alone after she first pitched to be my lawyer. But I couldn't.

Who am I kidding? She'll have moved on. I'm the fucking idiot still pining after a woman who I knew for a matter of weeks. Soon, I'll have been without her for as long as I was with her.

A sudden ache strikes my chest and I hold my fist against it.

'Do you have a view, Gregory?' Zara is watching me expectantly when I turn to the table.

'We've discussed this before,' I tell her, forcing myself to remember her last item on the agenda. 'Your role is to head up Corporate Social Responsibility within the remit I give you.'

'I appreciate that, Gregory, but we've followed the same charities for four years running. I think it would be a positive message if we spread our funding to some other areas of need, open up to a fair procedure, ask charities to pitch to us.'

'No. We stick with the children's hospital and domestic violence in Africa. Consider that item closed.'

Her mouth opens and for a split second, I think she considers challenging me but wisely backs down.

She thinks I'm a dick. Good. I am.

Lawrence closes the AGM and dials reception to have lunch brought through. I don't hang around for small talk.

Loosening my tie a notch, I take a seat behind my

desk. The live feeds to the Dow Jones, FTSE and other markets in which I dabble are playing on flat screens around the room. On my screen saver, Scarlett looks truly mesmerising in her black gown, the diamond choker around her neck outshone by those devastating eyes. It's a press shot. We're on the red carpet outside my mother's house. The annual gala. *That* night. I remember how awkward she felt, how she didn't want to get out of the Bentley. She was nervous that she wasn't good enough to be on my arm. What a joke! She was the most beautiful woman at the gala. Screw that, she's the most beautiful woman I've ever known, inside and out.

That fucking constant dull ache starts throbbing in my chest again.

'Greg.' Williams opens my office door and walks straight in. 'Where were you today? Because you weren't in the AGM.'

I sigh, not shifting in my chair. 'I'd already seen the papers.'

He takes a seat on the opposite side of my desk.

'I'm not in the mood, Williams.'

'Well, you're never in the mood, so now seems as good a time as any. Amanda speaks to her every day, Greg; she's a mess. She loves you. She's *in* love with you.'

She doesn't know me.

'It's over, Williams. Done. She's better off, she just doesn't know it yet. Now, we need to talk about that hair of yours.'

'Changing the subject?'

'Too right, changing it to something you *can* control. That hair has got to go before you're a dad. You look like a fucking gap-year student.'

He chortles and, despite myself, my lips turn up, too.

'Speaking of which. We had our first scan. Want to see?'

He pulls out his phone and shows me a black and white image, a picture of a picture of a large baked bean. But he's beaming at me, so proud he might burst, so I smile back. 'That's a very cute bean. I'm pleased for you.'

We talk for five minutes about the bean and how Williams is coping with Amanda moving into his place. Then he leaves and I can get back to staring at the image on my screen. Everything about her is perfect and effortless. She's a natural beauty, not like the women who bat their lids in restaurants, bars, wherever I go, or half the receptionists in this place. All those women see is my exterior and my money.

I came close to falling in love with her, too damn

close. But it could never be true. I don't fall in love. She made me want to be something I'm not. She made me want to be a decent person and, hell, I wanted to tell her the three words she was so desperate to hear. But it would've been a mistake.

I knew the night she got drunk and told me about the Dubai secondment, I knew then if she couldn't see it for herself, I had to make sure she went. We had to get the murder charge over with first. She had to see that the CPS wouldn't charge me, that we'd be free because no matter which one of us took the fatal shot, it was self-defence; my father would have killed us. She had to see that so she could move on knowing she'd done the right thing in the eyes of the law.

Then she told me she wanted to confess to sending my black past to hell. She wanted to save me, again. It tore me up inside. The thought of losing her. The thought of her locked behind bars for doing nothing other than falling in love with me and getting caught in my web of darkness.

When John Harrison called with the CPS decision, everything came crashing to me, everything I'd felt for the last twenty years. I hadn't cried since I was ten years old but holding her in my arms, knowing it was over, that she could move on and, yes, that I hadn't lost her, I sobbed. I couldn't stop the tears from fucking falling. I knew then. I knew I was going to send her away because I'd let it go too far. She's better than me.

I shouldn't have taken her to the opera. It was self-ish. I convinced myself it was for her, so she could have one night, the fairy tale. But damn it, I just couldn't let her go. And all night, I fought with myself. I had to remember the plan but, Christ, I wanted to say those three words she needed to hear. I wanted to say them so much that to not killed a part of me I didn't know was alive.

2

SCARLETT

I made the right decision to take the first flight out, checking into an airport hotel once I left the Shard. I held it together long enough to look sane at check-in. Then I got to my room and broke down. At some point, sleep took over, because when Reception called to wake me for my taxi to Heathrow early the next morning, I was still dressed.

That was five weeks ago. I've gotten better. Since the first week, I haven't cried myself to sleep every night. Now grief comes over me only in waves, though when it comes, it brings with it the same excruciating pain in my abdomen and the same crippling ache in my chest.

I've developed a routine in Dubai. Sunday through

Thursday, I'm in the hotel gym around five in the morning. I mull over the international newspapers in the main restaurant and take coffee with breakfast. Then I head to Mr Ghurair's office around eight. With two deals running concurrently, I have more than enough to keep me busy all day.

I've gotten used to the dry heat I'd found stifling when I took my first steps on Middle Eastern ground. Despite the winter, the temperature is in the mid-twenties Celsius and a dramatic hike from the below-freezing temperatures in England.

After work, I call Sandy or Amanda – or both – and head to dinner. I try to rotate between the four restaurants in the hotel so I don't get bored of eating the same thing, although half the time, I only push the food around my plate. In fact, the chef in Hoi An, the Vietnamese restaurant, has started giving me smaller portions so I don't insult him by leaving his food. After dinner, every night except Thursday and Friday when it's rowdy, I head to the outdoor pool bar. I order a drink and sip it, sitting on a white leather sofa staring out at the lights of the Burj Khalifa. The menacing spike of the building dominates the opulent skyline. Like everything in Dubai, it's big, it sparkles and it screams *money.*

On Thursdays and Fridays, I take my drink indoors, in Broadway, a 1940's New York-themed restaurant/bar. Quirky, dark wooden rails separate sections of the bar and there's a stage at one end of the room where theatre shows take place. It's different to the marble floors and elegance of the other public areas of the hotel. Tonight is Thursday, so I've enjoyed two small plates in the Michelin-equivalent Indian restaurant and now I'm making my way into Broadway.

I spot Paddy behind the bar and give him a half-smile, then hitch up the hem of my tight-fitting dress and slide onto a stool in the corner of the bar, placing the toes of my strappy heels on the rim. The lights are dimmed for a production of *Chicago* that's about to start.

Paddy finishes making a Manhattan by topping the drink with a Maraschino cherry, then slides it towards a waiter to serve.

'Hey, lady,' he says with his cute Dublin accent as he makes a beeline for me, tossing a white cloth over his shoulder. With the back of his hand, he knocks a rogue brown hair back into his messy mass of chin-length waves.

He rotates shifts between the hotel's pool bar and Broadway. He doesn't like working in the pool bar when the DJs are pumping out tunes on Thursdays and Fridays, so he moves to Broadway those days. He's not, incidentally, why I rotate but I can't deny it's nice to have someone to talk to.

'Hi Paddy, how are you?'

'Not bad. Tired. I've already worked breakfast and lunch today. How're you doing?'

'Fine.'

He shakes his head on a short laugh. 'The lady is always *fine*.'

'I'm not in the mood for counselling, Paddy.'

'You never are, sweetheart, but one day, you'll tell me who broke your heart.'

I lean a forearm on the bar and turn my stool, subtly angling away from him. 'What makes you think I have a broken heart?'

'Oh, let me see. You sit alone every night looking miserable, nursing one cocktail for an hour, sometimes two cocktails on a weekend, heaven forbid. You never want to talk about it. You're always *fine* and those eyes of yours drift off to another place. Ex-pats come to Dubai for two reasons. One: tax relief. And you're not getting that whilst you're on secondment. Two: to cure a broken heart.'

'Mmhmm, well I drink alone because you're the only person I really know in Dubai. I am *fine* and I drift off because your conversation is monotonous.'

'Oh, she's feisty tonight. I like it,' he says with a cheeky wink, making me laugh. 'Dry or dirty?'

'What did I have last night?'

'Dirty last night, dry the night before that, dirty the night before that, dry the night be—'

'Okay, I get the point. Dry then, please.'

'Sure thing.' He moves down the bar, pulling a bottle of Tanqueray and a bottle of vermouth from the mirrored wall. 'My finest,' he says when he places the cocktail on a black napkin in front of me. He plants his hands on the bar, waiting for me to taste test.

'Fine,' I say with a smirk as the first sip travels straight to my head.

'You're a tough woman.'

'Thanks. So, what about you? Tax or heartbreak?' He flashes me a look that says he's not giving me an answer, so I change course. 'What's your real name?'

'Why do you keep asking me that?'

'Because I don't believe you're really called Paddy. Too stereotypical.'

He laughs and moves off to serve.

I sip my dry martini as the curtain rises on the opening scene of *Chicago*.

This is the most dangerous time of my day. It's the time, without fail, that my mind finds Gregory and the pain comes back: my stomach, my chest, my head. It's when I think about how lost I am, how nothing makes sense without him.

I miss everything about him. *All* his personalities and quirks. The way he would pull the cuffs of his shirt slightly lower than the edge of his suit jacket. That stance. His hips flexed slightly forward so his strong calves pull the material of his trousers taut. His shoulders back, tall and broad. That half-smile. God, he could liquefy me with that half-smile. The way his hair feels like silk through my fingers when we're making love.

I stroke my lips where I wish I could feel his soft skin again. The familiar lump is building in my throat. I swallow it away with a sip of dry martini. He could drive me wild with just a single touch. And his scent. Rich, fresh. I close my eyes, remembering.

The stage darkens and a spotlight shines on the actress playing Roxie as the band strikes up 'Cell Block Tango'. Her soft, blonde bob bounces and her innocence disappears as she sings, 'He had it coming.' There's a sinister edge to her stage voice. *He only had himself to blame.* She's captivating. It's not enough to distract me from my thoughts.

What I crave more than anything is the feeling of completeness. I never realised I needed something else in my life. I don't think I did, anyway. Not until I met Gregory and, maybe for the first time, felt awake, alive, truly alive. Being near him was an adrenalin rush. Blood pumped in my veins, the way it does now. Just thinking about him raises my heart rate and sparks something low in my abdomen.

I knew he was flawed. I just didn't think he was... Well, I guess I just didn't think. I lost all reason with him. I became a different version of me, a Scarlett Heath who operated in the grey. I struggled to move away from right and wrong, the black and white I'd always known and clung to. I've had five weeks to realise that I prefer that version of myself. I prefer the grey. I prefer who I am when I'm with him.

Confident. Womanly. *Sexy.*

Our relationship was a mess, doomed from the beginning. We didn't do anything in the conventional way. The takeover. My dad. Murder.

'Scarlett.'

I jump as Paddy's voice brings me back to real time. 'Yes?'

'Here.' He slides a dry martini next to the one I'm currently drinking. 'From table fourteen.'

'Thanks but I don't accept drinks from strangers.'

'That's what I told her.'

'Her? That's new.'

'She told me to tell you it's from Trina.'

I try to locate the name, then the face in my mind. 'Trina. Katrina Martin?'

Paddy shrugs.

'It's nice to see you again, Scarlett Heath.'

She's standing over my left shoulder. Her ill-fitting black suit and scuffed leather flats have been replaced with linen trousers and royal-blue deck shoes. The belt that would normally host her police badge has been switched with a dark-brown buckled belt that's too big and chunky for the delicate fabric of her trousers.

If I were to judge her on appearance alone, I'd say she's a woman who wants to exude a sense of authority, severeness, unkindness and a *fuck you* attitude. Wait, that's my *actual*, informed view.

'I wish I could say the same,' I mumble. 'I suspect it isn't coincidence that you happen to be at the Crystal Grand in Dubai.'

'I knew you were smart.' She smirks and pulls a neighbouring stool close to mine, uninvited, definitely not welcome, but sitting nonetheless. 'That's why I knew you'd leave him eventually.'

I take a sip of my cocktail, a delay tactic whilst I muster some composure. 'What do you want, Trina?'

'I wanted to let you in on a secret.' She leans towards me, forearm resting on the bar, fingers wrapped around a half-pint of beer.

'Yeah, well, I've had my fill of secrets. Thanks anyway.'

She leans back and pushes a hand into the pocket of her trousers. 'There I was thinking Scarlett Heath is a good girl. That she was lured into something she didn't understand. I guess I was mistaken. You were in on it all along.'

I drain my glass and step down from my stool. I make to walk past her but she clamps a sweaty palm on my wrist. 'If I'm right, your career as a lawyer will be over.'

Does she know?

Snatching my wrist back, I growl through my teeth. 'If you've got something to accuse me of, do it. Give me your best accusation.'

She smiles. A sadistic grin. Then takes a swig from her beer. 'Sit.'

'I'll stand.'

She wipes her lips with the back of her hand and covers a belch. 'I think your billionaire boyfriend paid off DI Barnes. And I think one or both of them paid off the CPS.'

I shake my head, trying to make sense of her words. 'What are you talking about?'

That sardonic grin is back and I want to slap her face. 'I was right. You didn't know.'

My heart is pounding in my chest as my brain makes sense of her statement. *Gregory paid off DI Barnes?* I don't want to believe it. I *don't* believe it. I snatch up the drink Trina bought for me and take a gulp, then lean into her ear. 'Katrina Martin, you're full of shit.' I place my glass to the bar with a thud. 'Enjoy the rest of your stay in Dubai.'

'Scarlett.'

I'm walking away but, for some unbeknown reason, I turn to face her.

'I think you know I'm not talking shit and I think your breathing has quickened and the skin around your neck flushed pink because this is the first you've heard of it. Bribes, Scarlett. Bribes of the most corrupt sort. Bribes with government officials. Bribes that would ruin your career and put you all behind bars for a *very* long time. Unless, of course, you wanted to make a statement. I could get you leniency.'

'Fuck you.' The words grate through my teeth and locked jaw.

She throws her head back on a laugh. 'Yep, fuck me. But you just think about it. The CPS didn't bat so much as an eyelid over a murder and, moreover, a murder with a gun? Two ballistics reports are ordered for no good justification and what d'ya know, they conflict.' It's her turn to drain her drink. 'You're a smart girl.'

With that, she leaves and I stagger back towards my stool where I down the last of my second cocktail in one.

I want to think she's a liar but there were things I brushed over, things I didn't put my mind to. Like DI Barnes's connection to Jackson. The way he was nice to me when he turned off the tape during my questioning. How pissed off he got when Trina started badgering me, digging deeper for answers. He shouted at her. He ordered her out of the room.

Sunday night, after Gregory and I had returned from that godawful foxhunt, DI Barnes turned up unannounced at the Shard to tell Gregory and Jackson about the ballistics report. *How? Why?* I'd thought he was just forewarning Jackson, being a good friend. But I remember now that he was angry. He said they'd been lying to him, Jackson and Gregory, that they'd hidden things from him.

I raise a hand until I have Paddy's attention, then I gesture to my empty glass.

'Three in one night,' Paddy says, sliding the third martini in front of me.

Without even thinking, I drain it. 'Make it four.'

'Whoa, steady on. Is everything okay? Do you want to talk about it?'

Whatever look I give him makes him hold up two flat palms. 'To be sure. Number four's coming up.'

I can't believe I was so blind. So intentionally blind to what was happening. Gregory said he went to the police for me, so I could move on. He made me promise that if the Crown Prosecution Service made a decision not to charge him, I would accept that shooting Kevin Pearson was the right thing to do. That I would accept the decision meant *I* shouldn't be charged, that *I* did the right thing. If Katrina Martin's theory is true, it was all a lie.

Five weeks ago, I had Gregory. I deserved to be punished for what I did, for killing a man, but I thought I could get over it because I'd saved Gregory's life. For the last five weeks, I've been trying to make sense of everything that happened and the only conclusion I've drawn is that nothing makes sense without him. Not my involvement in the hostile takeover, not my dad being murdered as a result, not my burning desire to seek revenge, and not my incurable need to touch and feel *that* man.

I've realised things may never make sense again without him. I'm ruined for anyone else. Forget anyone else, I'm ruined in my own right. But the one thing I've been able to cling to, the one thing keeping me from dropping off the cliff of sanity, is knowing that I didn't lose *all* of Scarlett Heath. I took that shot because it was the right thing to do. Gregory escaping prosecution, escaping twenty-five years in a prison cell. *That* was the world telling me *I* did the right thing.

Now it's all unravelled. I don't have him and I don't have confirmation that I was on the right side of justice.

3

'You son of a bitch.'

'Scarlett. Not exactly the first five words I expected to hear from you after five weeks of silence.'

'Here's another five. You. Are. An. Arsehole.'

'That's four words.'

'You are an arsehole, Gregory.'

He sighs, and despite my fury and trembling hands, I can't help wondering where he is, whether he's sitting or standing, whether he's in *that* pose and wearing *that* suit. A fact that adds to my rage.

'Scarlett—'

'No, Gregory. Stop with your fucking lies. It's my turn to speak.'

'Scarlett, I've never lied to you.'

'Withheld the truth, then. Frankly, I don't give a shit because they both mean the same thing to me. Deceit.'

I don't sound like myself. My level of hatred and the filth leaving my mouth are surprising even to me. I'm as livid as I've ever been and the four dry martinis I polished off are amplifying the effect.

'You know, for days after you ended us, I felt like my world had come crashing down around me. I did something sinful, something wrong, and something that the person I was before you would never have done. I killed a man. And as warped as it sounds, that made sense when I had you. When I could see you might finally be free of your dark and twisted world. A world you wouldn't share with me. You were alive and that was my justification.'

'Scarlett—'

'Shut up! I said it's my turn to talk.' I rise from the queen bed of my hotel room and look out to the orange glow of Dubai's skyscrapers against the dark night sky. 'When I got here and realised I didn't have you any more, I lost my justification for... everything. Pearson, my dad. I was a mess. Then I realised you might not love me but I love— *loved* you enough to know that, despite everything, I was right to take that shot because the alternative is unthinkable.'

I swallow the emotion that stings the back of my eyes, throbs in my chest, and threatens to unsteady my voice. He won't hear me break. Not now.

'As much as I don't regret saving your life, Gregory, I broke the law, and I deserved to be punished for that. At the very least, I deserved to be tried in a court of law.'

'Scarlett.' He sighs, his voice gentle. *God, I miss him.* 'You did the right thing. Pearson deserved to go to hell. We were cleared.'

'No, Gregory. *We* weren't.' I sit back onto the soft duvet and put my spinning head into my free hand. 'You told me once that I had to trust you. You told me you got the police involved so that I could move on. Properly. You told me that I had to promise you, if you got a verdict of no charge, I would take that as *our* verdict. That we would both be free.'

'And we are, Scarlett. The CPS didn't charge me.'

'But it was bullshit, wasn't it? It was *all* fucking bullshit. You never had any intention of letting the law make that decision.'

'What are you—'

'Katrina Martin just paid me a visit.' I hear his sharp intake of breath. 'Tell me it isn't true.'

'Tell you what isn't true?'

'Don't fucking bullshit me, Gregory! I was an idiot.

So blinded by you, by not wanting to lose you, that I didn't see what was right under my fucking nose. Jackson and Barnes weren't just friends, were they? He didn't just forewarn you about the ballistics report; he gave you a chance to fix it. You were paying him off.'

'Scarlett—'

'Say it! You bought the CPS decision, Gregory. For once, tell me something true.'

There's a bang down the line that makes me jump. 'Damn it, Scarlett, it wasn't all a lie.'

'Say it. Tell me Katrina Martin is lying. Tell me I'm wrong.'

He's silent for seconds, eternal seconds that cause my heart to pound and my breaths to shorten.

'You're not wrong.'

From the moment Katrina Martin told me, I knew it was true. That doesn't stop his admission taking the weight from my body, my knees crashing to the floor. 'Then I'm not free. I never was.' The phone falls from my hand. His voice is a quiet mumble in the background as I stare at the reflection of a corrupt, broken woman in the wall of windows.

4

5.40 A.M.

I haven't slept. I've tossed and turned in the heat of my bed, too lethargic to move the ten steps required to turn on the air con. My mouth is dry and my body feels the wrong side of thirsty, the hungover side.

What am I supposed to do now?

That's the question I've been asking myself for the six hours I've been staring at the ceiling.

It's not like I can hand myself in to the police and request a trial. I'd put everyone else in jeopardy and I don't know if I could stand the uncertainty of another investigation, the police interrogating people I love. And whilst I'm raging at him for what he's done – *everything* he's done – there's no way I'd turn Gregory over for corruption. I'd never want him to risk his freedom again. He took the blame for me. He committed multiple crimes but he did it for me. Living with what I've done is my penance.

I grab the TV remote from the bedside table.

Crystal Grand homepage: teasing pictures of Crystal Grand Singapore, Crystal Grand Sydney, Crystal Grand...

Dubai news, in Arabic...

Dubai early-morning soaps... whoa... not soaps... stuff that should *not* be shown on TV in my room!

With a grumble, I throw the remote to the opposite side of my bed, where the duvet is in a ball from a heated tantrum about two hours ago. Peeling the thin cotton sheet from my clammy body, I shower, rinse off my unsettled night, then pull on my gym clothes and head to the ground floor.

The gym is empty but for one other ex-pat, a muscle-bound fitness trainer. I have free run of the machines as I watch BBC World News on the screens.

Cranking the treadmill up to a run, I hammer the belt with my feet and I try to focus on nothing but the sound of my breathing and the images of stock markets around the world.

It's around two in the morning in London. Gregory

should be sleeping. I wonder if he's alone. My stomach churns at the thought of anyone, ever, being in his bed with him. I hold my blink for seconds until the only image I see is of him, naked in his satin sheets. I wonder if his nightmares have stopped.

The tread automatically cuts out at an hour, so I move on to the stepper for twenty minutes, then the bike for a ten minute cool down. Any other Friday, I probably would have hit the outdoor pool for a few lengths too, but my dry martinis and lack of sleep are catching up with me.

Instead, I stand on the poolside and dip my toes in the water.

'Mind if I join you?' Paddy appears next to me wearing white trousers, shirt and shoes.

'Of course not. Why are you here so early?'

'Volunteered myself for pool duty today,' he says, leaning down to scoop a sample of water into a clear test tube.

'So, you're here for tax breaks, then?' My very slight smile is more for his benefit than my own.

Unusually for Paddy, he doesn't return the gesture. He puts a lid on his test tube and gives it a shake. 'Actually, no. Woman.' He shrugs. 'I'm over it now.'

'Mind sharing your secret?'

He offers me a pitiful curve of his lips and I can't help but think how much I wish it was Gregory standing in front of me with *his* half-smile.

'I take it your guest was unwanted last night?'

I scoff into the sports cap of my water bottle. 'You could say that.'

'Want to vent?'

'I really don't.'

'Well, if you change your mind, I'm around all day. They say we Irishmen make the best listeners.'

'Really? Who are *they*?'

He winks, a cheeky, very Paddy-like wink. 'Women. *All* women.'

I chuckle as he walks away, thankful for the only interaction I'm likely to have today besides cleaners and maybe a waiter at lunch.

I spend most of the day working from my hotel room, preparing additional enquiries of the construction company Mr Ghurair intends to acquire, venturing as far as the lobby café. This is one of the most mundane parts of a corporate lawyer's job: endless due diligence. Who owns the company? Who owns the assets, the machines, the tools and the cement? Will the company be in breach of any contracts with suppliers or customers if the acquisition goes ahead?

Are there any hidden red herrings that could impact the value of the company?

I'm the lawyer on the ground in Dubai but there's a team back at Saunders, Taylor and Chamberlain in London. Amanda is leading the due diligence from there, which has worked out great. She needed work and really could use a big deal before she goes off on maternity leave and her career flatlines for a couple of years. I needed support. And working together gives us more reason to talk regularly. As virtual as our relationship might be, she makes me feel less lonely out here.

The downside is that Friday is supposed to be my weekend in the Middle East but everyone is working in London so I am, too. The distraction probably isn't a bad thing.

I shut down for the day at four and head out to wander the dry streets, which are practically empty because everyone is chauffeured in Dubai. The late-afternoon heat is surprisingly welcome after the chill of the air con in the hotel. I soon find myself barefoot on Jumeirah Beach, water lapping at my feet and sand gritty between my toes as I look out across the turquoise sea. A burnt-orange haze lingers in the air, adding character to the horizon and serving as a constant reminder of the yellow dessert beyond the wealth of the city.

I'm so lost.

* * *

A now familiar waiter clears the dinner plate from my table on the balcony of Broadway, visibly disappointed that I've only eaten half my fillet.

As the first act of a 1950s-style rock 'n' roll medley draws to a close and I finish the last dregs of my dirty martini, Paddy appears. His bicep is tight under the short sleeve of his white cotton shirt and his messy dark waves are tucked behind his ears. There's a full glass of what looks like champagne, golden and lightly effervescent, on his tray.

'Hey lady, you look better than you did this morning.'

'Wish I could say the same about you.'

He shakes his head with a short laugh. 'So listen, your man there asked me to bring this over.' He gestures to the full flute with a flick of his head.

I look to the bar and see a gathering of six people – no obvious drink-gifters. 'Thanks, but—'

'No drinks from strangers,' he says in a mocking,

bored voice that sounds almost mid-yawn. 'I told him what you'd say.'

'Yet you're still standing here with a drink for me?'

'He tipped me more than I'll earn in my shift to bring you this particular drink.'

'What is it?'

Hand on the stem of the glass, he flashes me a mischievous grin. 'Before I tell you, I've got to know. If I'd asked you on a date, would I have had a chance?'

I feel my cheeks heat as I smile. 'You mean, would I have been your rebound ex-pat?'

He laughs. 'To be sure.'

'I don't think two broken hearts make a whole one, Paddy.'

He nods, one curt move. 'It's Pol Rodger 2002,' he says, placing the drink in front of me with a small napkin that's been folded into a triangle.

My stomach tightens as I unfold the tissue, and I'm holding my breath as I read the one word written there.

Aurora

My heart is pounding so hard, it could break my ribs – it feels like it might have – as I look back to the bar.

And I find him. He's here. Leaning on one forearm, sipping from a glass that I know is filled with Scotch, as if the world isn't spinning on its axis faster than Louis Hamilton laps Silverstone. His white shirt is rolled up to his elbows, three buttons open at the top. His muscles flexed beneath the silk. With one leg bent and resting on the low rail around the bottom of the bar, his cream chinos are pulled tight across his firm arse.

And those intense brown eyes lock onto mine, making the spinning stop. Making the world still and the room fade to nothing around us.

God, I love him.

'I take it you're good with Pol Rodger?'

'Hmm?'

'The Pol Rodger?'

I drag my attention from Gregory to Paddy and process his words. 'Yes. Sure. Fine.'

'And I take it that's your heartbreaker.'

I don't know whether I shake my head or nod or do neither. Paddy moves away as the most mesmerising man I've ever met walks towards me.

I'm looking up through my lashes as he reaches my table.

'Scarlett.' I'd forgotten how my names rolls off his tongue, smooth as velvet.

I subtly drag air into my lungs, holding his stare. I won't blink first. 'Gregory.'

'You look tired,' he says, finally breaking eye contact, giving me permission to close my lids.

'You flew five thousand miles to insult me?'

He sweeps up my champagne flute and sips. I watch his throat as he swallows the bubbles and my own lips part.

'Actually, it's more like three and a half thousand,' he says, placing the flute down on the table and sliding it my way. 'And no. I flew here because I don't care to be called a *son of a bitch*.'

I scoff. Seems like he's one millionth as pissed at me as I am with him. 'That's right. You don't like the truth, Gregory, do you?'

The faintest sign of a smug-as-hell smirk rises on his tantalising mouth that I suddenly remember can do the filthiest of things to me. 'It's funny you should mention that because the truth is one thing I came here to address.'

'That would be a first.' My words are much more confident than I feel. He's rugby-tackled me sideways, but I sit back into my seat and cross one leg over, sipping my Pol Rodger.

His brows furrow and he pouts. *God, I want to bite*

his lips. 'The other thing I came to address is that god-damn attitude of yours.'

I stand abruptly, my chair scraping against the floor, cutting through the ambience of the bar with something distinctly less favourable.

'Thanks for the champagne, Gregory, but you're wasting your time if you think I'd believe a word you say.'

Strutting past him, I make it out of the bar to the landing. Thumping the lift button, I glance nervously between the exit and four lifts. 'Come on,' I say whisper, foot bouncing, arms folded.

'Don't walk away from me, Scarlett.' His presence makes every last hair on my body stand on end, my nervous system attuned to him. 'I came here to set you straight on a few things and you're going to listen to what I've got to say.'

I squeeze my eyes shut so I don't see but I sense that he's moving closer to me.

I can't let him see me breaking on the outside even though I'm shattering on the inside.

The pain I've tried to kill since leaving London has come crashing back and it's striking me in the gut, crippling my body.

'Leave me alone, Gregory.'

He's next to me now. Too close. I can smell his fresh, rich scent. Feel his heat.

'I will, once you've heard what I have to say.'

I turn to him, reluctantly looking up to find his gaze already on mine, reading me, breaking down my façade.

'You lost the right to demand things from me when you lied to me and then sent me away.'

'Two minutes. That's all I'm asking. I'll tell you what you want to know.'

He has a point. This is for me, not him. 'Two minutes.'

'Outside, come on.'

He reaches for my arm and I flinch as flames ignites under his warm palm but he leads us through a fire exit and onto a quiet, desolate terrace. It's a side of the hotel I haven't seen but the frenetic lights of Dubai still shine in the night around us. I break our contact and move away from him, leaning forward on the railing.

'Your two minutes have begun.'

With a heavy exhale, he comes to mirror my pose. I inch away from him and in my peripheral vision, see his shoulders sag. 'You didn't let me finish last night.'

'That's because there was nothing left to say.' I can't

contain my anger and rise to stand. He straightens –
bigger than me in every way. But I *know* him, at least
enough to know that there are many facets to his per-
sonality and none of them intimidate me. 'You made me
promise, Gregory. You made me swear that I would accept the CPS decision, that I would see that as *my* justice. But it wasn't justice at all. You *bought* your own law.'

'That's rich,' he growls.

'What the hell is that supposed to mean?'

'You said yourself, a good lawyer bends the law.
That's exactly why you told me to hire John Harrison.'

'*Bends* the law, Gregory, not fucking evades it.'

'Curb the attitude, Scarlett.'

'No.' I'm leaning towards him, finger on his chest.
'You don't get to call the shots here. Not with me. So
tell me what you came to say because you have about
thirty seconds left before I walk away for the last time.'

He rakes his fingers through his hair. *Damn, I want
to do that.* Turning my back on him, I try to focus on
anything in the distance to distract me.

'I paid off some people but it's not what you think.'

'Who?'

'The CPS.'

A weight crushes the air from my lungs for the
second time tonight and I press my fingertips to my
lips.

'But *not* for the murder charge, Scarlett. Look at me.'

I shake my head but he gently tugs my shoulders, forcing me to face him.

'Look at me.'

I shake my head again, faster. His index finger is under my chin, lifting it in a too familiar way.

'*Not* the murder charge,' he says gently. 'The CPS didn't charge the murder of their own accord. That decision *is* yours. That was real justice. A decision they made because the right man died that night.'

I close my eyes both to break the intensity of our connection and to help me process what he's saying.

'I've *never* lied to you, Scarlett. I may have withheld information but I've never lied to you and I'm not going to start now. You can trust me because I'm telling you this... I *did* bribe the CPS to get rid of any possible gun charge but that had nothing to do with the murder charge. I swear on my—'

'Don't. Don't you dare swear on your life.' I open my eyes to find those precious gems looking into my hazel-greens.

He nods. 'I promise. I'm not lying about this. I flew here because I know you'll have spent the last twenty-four hours thinking you did something wrong but you didn't. This is the truth, Scarlett. Believe me.'

It takes three long breaths before I can admit that, 'I do.' But my relief is masked by the pain of his betrayal. The hurt of him sending me away. If I don't get away from him now, I'm going to crumble.

'Thank you. For coming here. For telling me.' Digging deep for all the confidence I can muster, I straighten my back. 'Goodbye, Gregory.'

I move past him as fast as my heels allow and head back to the landing. Once again, I'm thumping the lift button and willing it to come.

The fire exit door slams to a close, the sound of metal meeting metal echoing in the foyer, and I can feel his presence. 'Scarlett—'

'Please. Don't. You said everything five weeks ago and I— I'm not strong enough to do it all again.'

The lift pings and I finally drop my shoulders from my ears. Inside, I hit the button for the fifth floor and start to breathe.

But two hands crash against the closing doors, prising them open. He's staring right at me. Into me.

'Scarlett, I love you.'

My lips part as I stagger back against the wall of the cart. There they are. Those three words I've been desperate to hear. The words I imagined him saying to me weeks ago.

But he said he couldn't. He said he wouldn't.

'Why? Why now?' My words are barely audible.

He's motionless and he looks... afraid. 'I didn't come here to say that. But when I saw you...'

I shake my head as an overwhelming sense of confusion, of pain, love and anger, bears down on me. 'I can't do this again, Gregory. I can't. No one has ever hurt me like you.'

He drops his head towards his chest. *God, I want to hold him.*

'Please, Scarlett.'

My world begins to blur as tears fill my eyes. He looks so vulnerable. A shell of the man I have fallen for. The man who has ruined me for all others. But... 'Nothing's changed. We didn't end because of the case, or even because you made me leave. We broke because you won't let me in.' The lift doors tremble and begin to close once more.

He doesn't stop them, and I hear his words, almost exhaled, 'I can't.'

* * *

Why? Why now? After everything.

The hot spray of the shower caresses my skin and washes the salt of my tears from my cheeks.

Nothing's changed. It's true. I still don't know that

darkness within him. The real darkness. The black that broke us. It's still there and if he won't share it, we don't work. I'd spend every day wondering if it was the last. If he would do something deceitful. If he'd push me away. I can't do it again. I won't survive him a second time.

Water trickles down my face and into my mouth. *I want him so much.* My legs feel weak under the weight of his words, replaying in my mind. I press my hands onto the tiled wall in front of me and watch the water drain away.

What if?

Maybe we could make it work. Maybe I never know his darkest secrets but he accepts that I love him regardless. I convince him that he deserves to be loved, that he won't hurt me just by loving me back.

No. It's not enough. I need all of him. Living in fear of his next breakdown, incomplete, isn't a way to live my life.

After drying my hair, I lie back into the soft sheets of my bed with a towel still wrapped around my body. He was supposed to be justifying his corruption, that's all. It's not fair of him to ask me to do this. *Has he actually asked me to do anything?*

Hours pass by as the questions whir in my mind, keeping me from the sanctity of sleep. My confusion and desire are losing the battle against my sensibility, and what I'm left with is frustration and anger. He can't just fly to Dubai after everything and throw out those three words like, like, like I don't know what. He can't just do that. He said he's not willing to let me in. Right before the lift doors closed, he said *no*. And he sent me away; how could he love me and still send me away? And he *did* lie. He can call it what he likes, but he bribed the CPS.

Did they really accept self-defence? Were we honestly cleared?

I close my eyes and try for sleep again but it won't come. The alarm clock at my bedside, tells me it's 05.55. I give in.

I dress in my swimsuit, then cover it with leggings and a T-shirt and head down to the ground floor.

I'm rinsing in the poolside showers when he steps out of the male changing rooms in a pair of swim shorts, the sight of his naked torso making me wetter than the hot spray.

I ignore the dull throb between my legs and I dismiss him, moving into the pool. I take a sectioned lane in case he tries to swim near me, and I set off swimming a mile.

I've front-crawled three lengths before I realise he's

taken up the swim lane next to mine and dropped perfectly into rhythm alongside me.

Well that's just pissing me off even more!

He's fitter than me but I've been swimming almost every day for the last five weeks. I'm up to this challenge.

We power on. After forty lengths, he's still matching me stroke for stroke, breath for breath. I'm starting to think what's infuriating me more is that, whilst he's beside me, I can't watch his muscles move beneath the water.

Just because I'm pissed doesn't mean I can't appreciate him from a distance.

The only tantalising flash of him I catch is when we turn. We summersault in time and both kick off the end of the pool but his power moves him feet in front of me, until he drops back into my rhythm. In those brief moments, I watch him move, from his toes, through his legs, his flexing core, right to the tips of his fingers. His power driving forward. He really is something else.

And he loves me. *Me.*

Shake it off!

At fifty lengths, he's still mirroring my moves. At sixty-four, I don't waste time pushing up on my hands at the head of the pool and climbing out of the water.

Stomping to the showers, I rinse off. For a moment, he looks like he's going to talk to me, so I shut down the shower, grab my towel and head into the ladies' lockers where I switch into my gym kit.

And, of course, he's already in the *fucking* gym when I get there. He feigns stretching though I know he's actually waiting.

Oh, it's on, Gregory Ryans.

After a quick stretch, I get on the treadmill, set the time to forty minutes and hold my finger down on the speed button until I'm running at a decent pace. I have to fight to contain my temper when he climbs onto the tread next to mine and sets his bloody machine to the same settings.

It's a stand-off. A protest. A test of will. He wants me to concede. Like somehow beating me on the treadmill means he wins. He doesn't win. He won't win.

You can't just swan back into my life and throw around 'I love you,' Ryans. You sent me to Dubai.

We may have been cleared of one murder, but there's a good chance there could be a second any moment now.

At twenty minutes, I ramp up the speed further and the arsehole matches me. Damn my body for starting to tire. I need a different beat. Unhooking my phone from my bicep, I scroll through my tunes and, without thinking, select a song that's become one of my favourites. It reminds me of *us*, of being happy on our way to the opening hunt of the season. As Thirty Seconds to Mars's 'Kings and Queens' blasts in my ears, I cock one eye to Gregory's phone, resting on the lip of the treadmill screen.

He's listening to 'Kings and Queens'?

Thank God for reflexes. As my feet stumble and lose rhythm, I throw my hands on the side rails and take my body's weight until I'm composed enough to drop my feet back down and into my run. I can't resist a glance at him.

He smirks. *Arrogant arse.*

It's the last straw. My body has had enough and so has my mind. I slam my hand on the big red emergency stop button and roll backwards with the belt until the machine draws to a stop. Then I plonk myself down on the end of the belt, catching my breath.

He does the same.

Panting, I look up to him. A moment of weakness. Those chocolate diamonds are staring right back at me as he leans forward on his knees.

'Have dinner with me tonight. Please.'

'Gregory—'

'I've thought about it. Damn it, Scarlett, I've been thinking about it, you, *us*, all night. And you're right.'

I open and close my mouth without words.

'Have dinner with me tonight and I'll tell you everything. If you want to walk away from me after that, I'll understand and I'll never ask you for anything more. I'll leave you to move on, with someone who can treat you the way you deserve.'

I watch him with an overbearing urge to wrap him up in my arms and slap his face all at once.

'I know I hurt you. Maybe I should have told you about Barnes and the CPS but you would never have let me go through with it and I'll be damned if we were going to prison on a gun charge after everything we'd been through. And I know now that I shouldn't have sent you here. I went behind your back but I swear that I did what I thought was right by you. I'm no good at this, Scarlett, any of it. You, us, it's... I've never had it before and I know I keep fucking up at every turn.'

'You do.' Yet, on some level, I think I believe that he was trying to do right by me. The wrong thing for all the right reasons.

'Come tonight. Let me try. Otherwise I'll spend the rest of my life wondering about what could have been, what I threw away. Give me a chance to beat my past,

Scarlett. Please. I can't promise you'll stay and if you do, I can't promise things will always be perfect, but I can promise you that I'll try my best to be a man worthy of you. I'll spend every second for the rest of my life trying to be what you need.'

Like he always has the ability to do, he takes my breath away.

'Okay.'

'Okay?'

I nod. 'Okay.'

That half-smile I've missed so much draws on his lips and just like that, although I didn't think it possible, I fall deeper.

5

'Is this a good idea?' Amanda asks through a mouthful of popcorn: her pregnancy craving, so she says. Williams is so giddy about being a daddy that he just caves, driving around London at all hours to find the particular brand of sweet and salty she likes.

'Probably not,' I admit.

Brows raised on my phone screen, she asks, 'Do you *want* to know everything?'

'That's the million-dollar question,' I confess, moving from my hotel bed to the mirrored wardrobe doors. 'It feels like a first date.'

She sighs. 'Just be careful, okay? Don't forget he's the reason you're over there, alone.'

My best friend makes no attempt to conceal her

dislike of Gregory. 'You're getting in some practice at playing Mummy here.'

She smiles but it's fleeting. 'Seriously, don't fall for his shit; keep your wits about you.'

I nod at the phone.

'All right. Well, off you go, have fun. Don't wear anything too short and definitely do *not* put out.'

'This conversation just ended.'

She laughs, a belly chuckle, then I hang up and cast the phone onto the bed.

I scrutinise my reflection one last time. The cream dress I rushed out to purchase from one of Dubai's extravagant malls is demure at the front. A high, square neck, nipped in at the waist, resting an inch or so above my knee. I bite my lip as I turn to look over the open back, held together by two gold chains, one between the shoulders, the other midway down, the drooping fabric finishing just above my coccyx. I've curled and pinned up my hair and now, looking at myself, I feel silly. I've dressed up to find out the worst there is to know about the man I love. I've let myself get that whirling sensation in my stomach that only Gregory has ever caused.

He broke your heart, I remind myself.

He's talking to Paddy at the poolside bar on the fourth floor. The night is warm but a light breeze chills my back as I watch him. His shirt is unbuttoned just enough to tease me with the olive skin of his chest. The sleeves are rolled up hench forearms, like they were last night. Grey trousers hug every part of him they should and he looks tall, strong and suave. His chiselled features tighten when Paddy inclines his head in my direction. Gregory turns and watches me walk across the bar towards him.

'Good evening.' He holds out a cocktail glass for me to take.

I cast my eyes to Paddy, then back to the glass that Gregory is offering. 'There's an olive in my glass.'

'It's a dirty martini,' Gregory says, stating the obvious.

I turn again to Paddy. 'It's not a dirty martini night.'

'That's what I said,' he says, throwing his bar towel across his shoulder. 'I said it's a dry martini night but your man there said you'd like it dirty.'

Gregory smirks, smug and supercilious.

I take the cocktail stick with two olives from the glass Gregory's still holding. 'Did he?' I put the stick in my mouth, locking my lips around it then draw back slowly, pulling off the olives.

His lips part slightly. Mission accomplished, I drop the used stick back into the glass. 'I'd like a dry martini, please, Paddy. There'll be nothing dirty about tonight.'

Paddy throws his head back on a laugh and Gregory rolls his jaw, the ghost of a smile on his face.

'God, I've missed you,' he whispers. His words knot a rope in my stomach.

'Don't, Gregory. I came here to talk, that's all.'

He nods. 'Let's have your drink brought up to my room.'

'Ryans, you can think again if you think—'

'Scarlett, I've promised to tell you everything but I'm not sharing with the world. I've arranged for dinner in my room. I'm not suggesting you stay; I just don't want to do this here.'

He leans over the bar and relays the message to Paddy, then he's back by my side, smelling truly divine. He leans into me so I can feel his breath, an intoxicating blast of hormones on my neck. 'You look stunning in this dress.'

I clear my dry throat. 'Thank you.'

He gestures to the exit of the bar. 'Shall we?'

I start to walk and falter when the flesh of his palm grazes my bare back. 'Please, Gregory, don't fuck with my head.'

I'm grateful for the group of four men and women who ride the lift with us. 'Flutterflies,' I almost inhale to myself, hands containing what threatens to fly right out of my torso.

'Flutterflies?' Gregory asks on a whisper.

I let out a short nervous laugh. 'Fluttering butter-flies. Witty, huh?'

'Took the words right out of my mouth.'

We ride the final three floors alone, the lift's arrival ping breaking the palpable tension between us.

He gestures for me to exit first. He swipes his key card at the large double doors of his room – the only one on the floor – and holds one open for me.

'Naturally, you have a penthouse suite,' I say, step-ping into the vast lounge.

'High and fast, baby.'

I turn my head quickly back and see his startled face. It's scary how right it feels to hear him call me baby. *Dangerous.*

'This is nice.' I wander the mock marble tiles onto a soft cream carpet, the stem of my heels dipping into the floor.

An L-shape sofa sits in the middle of the lounge in front of an electric fire. Heatless flames are alight in a deep red feature wall. The room is warm and luxu-rious in every way: the fabrics, the colours, the out-standing view across the city and out to sea.

'The dining room is this way.' Gregory moves

through an archway into a separate area backing onto the lounge.

In the middle of the space, there's a table large enough for six suede chairs. Abstract art decorates the walls and makes the whole room feel contemporary. The table is set for two: one setting at the head of the table, the other to the side of the table. *Too close.*

A butler appears as if by magic. 'Miss Heath,' he says with a dip of the head, before pulling out the chair at the top of the table. 'My name is Roshan and I will look after you tonight.'

'Thank you.' I offer a soft smile as he pushes me in and places a napkin across my legs with gloved hands.

As he makes a similar fuss for Gregory, I enjoy the panoramic view.

We sit in silence as Roshan makes quick work of pouring water, filling our white wine glasses with the Sancerre Gregory has picked for our first course, and placing fresh bread rolls on our side plates.

'Are you ready for your appetiser, sir?'

'Yes, thank you.'

With another dip of his head, Roshan leaves us in our awkwardness, his movement causing the intricate table lanterns to flicker. The soft light dances across Gregory's face and knots the rope in my stomach tighter.

'How do you see this playing out?' I ask.

There's a shift in his demeanour that's reminiscent of the little boy from my dreams. Young Gregory is sitting at the table with me, reminding me what tonight is about. He's going to reveal everything to me and the thought must scare him because it's terrifying me.

He turns the base of his wine glass with his fingers, then slowly raises the frosted glass to his lips. 'Like I said, I'm going to tell you everything. The bad, the ugly, for as long as you want to listen. I've never told anyone, not everything. I don't talk about it. I'm not sure how to say it out loud. All I know is that I have to try because the last five weeks have been hell. I don't want my life without you in it and I know you need to hear this if you're ever going to understand why I pushed you away.' He takes another sip of Sancerre. 'I'm praying that once you've heard it, you won't run. But I'll understand if you want to. You should know that. I wouldn't blame you. God, I'd probably think you made the right decision. I've brought so much shit on you and I— I couldn't hurt you any more.'

'You *did* hurt me more, when you left me with no choice but to move halfway across the world.'

'I know. I do. But I did it because I thought I was protecting you, Scarlett. I did it to keep you away from what I'm going to tell you.'

'Your appetisers,' Roshan announces as he re-enters the room, placing a trio of seafood in front of us both. 'You have spiced crab cake here. In the glass, salmon mousse with cucumber garnish. In the bowl, cold fish soup with tomato base.' He beams at me and tops up Gregory's wine before leaving us alone.

Gregory leans back in his seat with a long inhale and twirls the base of his glass with his fingers again, staring down at the table.

'I've only ever loved two other people.' His eyes close and slowly reopen. 'My mother. And my sister.'

'You have a sister?'

'I had a sister.'

He sips his wine and his shoulders drop a little. That's the first admission and I don't know if he started with the easiest or the hardest.

'I'm sorry.'

He nods and stares back to the table. 'Her name was Elsa. She was older than me. Four years older.' He smiles sadly. 'She was beautiful. Sweet. Smart and funny.' His eyes flick up to mine and away again, just as quickly. 'I adored her.'

I swallow as he makes the first chip in my heart. *Pull yourself together, Scarlett; this is about him.*

'She— She ah—' He drags a hand through his

thick, brown hair. 'She killed herself. She was fourteen.'

I dig my teeth into my gums, the pain a distraction from the lump building in my throat.

'That's why you were worried I might've harmed myself the night I didn't come home from the office.'

He lifts his head to face me. 'Yes.'

'I'm sorry, Gregory, I really am.'

He moves back to turning his glass. 'She killed herself because of me, Scarlett, because I couldn't protect her.' He rubs a hand roughly across his mouth and chin.

'Your father,' I whisper.

'Yes.'

Roshan comes back into the room and removes our all but untouched plates after we assure him the food is good but we're leaving room for the main course. He pours Pinot Noir into our red wine glasses as I watch Gregory. He's left the room, gone to a place only he knows. I have to fight with myself not to go to him and fold my arms around his neck.

'I don't remember it starting,' he says. 'It seems like he just always beat us, for as long as I can remember. I see new things sometimes, in my sleep. Mostly, I remember the physical stuff but I saw a lot.'

I want to tell him to stop, that I don't need to know, but the words don't come because deep down, I know if we have any chance, he has to keep going. For us. For him.

'He would beat my mother raw. At first, when we knew he was coming home or when we heard his car, my mother would get Elsa and me in bed. She told us to pretend we were asleep and we did. But we heard. We heard every punch, every scream. I didn't do anything about it.' He takes a gulp from his Pinot Noir.

'You were a baby.'

He shakes his head. 'Sometimes, Elsa would come into my room, or I'd go to her, and we'd hide under the duvet, listening, crying, afraid, until it stopped. We'd get up the next day and it would be like nothing happened. He would go out to work and my mother would smile, make breakfast. Christ, and you know, that was easier. It was easier to be normal and pretend like life was fine. So I did.'

Almost reflexively, I reach out across the table and rest my hand on his.

When Roshan returns, we break our brief contact. He places two plates of thinly sliced rare beef with grilled asparagus and tomatoes in front of us, then leaves.

'Please eat,' Gregory says.

I find myself cutting a mouthful of meat because I

don't want to antagonise him. Not now. He also takes a forkful of food, then washes it down with wine.

'When I got older, six, seven, I couldn't lie in bed. I used to goad him. Trying to keep him away from my mother. It would work. He'd turn on me instead. He'd beat me, he'd say... fuck, all kinds of shit about my mother. Things I wouldn't repeat. One night, he— He was standing over my mother when I came downstairs. He'd been screaming at her because he was out of drink or she'd gotten rid of it. He was holding a broken bottle and it was— It happened in slow motion. She was on the floor, curled up like a foetus. When he lifted his hand, I ran, screaming, and got in his way.' He shakes his head. 'There was so much blood. I think he shocked himself sober.'

My eyes are stinging. 'The scar on your back.'

He nods and gulps down more wine. 'It worked that night. So the next time, I did it again. Then again and again. He didn't leave my mother alone but we shared the beating. She used to come to my room after he'd passed out and she'd cry, sob, saying thank you, over and over.'

'God, Gregory, I—'

He looks up to me. 'Do you want me to stop? Do you want to go?'

'No. I want to be here. With you.' I take his hand

and stare down at it until I've forced the building water from my eyes. I roll my fingertips across the burns on his wrist.

He interlaces his fingers in mine, watching our hands entwine. 'He made me do it to myself. He lit a cigarette and handed it to me and watched me stub it out on my skin.'

I wince and grip him tightly.

'It was me or my mother. She was on the floor. She could barely move. I thought he was going to kill her.'

I lift his hand and press my lips to his burns, trying to cover the memory. He pulls away from me and goes back to fiddling with the base of his wine glass.

'That night was the beginning and the end. Something changed in me. I begged my mother to take us away. Her, Elsa, me.'

'She wouldn't go,' I croak with closed eyes, fighting against the pressure behind my lids.

'No. I spent years trying to make sense of it. I'm still not sure I understand it but I've made peace with it. There was a time I thought I'd never forgive her for keeping us there. I guess now I see I was blaming the wrong person.'

Roshan is back, clearing our half-eaten plates again. Gregory asks me before cancelling dessert and dismissing Roshan for the evening. When we're alone, he pushes out his chair and moves to stand in the window. There are so many thoughts spiralling through my head, I can't get a hold of anything, so I stay in my seat and watch his reflection in the glass panes.

'When my mother refused to leave, I stopped going to her. I stopped making him turn on me. Christ, I just left him to beat her because I was so fucking irate. He could've killed her and I just sat in my room, hiding.' His back expands with his breath. 'My mother wasn't enough for him then. She wasn't enough satisfaction. That's when things changed. Then he'd come looking for us, Elsa and me.' He turns. 'This is what you need to know about me, Scarlett. You know what I did when he came for me and my sister? I hid from him. I *fucking* hid!'

His barked words make me jump.

'I stood behind doors, in wardrobes, under beds. He went to Elsa and he didn't just fucking beat her, Scarlett; he—'

His face is full of anguish as he drags both hands through his hair and holds them to the back of his head, his fingers interlaced, his knuckles white.

A silent tear streams down my face. 'He abused her.'

He's shaking his head, then nodding his head, all the while balling his hair in his fists. I've never seen him like this: losing control. 'Over and fucking over. At first, she'd fight and scream, then she used to take it. Silently. But I could hear it. The bed, the sound of him.'

I can't move. I'm rooted to my chair, tears pouring down my face.

'It went on for months before I couldn't sit back any more. I would go to her. Christ, I can still see it in my head every day. What he did to her. The look in his eyes. He wasn't bothered about me any more. It was like he'd stepped up to a whole other level. I'd goad him, shout things and fight him. But he'd knock me down, lock me out of the room. I couldn't help her and I'm the reason it fucking started.'

His hands move back over his face and he drops his head. Then his body jerks and he smacks a fist so hard into the wall that I'm surprised it doesn't leave a hole. I move to him, despite my leaden legs, desperate to comfort him.

'No.' He turns and I see his red eyes, desperately fighting, unwilling to let go. 'You need to hear it.' He takes a deep breath. 'She went away for a while. I don't know where. I was just relieved that my mother had seen sense. The beatings got worse for us but I didn't care. By then, I wanted them to be worse. I wanted to die. I prayed every night but not for him to stop. I prayed for him to go too far and end it, end everything.'

Tears drip from my chin.

'She came back. Elsa. He made her come back. I don't know how or why, I just remember coming home from school one day. I was ten. She was back, and it started again.'

I reach out to touch his arms but he backs away.

'The next day.' He pulls air through his teeth and rolls his tight jaw. 'When I came home from school, the police were at the house. She slit her wrists. She killed herself and it was all my fault.' His eyes close, masking his pain. 'I let him beat my mother and rape my sister. Do you hear me? My sister killed herself when she was fourteen years old because I didn't help her. I stood by and I might as well have killed her myself.' He slams a flat palm against the window and holds it there. 'I hurt people I love, Scarlett. And when I met you, it started all over again. I hurt you. I couldn't protect you. You had to get out of London. You had to get away from me because I'm a monster, Scarlett.'

I'm stuck to the spot, unable to move or think, staring at the broken man in front of me. I don't know what I expected but I didn't expect *this*.

He turns. Eyes red, raw and fixed on mine. 'So now you know.'

My lungs have an overwhelming need to catch air and I realise I've been holding my breath.

'You should go,' he says softly.

I just keep staring at him, images and thoughts confused in my mind.

'It's okay,' he whispers.

I move my head from side to side, slowly, then faster, then violently. 'Gregory, this, all of this, it's *not* your fault. Do you hear me? You didn't ask for that sick bastard to be your father. You were a boy. A baby.'

'I let him rape her, Scarlett.'

'No!' I go to him now and throw my arms around his neck, pulling him into me. 'No, you didn't.'

He wraps his firm arms around my body, holding my head to his shoulder, and rests his chin on my scalp.

'You're a good man, Gregory Ryans. You're the best man. You're kind and brave and that little boy didn't deserve to be born into that life. Are you listening to me?'

'I love you.'

Those three words. Through all his pain and torment, his says those three words.

'God, Gregory, I love you, too. So much, it hurts.'

He squeezes me so tightly, I can't breathe. I tell him so and he laughs. A short-lived break but I'll take it.

He releases his grip and pulls back. 'Will you stay?' His voice is barely audible. It's not the Gregory I know. It catches me off guard.

'Gregory, I, this is all, we—'

'It's fine. I get it.' The expression in his tortured eyes strikes my gut with a dagger and twists.

'Don't do that.' I step into him and grip the tops of his arms. 'Don't put walls up. I'm not walking away. I'm not afraid of what you've told me. It's a lot to take in.' I sigh, dropping my arms to my sides. 'I just need to process everything, get my head straight before you invade it again. I'm trying to understand you and I'm grateful, so grateful, that you've let me in. But you *hurt* me, Gregory. Sending me away *broke* me. And you did it intentionally. For good reason or not, I can't just forget that.'

'I get it.'

'Do you?'

'I do. But I'd like you to stay. Just to talk. There are two bedrooms; you could go to your own room when you're tired.'

'I really don't think it's a good idea.' I walk towards the door, trying not to let the emotion balled up in my throat surface.

'Scarlett, please.' His plea makes me stop and to my horror, he's on his knees when I turn around. Gregory Ryans, powerful CEO, the man whose presence can silence a room, the man who demands control, *my* Gregory, is on his knees.

'Get up. This is not you, Gregory; you don't belong on your knees, not for anybody.'

'You're not anybody, Scarlett; you're the only person who's ever wanted to climb walls with me. You're the *only* person who could bring me to my knees. I'm begging you to accept me because I'm miserable without you. You can have all of me, baby. You can own me.'

'I don't want to own you, Gregory. I want you to be on the same page as me, part of a team that faces everything together. Not a team where one person runs when things get tough.'

'I can't promise I won't fuck up. I will. But I *want* to be everything to you. I won't ever push you away again. And I'll talk to you. Damn it, I'm *trying* to talk to you.'

'And I'm grateful, I am, but I need to go back to my room.'

I leave him there, on his knees, an image that threatens to tear me apart all over again.

* * *

My eyes sting as I ride the lift to my floor and walk with weightless legs to my room. In his suite, it was less what he said and more the look on his face: years of torture, abuse and anguish. Now, the enormity of what he told me is sinking in. Gregory had a sister. His father repeatedly raped her, beat Lara, beat him. He was helpless.

The weighted door to my room bangs heavily behind me and I fight back tears as I grab the silk shorts and cami that have been folded on my pillow. I suddenly have no energy and slump onto the end of the bed. Then like a raging storm, pain strikes my abdomen. I see his face, see him kneeling in front of me. Thirty years of torment flood my mind and the lump I've been fighting in my throat bursts. With a yelp, my tears come and I cry into my hands. The onslaught is uncontrollable.

How can a human being do that to another? How can a father *do that to his daughter, his son, his wife?*

And he saw. He saw it all.

He felt every blow.

His own father stabbing his back with a serrated bottle.

He was only a boy.

I strip down and climb into the shower, desperate to wash away everything I've heard, wishing I could do that for Gregory. I've left him there, alone.

But the pain he caused me. I slide down the wall and sit on the floor of the shower, my knees pulled into my chest, and let my tears fall. He can't undo the past, not Pearson, not Elsa, not bribes and not the deceitful way he got me to Dubai. But now I at least understand *why*. As perverse as it might seem, he bribed the CPS for us, for me, so that a gun wouldn't be the reason I went to prison if the murder charge disappeared. And as much as I hate him for sending me here, he thought he was protecting me. He was afraid to love me, to hurt us both.

I get out of the shower and dry my body, then my hair, staring at myself in the mirror. *This isn't me. How could I walk away from him when he needs me?*

I love him.

I slip into my nightwear and wrap the hotel's white towel robe around me and head back to Gregory's suite.

My heart and head are heavy again by the time I reach his door. I have to put my own thoughts aside. With a deep breath, I lengthen my spine and knock.

He answers the door with a towel around his waist, wet hair and a glass of Pinot Noir in his hand. As inappropriate as it might be, my sex twinges and my mouth dries.

'You came back.' His voice is stronger now but he's still not my intense, sexy billionaire CEO. He steps away from the door for me to come in. 'Would you like wine?'

'Yes, please.'

I curl my feet under me in the corner of the L-shape sofa. Gregory hands me a glass of Pinot Noir then hesitates before sliding down to the sofa next to me, his bare chest just inches from my arm. I swallow as subtly as my rising temperature and pounding heart will allow and thank God for the white wool keeping my skin from his.

'Tell me about her. Tell me about Elsa.'

He drains his glass and leans forward to pour another, then settles back, resting his elbow on the back of the sofa, his head close to mine.

'She had long, dark hair, like yours. Big, brown eyes. She loved to read. She was always reading. She would tell me about her books and pretend...' he shakes his head, '...pretend she was one of the characters, living someone else's life.'

'Did she have a favourite?'

He shrugs. 'I wish I knew. There are so many things I didn't listen to or that I've forgotten. I wish I could remember the good things but all my memories are tainted. I can't think of her without seeing him and what he did. I want to remember how happy she was when we were away from him.'

Instinctively, I stroke his cheek. He swallows, his lips parted slightly, and I take my hand back.

'She had this doll. A rag doll. She used to pretend she was feeding it. Christ, what was it called? I can't remember its name. She took it everywhere. Before— before things changed.'

'For what it's worth, Gregory, I'm sorry. More sorry than I can put into words. But I'm pleased you told me. I'm glad you trust me.'

His gaze falls to my lips. I close my eyes and sip my wine.

'Tell me there's a chance, Scarlett. Not tonight. Not now. Just a chance.'

I take a sharp breath when my lungs cry out. 'There's a chance.'

He reaches a palm towards my face and I want to feel his touch but I whisper, 'Don't.'

He moves the ball of his hand back to his temple, propping himself up.

'Can I ask you something?'

'Anything,' he says.

'The night I came home and you were on the

phone to Lara. The night she'd been questioned by the police. You were talking about a woman, someone the police had brought up and questioned your mother about. It was Elsa, wasn't it?'

'Yes.' Another gulp of Pinot Noir. 'The night Elsa killed herself, everything came out. It was as if my mother finally opened her eyes. I don't know every-thing. I was ten but I still had to give a statement. It's the only time I've talked about what I saw before tonight.'

'What happened to your father?'

'He was convicted of sexual assault. He was sen-tenced. Then Lawrence was on the scene.'

I raise my eyebrows.

He shrugs. 'I've never asked. It doesn't matter any more and I'll always be grateful to him.'

'That's when he brought you to England?'

'Ja. He's a good man. He loves my mother. Those are the only things I care about now.'

I slowly draw a deep breath.

'Heard enough?' he asks with a short, troubled laugh.

'I think maybe for one night.'

He takes my wine glass from me. 'You've got work tomorrow. I'd still like you to stay... in your own room... if you want. I'd like to wake up in the same place as you.'

I nod, biting my lip nervously, unsure whether I should stay but not wanting to leave.

He lifts his fingertips to my temple and I close my eyes under his gentle touch. 'Until tomorrow then.' He bends and I gasp as his soft lips press against my cheek.

'Tomorrow,' I manage.

6

So many things make sense now that didn't before. His violent overprotectiveness with me and with Williams's sister. His explosive reaction to my old boss, Jack, who cornered me but never outright touched me. Gregory went out of his way to dig into Jack's past and make sure he was put behind bars, where he couldn't hurt women any more. How he nearly lost his mind when I fell asleep in my office and didn't call. That he was genuinely afraid I would have harmed myself. It seemed ridiculous then but not any more. His fear of being loved and being *in* love. All he knew was that people he loved, people who loved him back, got hurt. And he blamed himself.

There isn't a clock in my room but I've been lying

under the gold satin sheets for what feels like forever, a thousand thoughts spinning through my mind. Images of him as a boy. Wishing his own father would kill him and put an end to it all. Tears. Blood.

If I'd seen those things, if I'd felt the way he must have, I'd wait for the first opportunity I had and I'd kill the bastard who dared to lay a finger on me and the people I love. As I lie here, I'm glad I killed Kevin Pearson.

Finally, Gregory can be free and truly free. He told me. He let me in. He's been terrified of letting someone get close to him for twenty years and now...

I slip out of the covers, pull my hair across one shoulder and go where I should have been for the last hour.

I bend the handle and slowly push open the door to his dark bedroom. The dim light of the moon and the twinkle of Dubai's lights cast a gentle hue across the space. The satin sheets of his king bed are pushed onto one side, the bed empty, and Gregory stands in silhouette before the wall of windows. His arms folded across his naked chest, dark loungewear hanging low on his hips.

My heart races as I move towards his back. He flinches when I slide my hands down his toned biceps as if he hasn't heard me come in, then he sighs and unfolds his arms to his sides as my lips brush his shoulders, one then the other.

God, I've missed the feel of his skin on mine.

I press my chest against his back, my pelvis to his firm arse. With a sharp inhale, he turns, pulling me into him. Even in the darkness, I feel his mesmerising stare, connecting with every nerve in my body. His fingertips stroke my temple, down my cheek, then slide to the back of my neck.

His breath teases my lips. 'Aurora.' That one word makes my stomach flip.

He presses his mouth to mine and my body melts into his kiss. Greedily taking his lip between my teeth, I groan under the touch I've missed so much. His tongue matches the swirling desperation of my own.

He holds my cheeks as he whispers my name and takes my mouth again. My hands roam hungrily over the skin of his bare back then I slip my fingers into his hair, pulling him to me like I can't get close enough.

'I've been dreaming of this for five weeks,' I say.

'Baby, I've thought about you every minute of every day.'

'How can you hurt me so badly and be the only person who can fix me?'

His forehead meets my brow and the tip of his nose grazes mine. 'Because we're meant to be together, baby. I knew that the first time I met you. I think I knew I loved you the second I saw you in my board-room. It just took me a while to get here and I'm sorry it did. I'll never hurt you again, Scarlett, I promise.'

'I know.'

'I'll spend every day for the rest of my life pro-tecting you.'

'I know.'

'You're the only woman for me. You're the only woman I've ever loved, plain as night.'

I smile, genuinely, for the first time since he's been here. 'Plain as day.'

His chest chugs as a short laugh escapes his de-lectable lips. A sound I'd like to hear every day for the rest of our lives: his happiness.

Our mouths meet and he lifts my legs around his waist and takes us to the bed. Sitting me on the edge, he slides my cami up my body, his fingertips teasing my skin. I raise my hips as he slides the shorts down my legs before standing to push his own bottoms to the floor, revealing himself, proud and ready.

Raising my chin with his index finger and thumb, he pushes his lips against mine, then lifts me back up the bed. My legs fall wide as he crawls between them. The weight of his body between my thighs presses his hard length against my stomach, a feeling I savour. He leans forward, resting his forearms either side of my head, and strokes my hair back from my brow.

'Kiss me,' I beg.

He does. At first, soft and tender. Then his pace quickens, the force of his mouth, the turn of his tongue, and I match him, stroke for stroke, both audibly drowning in each other.

'I've never wanted anything so much, Scarlett. You own me,' he whispers, grinding against me.

I shift my head to one side as he sucks and nibbles my neck, working his way to my collarbone, gently blowing warm air across my skin. Taking his weight on one arm, he cups my breast in his other hand and tweaks the already hardening nipple. I close my eyes when his mouth wraps around the sensitive tip, a feeling that speaks to my entire body. I squeeze my thighs around his hips as his teeth take over and pull my flesh, somewhere between pain and pleasure, sending my insides into turmoil.

He kisses my sternum and starts working a line down my navel. My back arches as he reaches the bottom of my stomach. In my mind, I'm begging him to move three inches lower but my words are lost in heavy pants as I squirm beneath him.

He waits, hovering, not touching me, sending me

into a frenzy. Then he blows gently from the bottom of my stomach. A line. Down. Down.

I gasp as his breath caresses the top of my sex. He parts me with his fingers and continues his trail of hot air, my hips jolting forward when he strokes my swollen clit.

'Gregory.' His name leaves my mouth as a desperate plea.

'Tell me what you need, baby.'

My fevered muscles respond to his words, tightening.

'You. I need you.'

He leans forward and offers two fingers to my mouth. I take them slowly from the base, sucking them like I would his cock as a low rumble escapes his chest. Then he shocks me by moving his wet fingers straight to my arse, stroking them over my hole. He bends towards me and my entire body stills in anticipation. He makes me wait, enhancing my yearning to have him. Then his tongue meets my clit and he pushes his fingers into my aching sex, the double assault making me cry out, my back arch higher, my head dig back into the bed.

'You're so wet, baby.'

He moves his fingers, working me in circles, stroking my spot in time to the whirl of his tongue around my bud, building me to an orgasm I've desired for too long. My hands move to his hair, keeping his head right where I need him to be. He removes his fingers and slides his tongue down, dipping inside me, tantalising the charged skin of my entrance. My breaths speed up, coming fast and heavy, my mind clouding in a heady euphoria.

My insides tense, craving his depth. As if reading my mind, his fingers are back inside me, two, then three, taking me higher. As his tongue strikes a line over my clit, my shoulders rise from the bed, I reach out my hands and grip the bedsheets.

'Gregory!'

'Come for me, baby. I want to see what I do to you.' He rams his fingers hard into me. His tongue continues to swirl my clit. My muscles spasm and he grates out a wild sound I feel against my sex, my undoing.

I call out his name as I unravel around those magic fingers on an earth-shattering orgasm.

Before I even open my eyes, his mouth captures my heavy pants. His hips push into mine, his body rests on one firm arm and the fingers of his other hand stroke hair from my damp temple.

'How could it have taken me so long?' He inhales the words like he's asking himself the question.

My heart is pumping blood through my veins so hard and fast, I think it might explode. I couldn't love him any more than I do, physically, mentally. Despite everything, I never want to be apart from him again. I want him, just as he is, flaws and all.

Hooking my arms around his waist, I pull his body closer to mine, seduced by his guttural murmur. 'Make love to me, Gregory.'

'Baby, you don't have a choice.'

He slides one hand between us and guides himself to my entrance. My legs part further and he slides slowly into me, stretching me, filling me, making me whole again. As he draws out, his tongue wraps around mine and takes me to a world where only Gregory and I exist. A place where nothing and no one can wound us.

He moves slowly, his hips rotating with every delicious drive forward. My still-high insides work up again.

He rolls us, his hot, damp chest pressing against mine until he's lying under me, his hands roaming every inch of the skin on my back. I drop my mouth to his neck and taste his saltiness, smelling sex on his flesh. I rise to my knees, pushing him deeper into me as I keep his rhythm and move in circles around his erection.

He grabs my breasts, cupping, stroking, tweaking the ends. My hips quicken, and I dig my hands into my hair as he lifts me higher. Then his hands are on my hips, slowing my rotations around him.

'I don't want this feeling to end,' he whispers.

He's so damn beautiful, I can't resist him. I get lost in his kiss, unable to stop myself from building to the brink. My walls grip his thick cock.

His low growl into my mouth drives me higher as he rolls us again, quicker this time, and he's back on top of me, my legs locked around his waist. His controlled thrusts intensify, until he's pounding relentlessly and I feel him swell the last bit. He's close and the thought sends my muscles into spasm.

'Gregory!'

'Together, baby.'

I squeeze his hips with my legs as my climax courses through me.

'Jesus, Scarlett!'

He fills me, pulsing and thrusting, over and over, until his body trembles and he falls onto my chest, gently rotating his hips until every last drop of pleasure is taken from us both.

He rests his cheek against my sternum and strokes lazy fingers up and down my arm. This is right. This is exactly how things are supposed to be.

I wake in the night and smile when I feel his arm wrapped around me, pulling me onto his bare pec. I watch him peaceful, beautiful sleeping beneath me, until a contented sleep finds me again.

* * *

He sits at the head of the dining table, multiple cloched dishes surrounding him, a jug of fresh orange in the middle of the table next to a large cafetière of coffee. His hair looks roguish and bed messy in the hottest way. His captivating half-smile pulls on his lips when he spots me.

'Good morning, Miss Heath.'

Standing behind him, I pull my fingers through his hair then press my lips to his scalp, inhaling his scent. 'Mr Ryans.'

He takes my hand and presses my knuckles to his lips. I waste no time in stealing a kiss, enjoying the reminder of just how tender my own lips feel.

'What do we have here?' I ask, looking around the table. I take a cloche from the plate at the setting next to Gregory and grin.

'Your favourite.'

I slip into a chair as Gregory pours me coffee, then

I dig into my pancakes with crispy bacon and syrup. I can feel his eyes burning into me.

'What are you thinking about?'

He takes my hand and turns his thumb slowly across the top. 'Come home with me.'

Mr Ghurair. Two deals. The firm. These are the things that sense should bring to the front of my mind but all I see is him, us.

'You're everything to me, Scarlett. My whole world. Come home with me.'

'If you remember, I never wanted to be here in the first place.'

He rolls his jaw as he resumes his seat at the table. He's keeping a lid on his temper and so he should, too; he has no right to be angry in this.

'I don't know if I can leave. There are some conversations I'll need to have.'

He nods. 'Your firm.'

'Yes. And of course, thanks to you, I'll have to deal with Neil Wallace and undo the commitment you made on my behalf. God, imagine what he'll say. It's probably a good time to share with you my sincere gratitude for limiting my career progression.'

People don't stand up to Gregory. I can almost feel him fighting to find a response that isn't to wipe the floor with me. He takes a breath. 'You're a good lawyer, Scarlett. The firm knows that and so does Neil.'

'Is that what you'd say if it was one of your employees?'

'No. And I take your point. So... if you want to stay, we'll make it work. I'll fly out, be here whenever I can.'

The bloody arse has called my bluff. He might be wearing his poker face but he knows it, too.

'As it happens, I have actually been thinking about trying to move back to London sooner than planned. But that does *not* get you off the hook. I, erm, I've sold my dad's house.' I search his face for concern, waiting for the realisation that I'm about to be homeless to hit him, but his lips are straight.

'I know.'

'How do you— Jackson?'

'Yes, and I think what you're doing for Sandy is incredible.'

The money. 'Well, it's no more than she deserves after all the years.'

'Still, two hundred and fifty thousand pounds when you're not— It's extremely generous.'

I shrug. 'I was hoping she'd use some of it for the wedding. I think she and Jackson are only waiting because of the cost but she won't use it. I can't manage to convince her that my dad would be happy for her to use some of it on a wedding. I just want her to be happy.'

'They aren't *un*happy, Scarlett.'

'I know. It's just, there's something nice about being married, I think. Sandy's a purist. There's a commitment behind a marriage.'

'You don't have to be married to be committed to someone.'

'No, of course not, but marriage just feels more definite.' I wave a lazy hand in the air. 'Anyway, the house sold sooner than I thought it would. It doesn't make sense for me to keep it. I'm going to buy an apartment closer to work.' He watches me without the semblance of a reaction. 'I was supposed to be out here to complete two deals. The first is around three weeks from completion. The second will be more like the end of March. I'll have to at least stay to complete the first but I need to clean out the house, so I'm hoping I can convince Mr Ghurair that the second deal can be completed from London and maybe I can just fly out once every week or two.'

I can tell he's trying to suppress a smile and he does right to keep it hidden.

'So you'd come home in three weeks?'

'That's what I'm hoping, yes.'

'Three weeks.' Now his lips curl and my anger

wanes because he's just too damned cute. He tears a bite of pastry from a croissant. 'Good. But Scarlett, you won't be getting an apartment in the city. You'll come home. To *our* home. Where you belong.'

I watch him eat the pastry, his face perfectly serious. And I want to give him some whip-smart retort but what I actually feel and say is, 'I'd like that.'

He lifts my knuckles to his lips again. 'Settled then. Three weeks. I'll keep the suite here. You can stay full-time and I'll come back whenever I can.'

He's back to Mr Controlling and for some reason, that makes me significantly happier than seeing him on his knees, for me or anyone. 'You're such an arse,' I tell with a laugh. 'But I have a room here. The firm pays.'

'Fine. I'll pay the upgrade rate. I'm not staying in a pokey little room and I won't have my girlfriend staying in a pokey little room whilst I'm gone.'

'You haven't seen my room.'

'And I don't want to. It'll be pokey.'

I laugh again. *I've missed his crazy.* 'Right. I have to go to work. I have some discussions to have with my client that I'm pretty sure he's not going to like.' I plant a chaste kiss on Gregory's brow and make for the door.

'Hold up, firefly. You might need this.' He dangles a key card to his room in front of my face. As I reach for it, he pulls it away and drops a kiss on the tip of my nose. 'What time should I expect you?'

'Eight-ish maybe.'

'We'll have dinner together here.'

With a sigh, I grab the key card. 'That's not a question.'

'It wasn't intended to be.'

'You're not forgiven!' I call back across my shoulder as I walk away.

7

My day started with a call about Mr Ghurair's latest deal. I was supported by Amar – Mr Ghurair's cousin and closest confidante – as we discussed the financials of the acquisition with the seller's lawyers. After that, I set to work on the next turn of the asset purchase agreement.

No matter how hard I tried to focus on drafting amendments to the document, I couldn't stop thinking about my sore lips, the lingering satisfaction between my legs and the tenderness of my breasts. My morning was consequently protracted but it was a damn sight better than my afternoon spent regretting convincing Mr Ghurair that my completing the second deal remotely could have cost benefits. Now I get to piss off Neil Wallace *and* work my arse off.

I'm thankful for the end of the day and even more thankful that tonight, I won't be eating alone. I won't be nursing a cocktail because I have nothing better to do.

Tonight, I'm heading back to Gregory.

I reapply my red lipstick, ruffle my hair and straighten my fitted dress in the hotel lift.

When I open the door to the penthouse, I'm welcomed by dim, flickering lights. There must be hundreds of votive candles decorating the suite. Two parallel rows lead from the door and I follow them through the lounge, passed the master bedroom and into the en suite. More candles decorate the corners of the bathtub and line the marble sink unit. Vanilla fills my nose, warm and sweet.

'Good evening, Miss Heath.'

His words come from behind me, his breath on my neck. He moves my hair down one shoulder and I lean my head to expose the skin of my throat.

'Are you coming home with me?' he asks through sensual kisses.

'In three weeks.'

I feel his lips curve against my neck.

'But I'll never make partner. Neil hates me.'

'He'll come round. If I was your boss, I'd come round.'

I turn to face him, pressing my chest against his crisp white shirt, raking my fingers through his thick, dark hair. 'You might be a little biased.'

I feel his smile against mine.

'There's also a catch.'

He pulls back from me but keeps his hands on the small of my back, gluing our waists together. 'Share.'

'I told Neil that a big client of mine needs my help in London.'

'The CEO of your big client being...'

I dab a finger against his firm pec. 'Exhibit A. And you owe me.'

'Ah, well, perhaps now is a good time to talk about the real reason I flew to Dubai.'

I pout playfully.

'I needed a lawyer.'

'Right, and you could only find one working in the UAE?'

'Exactly.'

His tongue parts my lips and I drown in his taste, pulling him to me with my hands around his neck.

'I'm coming home,' I whisper.

'Where you belong, baby. Until we're grey and old.'

Unwilling to move my mouth from his, I unbutton

his shirt and push it back over his shoulders, indulging in the feel of his chest that might even be firmer than it was when I left London. I gently bite his pec.

I release his belt, the button of his blue chinos, the zip, then draw his trousers down to his bare feet and he steps out. I hold his gaze as I pull his boxers to the floor, his solid cock springing against his navel.

When I've sated my man and him me, we lie in the bathtub, his legs either side of mine, my back to his chest.

My entire body relaxes as he fills and squeezes a flannel across my chest and rests his cheek against my temple.

'How did we get things so wrong?' I ask.

'No more,' he says into my hair.

I run my hands up and down his wet thighs as he cleans my skin with warm, bubbly water.

'We need to talk about Katrina Martin.'

His chest deflates.

'She flew out to Dubai, Gregory.'

'She's just got a bee in her hat.'

Despite my want to be serious, I look to the heavens and tell him, 'Bonnet. She's got a bee in her bonnet.'

He chuckles.

'I'm serious. She came here to find out what I know about the bribes. She's not going to back off easily.'

'There's no trail. Even if there were, she'll be looking for a bribe around a murder charge.'

'She won't find one.'

He continues methodically bathing my skin. 'No. She won't.'

'How can you be so sure?'

'Look at me.'

I turn in the water to face him.

'She won't.'

I shouldn't have looked into those irresistible eyes. My body moves before my mind has time to think. My hands lock into his wet hair and I attack his mouth. He willingly accepts, his hands moving to my arse, pulling me against his pelvis. He starts to grow beneath me. Then he's lifting us out of the bath, carrying me to his bedroom without stopping to dry.

'That was a good talk. A solid resolution,' I tell him.

'Solid being the operative word.' He bites my lips. 'Baby, this is five weeks' worth of hard-on. I'm going to be solid all night.'

8

In some ways, three weeks flew over. Gregory nights were easy. He kept me more than a little busy. He's been amazing. He's spent at least two nights in Dubai each week, working from the penthouse suite. Non-Gregory nights haven't been unbearable either. I've been crazy busy completing Mr Ghurair's deal, or I've been helping Sandy plan.

I'm told it's coincidence that just hours after Gregory returned to London three weeks ago, I received a call from Sandy saying she and Jackson have decided to get married. She explained away how they hadn't previously thought about holding it abroad and how Lara has contacts in St Lucia so they could marry soon and it wouldn't break the bank. And by *soon*, she meant four weeks.

So here I am, sitting in a chair on one side of Neil Wallace's desk, my first morning back in the London office. He's pacing the floor on lanky legs, trying to keep his temper, switching between folding his arms across his blue shirt and huffily pushing his hands into the pockets of his black pinstripe trousers. Not only have I cut my secondment short, I'm now going on annual leave for two weeks from Thursday, seventy-two hours after returning from Dubai. I'm not sure if it's the temperature of the room or the heat radiating from Neil that has my skin flushed and my hand fanning air against my cheeks each time he turns his back. Neil is a family man at heart but my explanation about having to be in St Lucia to walk my sub-mum down the aisle is falling on pissed-off ears.

'Disappointed would be an understatement, Scarlett.' He shakes his head of silver hair and halts in front of his desk, staring down at me.

One thing's for sure: my career ladder has snapped in two. Hours of effort, slogging my arse off for the firm, big wins, expedited promotions. They mean nothing now because I just pissed off the man at the top of the tower, two times.

'I'm sorry, Neil, honestly I am and it's not something I've done before but, well, sometimes, family has to come first.'

There's something I never thought I'd say to my boss.

He sighs, almost resigned, as if there's an outside chance my words have resonated somewhere in his brain. 'I won't lie to you, Scarlett. This hasn't done you any favours.'

I nod. 'I know.'

* * *

It's after eleven, dark, cold and wet when I leave the high-rise but I smile as soon as I see the Range Rover. It's the first time Gregory has ever picked me up from work himself. Jackson is already in St Lucia.

I wheel my large suitcase through the disabled access door and Gregory pulls up the collar of his navy trench coat as he climbs out of the driver seat.

'I had a feeling we might need boot space,' he says.

He takes the suitcase I've struggled to lug through my office block and makes quick work of throwing it into the car whilst I run with my mac over my head to the passenger side.

'Hi, you,' I say with an enormous grin as he climbs behind the steering wheel.

'Hi.' He cups my cheek with his warm palm and

presses his lips to mine. 'I'm sorry I couldn't meet you from the airport.'

'That's okay. I thought it would be best to face Neil sooner rather than later anyway.'

'How did it go?'

I let out a short laugh and flop back in my seat as Gregory fastens my belt around my tired body. 'I'm pretty sure my career with Saunders, Taylor and Chamberlain has reached a dead end.'

Gregory drops a peck to my brow, then buckles himself in and pulls out to the road too quickly. I press my body into the seat as heat climbs through the black leather, and I turn my head to look at my sexy CEO.

He casts me a quick glance as he takes a left turn. 'If it was so bad, why are you smiling?'

'Because something occurred to me whilst I was sitting in his office having my ears chewed off. Something I've never thought before.'

He glances to me again. 'What's that?'

'It doesn't matter what Neil Wallace has to say because at the end of the day, I get to come home to you.'

He focuses on criss-crossing with traffic over Blackfriars Bridge, heading south across the River Thames, but his lips turn up in a sexy half-smile and he reaches for my hand. He drives back to the Shard and carries everything for me, including my handbag, when we get out of the car.

'Are you tired?' he asks as we ride the lift to the sixty-fourth floor.

'Mm,' I say with sleepy eyes. 'It's almost four in the morning UAE time.'

'I know,' he whispers into my temple. 'I've been crossing that time barrier for three weeks.' He kisses my scalp. 'Are you hungry? Amy made extra dinner just in case. You should try to eat something.'

'No, thank you, sleep sounds much more appealing.'

He gestures for me to step into his apartment then follows, carrying in my suitcase. I stand for a minute, looking around the large, open-plan lounge, and give myself a moment to take everything in. The heated, dark wood floor, the expanse of windows overlooking London's twinkling skyline. The luxurious monochrome furniture and the abstract art on the walls that I used to think screamed *bachelor*. Now, I think it all screams Gregory. Gregory's home. *Our* home.

I don't let myself look at that spot on the floor that tries to draw me in. The spot where blood once pooled in the aftermath of my fatal shot.

'Would you like a drink?' he asks from the ultramodern, open kitchen area at one end of the lounge.

I focus on Gregory instead. 'No, thank you.'

'Just bed?'

I offer him an apologetic smile. 'Please.'

'Okay, let's get you upstairs.'

He lifts my suitcase upstairs and I follow, watching his back move beneath his white T-shirt, his arse flexing under his indigo jeans. *All mine.*

As we walk the landing towards our bedroom at the far end, Gregory slips the luggage into a spare room. 'I'll have Amy take care of that in the morning.'

'Thank you.'

'Oh, dear, we aren't getting much out of you tonight, are we?'

I shake my head. 'Sleepy.'

He chuckles. 'I know, baby. Before you shower, I want to show you something.' He takes my hand and stops outside another white door. 'This is your welcome home gift.'

He pushes open the door and when we step inside, he hits a switch, making ceiling spotlights illuminate the space. Turning on the spot, not knowing where to look first, my mouth falls open.

The double bed that used to be in here is gone. The space has been completely transformed. The walls are lined with mahogany, open-door wardrobes. All my clothes, other than the small stash still in my suitcase, have been hung under strategically placed lights. Short dresses. Long dresses. Trousers. Jackets. Each item of clothing has its own specific spot. Around the floor, a low-level shelf hosts my shoes, the pairs positioned just so. Four padded stools forming a square in the middle of the room and I kneel on them to peer into a glass-topped chest.

'My jewellery.'

Drawers in one corner are the only section of the wardrobe not on display. I assume my lingerie is in there.

On a dressing table beneath the window, I see Gregory's smiling reflection, where he's leaning against the doorframe.

'Do you like it?'

'Gregory, it's amazing. Thank you so much.'

'You're more than welcome, angel. Amy's already started to pack you some things for St Lucia. I didn't think you'd have much time, so I had Julia and Lucas send over new holiday clothes from Harrods. But I know how stubborn you get about your clothes, so let Amy know if you want to add anything else. I can arrange for different stuff from Julia and Lucas, too.'

Shaking my head, I go to him and run my fingers through his hair. 'How long are you going to be on your best behaviour?'

'I just want everything to be perfect for you.'

'Everything *is* perfect, Gregory. It's perfect because I'm here with you.'

After showering, I slip into a plum silk nightdress. Gregory is taking a call in his office, presumably to somewhere in a different time zone, so I tuck my tired limbs under the duvet and sink into his... *our* mattress. Amy has changed the sheets and although I miss his smell, the fresh linen scent on the Egyptian cotton is incredibly homey. Reaching for the remote, I switch the room to darkness and smile to myself. I'm here, in *our* bed, in *our* home.

I'm semi-comatose when Gregory's weight leans onto the bed next to me. He lifts the covers and wraps his body around mine, pulling me back into him, cupping my thighs and knees with his own. He trails a finger lightly up, down, across my arm and nuzzles into my neck.

'Welcome home, baby.' He continues to swirl his finger. 'I'm going to remind you every single day how much I love you.' He inhales deeply at my neck, then kisses the skin beneath my lobe. 'Always.'

* * *

'Your latte.'

Margaret hands over the blue cardboard cup then adjusts her glasses on the bridge of her nose.

'Thank you.'

'And here's your paper mail.' She gives me a stack of documents, already opened and sorted. 'Only the top three need to be actioned. Pop the others in your filing tray when you've looked at them and I'll scan them into files for you. Oh, and there's one more thing.'

She totters out of my office in her nude kitten heels, skirt swishing as she walks.

I'm sifting through last night's emails when a mass of bright white enters my peripheral vision. An absolutely gargantuan bouquet of flowers shields Margaret from my view, her head poking around one side to see where she's headed.

'These came for you not long ago.'

She places them down on my desk with an expectant look on her face. Rising from my chair to appreciate the bouquet in its full glory, I take the small red envelope and slip out the card.

I'm going to remind you every day how much I love you.
    Always. G x

Beaming, I breathe in the mix of white roses, lilies, Queen Anne's lace, chrysanthemums and a heap of other beautiful white flowers I don't recognise but which smell divine.

'Looks like you had more than one reason to come home early,' Margaret says with a mischievous glint in her eye.

I try not to confirm that she's hit on the *biggest* reason I wanted to come home, but I'm pretty sure my face is a dead giveaway because she's practically singing, 'Young love.'

Rolling my eyes, I move my flowers to the window ledge. 'We need to discuss my schedule, Margaret. I'm going to have a lot to juggle before I leave for St Lucia. I still have work to do for Mr Ghurair and Mr Ryans has sent across a new deal for one of his companies, Constant Sources. I'll be taking my phone and laptop on leave with me, so it's not a complete shutdown for two weeks, but I will be trying to work as little as possible whilst I'm away.'

'Well, luckily you were never supposed to be in the UK so you don't have any face-to-face meetings planned. You do have a couple of conference calls but they appear to be catch-ups more than anything, so I've already looked at times to rearrange for when you return.'

She comes round to my side of the desk, standing over my shoulder and I open the Outlook calendar to my screen. 'Who are they with?'

'Hugo Delaney of DDI International a week today.'

'Ah, yes, his father's retiring and Hugo is replacing him on the board of DDI. That can wait; I just want to make sure he knows who I am.'

'The other was Spencer Cromwell.'

'MD of Charleston Beverages. Hmm, I would prefer not to rearrange that one, actually; he won't take too kindly. When is it supposed to be?'

'Monday at twelve.'

'GMT?'

Margaret nods and moves my mouse to locate the appointment in my calendar.

'Let's keep that one.'

'Of course. Mr Ryans would like to schedule a negotiation meeting at his offices before you fly out. He's asked for tonight or tomorrow morning.'

'I can't do today; I have to draft a due diligence report for Mr Ghurair's final deal. Could you speak to his PA and arrange something for late afternoon or evening tomorrow?'

'Absolutely. Is there anything else?'

'Not just now. Thanks, Margaret.'

As she exits, Amanda swoops into the room in a

fitted, electric-blue dress that shows her growing bump, her red hair bouncing and thick, her skin truly glowing.

'Look at you!'

She rubs her tummy and her eyes fill with affection. 'Well, I don't have to hide my little princess any more.'

'Princess?'

'Meh, today, she's a she.'

I giggle as she flicks a hand flippantly through the air.

'I take it you've told Neil then?'

'Just. I figured he's so pissed at you over coming back from Dubai and going on leave that he won't care so much about me being pregnant.'

'What are friends for if you can't use their grave to dance on?'

'Exactly what I thought,' she says. 'I am *so* excited for St Lucia. My out-of-office reply is already turned on.'

'For Thursday?'

'No, silly. I have a half-day today and I'm off tomorrow, too. Packing time. When are you finishing?'

'About five hours before the flight?'

'You're insane.'

'Insane I may be but I'm trying to keep Neil and

Mr Ghurair happy and pick up a new deal for Gregory.'

'How is the neurotic arsehole?'

I cock my head to one side. 'Amanda, could you not, please?'

'Listen, I'm the one who had to see what he did to you, when you were together and when you were apart. I can drop *neurotic* if you like but he's still an arsehole.'

'You don't know what happened. Not everything.'

'Yes, well, I know all I need to know. If he wants my trust, he can earn it.'

There's an unlikely happening.

'Do you at least think the pair of you can be civil in St Lucia? For my sake, and for Sandy and Jackson. It is their wedding, let's not forget.'

'I'll behave if he does.'

I roll my eyes as she turns on her velvet stilettos and leaves.

9

Amy has packed; what she's packed for me is anyone's guess. Julia and Lucas from Harrods have apparently made sure I have the complete holiday wardrobe and all travel arrangements are taken care of. I've sent the due diligence report to Mr Ghurair and a list of additional enquiries to the other side, which means I should have bought myself a hassle-free week on that deal whilst they find the answers.

I take a final swig from the lukewarm coffee on my desk and shut down my computer.

'Margaret, I'm heading to the negotiation meeting at GJR's offices. Is my cab ready?'

'It's outside. Mr Ryans arranged it. Should I set your out-of-office reply?'

'Not yet, I'll be back in the office late tonight to finalise the details of this negotiation before I fly out in the morning.'

'Well, have a wonderful time, won't you?'

'I'll do my best. Remember, if you need me—'

'I know, I know, you have your phone. I won't be calling you unless I absolutely have to.'

I smile. 'Thanks, Margaret. You're a star.'

As I ride the lift to the ground floor, I check my make-up and adjust my black pencil dress.

When I step into the street, London's brisk air strikes me even harder than usual after the heat of Dubai and I pull my coat closed at the chest.

Kenneth – replacement Jackson whilst he's on leave – is waiting for me. I cast my handbag and laptop case onto the back seat of Gregory's Mercedes and slip inside. Kenneth closes the door behind me; he's either started to get this or Gregory has had a word about procedure. Something tells me the latter is more likely.

I flick through the information a trainee managed to pull together for me on the game Gregory wants Constant Sources to acquire. I can't personally see what all the fuss is about. In *substance, Black Diamonds looks* like other games I've seen before. A robber in jailhouse stripes runs across the bottom of the screen, occasionally jumping over traps set to catch him and avoiding the batons of red-faced, raging policemen. Meanwhile, black diamonds fall from the sky when buildings miraculously get blown up. The robber must catch the falling diamonds in a shopping trolley-type thing. My trainee tells me it's great but I translate that to mean he enjoyed playing on it all afternoon then calling it research and billing his time to GJR.

One thing that's undeniable however, is that mind-numbing though it may seem to me, this game's download figures are already showing big promise. The creator is a guy in his late teens, Stuart Culliton. He's new on the scene but there are one or two articles online, marvelling at his age, questioning whether he could be the next Mark Zuckerberg. I'm interested to meet him.

'Thanks, Kenneth,' I say as I step onto the pavement outside my dark knight's glass tower.

I ride the lift to the highest floor for Gregory's office block. When the doors open, I'm confronted by a young, slim man dressed in cleaning uniform. I recognise him from somewhere but I can't place him. As I move out of the lift and passed him, I do a double take, my mind struggling to connect the dots.

Then he beams at me. 'Scarlett.'

'Paul?' I'm used to seeing him sitting on the pavement outside my office block, pale and shaky, but now he has colour in his cheeks. His eyes have more life and his hair is clean. 'What? How?'

'I've been hoping for weeks that I'd see you again, so I can say thank you.'

'Thank me for what?'

'Asking Mr Ryans to give me a job.'

'He— Gregory employed you?'

He nods, his cheeks flush. 'You didn't know?'

'No. I— When?'

'Six weeks, four days ago.' He plants his mop in his red bucket and leans on the stem with pride. 'He sought me out, in the shelter. I knew his face from when he dropped you off at your office and that morning he was looking for you.'

Oh, yes, I remember, when you gave up my hideout. 'I suppose I can forgive you for that.'

He smiles. 'He told me he was doing it for you. He took me on. It's like a dream. No one ever gets a job from the streets. He gave me an advance on my wages so I could rent a room, said I have to earn it back, of course, but it covered my rent for six months and left some over. I won't let him down. I won't let either of you down, I promise.'

'I don't know what to say, Paul. I'm pleased for you. Really, really, pleased for you. You look well.'

He shrugs, bashful. 'Might pay my soup angel a visit now that I'm getting back on my feet.'

He used to tell me about a woman who served him in the soup kitchen. He swore she was giving him *the eye* and he called her his soup angel. 'I think you should. Listen, I've got to go but it's lovely to see you. And, Paul, don't stick to this for Gregory and me; do this for yourself.'

He nods and gives me a soft, proud smile that makes my entire body warm.

I pass Sue at reception and walk with purpose straight into Gregory's office. He lifts his head and stands as I cast my bags and documents onto one of the sofas. As soon as he steps out from behind his desk, I throw myself at him, hands locking into his hair, mouth crashing roughly against his.

'What have I done to deserve that reaction?'

'You, Gregory Ryans, are quite simply wonderful. That kiss was because I just passed Paul in the corridor. Thank you. What you've done for him is incredible. You've put your faith in him.'

He strokes a hair from my brow behind my ear in that way he does. 'No, baby, I put my faith in you.'

I lunge again, taking his mouth and twisting my tongue around his until he matches my pace and pulls me into him. We're both panting when we separate. 'That one was for the flowers.'

He drops his forehead to mine. 'You're more than welcome.'

'Erm, sorry, sir.' Sue clears her throat in the doorway. 'I'll close this for you.'

'Do so,' he says, turning my chin back to face him, his complete attention focused on only me. 'I wish I could take you home to my bed right now.'

Closing my eyes, I try to push those thoughts away. 'Me too but we've got work to do.'

He bites the tip of my nose. 'We have.'

We settle onto the two leather sofas in his office and a blushing Sue brings through coffee, setting out the pot and two saucers on the table between us. I offer her an apologetic smile, both because she walked into our embarrassing PDA moment, and because I remember she has a crush on my man.

After a chat through the background information on *Black Diamonds,* Gregory fills me in on what Tim and Jean-Paul have pulled together for Constant Sources. Gregory doesn't want to keep *Black Diamonds* available for gaming; he wants to buy it and take it off the market to stop it from putting a dent in the profits of *his* game, *Jail Run.* Tim, Jean-Paul and Williams have all looked over the finances. *Black Diamonds* is still in its infancy but if it continues on the current projections, it could take 50 per cent of *Jail Run*'s profit in twelve months.

'Is it so similar to your game that there could be an intellectual property claim?'

He twists one side of his mouth and shifts his head. 'Not similar enough. It's a popular concept. It's just a case of having the best.' He leans back into his sofa, spreading an arm across the back of the leather seat. 'It's pretty amazing though, what this kid's done. I mean, he's nineteen and from what I can tell from digging, this is his first venture.'

'Very entrepreneurial.'

'Indeed, but I wonder whether he's just the face of the game, to give it a story. The way he's got the game on the market and selling, it's like he's had support from someone experienced.'

'Or a case of first time lucky.'

'Possibly.' He glances at his Omega. 'Right. It's five to seven. They'll be here any minute. Let's get this done, then I can take you home and fuck you until you scream my name into tomorrow.'

I gasp, then he winks at me and I laugh, hard. 'I'm going to call your bluff on that, Mr Ryans.'

'I sincerely hope you do.'

Sue's voice comes over the intercom on Gregory's desk. 'Your 7 p.m. has arrived, sir.'

'Showtime, lady.' He stands and fastens one button of his blazer then lifts his head and corrects his silk tie.

'I like you in a three piece,' I confess, straightening my dress.

'I like you naked.'

Despite myself, I smirk. 'Gregory, that's not professional.'

'Apologies, Legal Counsel. I also like you in that tight little black dress. I like thinking about how I can take you out of it.'

'Game face, Ryans.'

'Sorry.' His lips straighten.

'Better. Now, before we go in there, I want to know your tactics.'

'Don't worry about my tactics, Scarlett; this is what I do.'

'I do worry, Gregory. This product might be selling now but as far as I can tell, there's no registered intellectual property in the game. If you intend to buy it and take it off the market, there's not much protecting you. If someone brings a replica to market, you could be right back to where you are now.'

'All right, all right. I get it. I'm going in at five hundred thousand.'

I contemplate that figure. *Seems reasonable.* 'And your upper limit?'

He leans his head to one side with a look that tells me I'm not going to find out the answer to that question. He holds open the door to the office for me. 'You'll know if I reach it.'

I grit my teeth. 'Good to know we're a team here.'

We make our way to the boardroom on twenty-seven. 'This one is bigger and more intimidating,' Gregory explains.

'You made me pitch in there the first time I came here.'

'I'm fully aware. How you handled that room told me everything I needed to know about how you'd handle other things.'

There's a sparkle in those dark eyes that tells me he isn't talking about business.

In the boardroom, we make introductions. Stuart and his legal counsel are sitting at the far end of the large board table. Stuart looks even younger than his age would suggest, almost drowned in his surroundings. His hair is almost black and ruffled. His eyes are a dark, deep brown. Striking. There's something about them, something I can't put my finger on, as I shake his hand. I watch him sit back in his chair and cross the ankle of one leg over the knee of the other. He's arrogant in a too familiar way. But when Gregory takes a seat opposite him, Stuart uncrosses his legs and his cocksure posture folds back to young boy as he sips from a glass of fresh orange. The legal counsel, Markus, is tall. His slim shoulders are hunched forward, a little potbelly resting over his belt. There's something reserved in his manner. Introverted, maybe. He *looks* like he'd specialise in IT and IP law.

Markus kicks us off. 'Stuart, why don't you share some background about *Black Diamonds*. I'm sure Mr Ryans will be impressed with the figures, to say the least.'

Stuart opens his mouth to speak but Gregory holds up a flat palm. 'No need, gents. I've done my homework. Let's just get to it. I'm going to make you an outstanding offer for *Black Diamonds*. Given the product is still very much in phase one of the marketing cycle, it really hasn't proved much worth. Do you know the percentage of start-ups in the gaming sector that fail in the first twelve months, Stuart?'

Stuart shakes his head and takes another sip of his juice. Nervous, I think. Gregory can be intimidating at the best of times but tonight, he's in full throttle.

'Over 80 per cent. That's full engine failure, complete crash and burn. And here's the thing, Stuart: young entrepreneurs like you throw everything you have, financially, physically, emotionally, into making a success of your venture. What that means, is your crash and burn stands to leave you grovelling to Mummy and Daddy or lining the streets with fellow failed entrepreneurs.'

Jesus, Gregory, calm down.

I wait for to see the timid reaction of the boy being talked but I'm surprised to watch him lean forward towards his counterpart.

'You're mistaken, *Gregory*.' Stuart spits his words in a thick Zimbabwean accent. He has a temper, though unsurprising given the tone of this meeting. 'I never met my parents and I have no intention of ending up on the streets, so this game will continue to be a success and I'll be one of the two in ten businesses that *don't* fail.'

I wait for Gregory's retort but it doesn't come. He leans back in his seat, hands forming a steeple. If I didn't know better, I'd say Stuart just struck a chord with the mighty CEO.

'Tell me, Stuart, what is it that will make *you* successful?'

The teen straightens his back but seems uncertain again. '*Black Diamonds* is unique.'

'Bullshit,' Gregory snaps. 'If you're looking to set your stall out, don't start with your weakness and pretend it's a strength. Lay your weakness on the table. Get it out there so your opposition can't use it against you but don't lie about it.'

He's giving him advice now? Aggressively dished out but advice nonetheless.

'You don't have a unique product. *Black Diamonds* is a knock-off of my own *Jail Run*, not to mention successful games produced by ten other well-known companies.'

'Is that right?'

I watch Stuart with wide eyes. He's either unable or unwilling to back down.

'Then tell me why in my first three months of trading, I've had hundreds of thousands of downloads and why I'm eating into your profit?'

Gregory unbuttons his jacket as if he's nonplussed but I don't think that's the case at all. 'You don't have a workable business model. You can't build and sustain a company on one game. What happens when people get bored, when technology moves on and your app loses functionality or users complete the game and go looking for the next? You fail. You don't have a marketing plan. You don't have financial backing.'

'How would you know that?'

'I have ways and means, Stuart, and I have those ways and means because I *do* have a sound business plan. I have money enough to look into a child playing from his bedroom at being a businessman. So, here's my offer. I'll give you five hundred thousand pounds tonight. I'll take your game and do as I please with it.'

'Half a million?'

'Half a million pounds to create a platform that allows you to grow.' Gregory relaxes into his seat beside me but my eyes are on Markus, my counterpart. No lawyer worth their salt would let their client take the first offer.

Sure enough, Markus leans into Stuart's ear and Stuart confirms, 'No deal.'

Gregory cocks his head to one side and smiles, then pours himself a glass of water before resuming his cross-legged position. I watch his reflection in the windows. His body moving against the indigo sky and city lights as he sips the water, strategically dramatic in the silent room, eyes fixed on Stuart. He replaces the water glass on the table then shuffles his leather chair back just enough to say, *We're done here.*

Or so I think.

'One million, and that's my final offer.'

He looks straight ahead at Stuart, who is somewhere between gobsmacked and smug. I have to dig my nails into my palms. This is Gregory's show; I'm just his lawyer. I've given him my advice and I need to keep my cool. But doubling the offer, what is he thinking?

More mumblings pass between Stuart and Markus. 'My client and I need to discuss your offer. May we take five minutes outside?'

'By all means,' Gregory says, his tone almost bored.

Once the door clicks shut, I whip around to face him. 'Are you kidding me? One *million*? That's insane.'

'Actually, Scarlett, it's not. The kid's got something and I stand to lose a lot more than one million if he succeeds in line with projections or if a bigger company takes *Black Diamonds* from him and gives it the right kind of support.'

'Even so, you doubled your offer, Gregory. That tells him your first offer was a joke and your second offer probably was, too.'

'Seriously, Scarlett, you're going to tell me how to conduct a business negotiation?'

'I'm going to tell you how *not* to conduct it.'

'Scarlett, this is my world. This is what I do.'

'You could have fooled me!' I rise and walk to the window, feigning looking out to the towers and twinkling lights but watching him regard me through the reflection, his smug smile frankly pissing me off.

He scoffs like I'm a kid taking a tantrum and *that*

pisses me off even more. 'I'm intrigued by the kid. I want to see where this goes.'

I do a one-eighty, arms folded across my chest. 'And you're willing to blow one million pounds to find out?'

'It's small fry. If it doesn't work out, it's an expensive mistake, but I didn't get where I am today because I shy away from risk.'

You shied away from one risk for long enough.

I'm glaring at him as the door opens, adding to my temper by forcing me to fake a smile.

Standing, I can appreciate just how un-lawyer-like Markus looks, with his unkempt appearance and all-round general manner and poise. He starts to speak before his arse even hits the chair. 'My client believes his product is worth more than one million.'

I bite down so hard on my gums, my mouth tastes metallic. Gregory raises one hand to his chin and I know he's going to make another offer.

I can't let him. I won't. 'It's a shame your client doesn't seem capable of speaking for himself, Markus,' I say. 'If he could, he might be able to justify to my client why in God's name this technically basic game that's similar to a lot of games already on the market and that has almost non-existent IP protection is worth even half a million pounds, let alone more.' I turn my attention to Stuart. 'Do you understand the real reason Constant Sources wants to buy your game? We want to remove your game from the market. Not because it's worth money now, but for the off chance that a company with enough time and energy might buy it and turn it into something more. Specifically, a company who knows how and has the money to protect the rights in the game properly. As a piece of technology, your game is practically worthless. But with no registered intellectual property portfolio, *Black Diamonds* could be recreated if it fell into the wrong hands. And do you know what you could do about that? Nothing. Unless you have a bottomless pit of money to step into a ring with wealthy businessmen, you can do absolutely nothing. Has your lawyer told you that?'

'My client doesn't need this,' Markus says, coming to stand. 'We'll find a new buyer. Come on Stuart, let's go.'

'Yes, of course, you'll find a new buyer,' I say with sarcasm that should be aimed at my unhinged boyfriend. 'Let me tell you how that goes. You sit around a table like this for hours, again, and the person you sit across the table from will know your offering is built on sand. That your international intellectual property portfolio is non-existent. So, let's say that person offers you half of what my client is offering and you accept because you've realised, *finally*, that your offering isn't as valuable as you'd thought. My client will go to your buyer and buy the game from him for *ten* million pounds. So, your buyer wins two times and you have half of what you have on the table right now.'

'Stuart, let's go,' Markus urges, eye-balling me as if I give a damn.

Stuart leans back in his chair. 'Wait, I need to think.'

I shuffle in my seat so that I'm looking right at him and in the most nurturing voice I can conjure, I reason with him, the final, gentle nudge across the line. 'Look, Stuart, your greatest asset right now is your mind. You can create something better than this game and with one million pounds, you could have the time and resources to do exactly that. Can I be honest with you?'

He nods.

'I advised against Constant Sources making this deal at all. In my view, the risk is just too high; I can't see beyond your not having registered your rights in the game. Now it's after eight at night and I'm wondering whether you want to sell this game at all. If you don't, that's fine. I'll gladly see my client walk away from this deal but I can promise you one thing: the offer on the table will not increase and you won't get a better offer elsewhere.'

I take the sale agreement out of my document folder and write *one million pounds* into the commercial schedule then rest my pen on top of the contract and slide it across the table.

'Take the deal, Stuart.'

He looks to his lawyer, who nods without a word.

Stuart takes the pen and turns it in his fingers.

'I had a figure in mind when I came into this room,' he says. 'You haven't met it.'

Gregory sits forward, resting his forearms on the table. 'Stuart, my lawyer has told me to walk away at one million.' He casts an eye to me and beneath his business façade, I can tell he's pissed that I've trampled his negotiation. 'I will walk away. But first, let me put something else on the table for you. You can take one million; that's my top offer. Or, you can take seven hundred and fifty thousand and come to work for me. At Constant Sources, from this office in London.' He leans back and re-crosses his legs. 'I think you've got something, a hunger in your eyes, business in your mind, and I like that. I also think that, with guidance, you could be a solid creator. You're nineteen; take this opportunity and come to me whilst you work out which you are: an entrepreneur or a designer.'

Stuart's entire body visibly softens and his eyes widen.

'I was once in your position, stuck between wanting to create something and making money. Making money was the right path for me but I had to find out the hard way. I'm offering you a chance to take five years to earn some money and make that decision in a risk-free environment. If in five years you want to set up on your own, great, you'll have the world at your feet with a good CV in your pocket.'

'I'd like to think about it,' Stuart says, his voice catching in his throat.

Gregory shakes his head. 'That isn't part of the offer. Sign now or walk away.'

The pair stare at one another for seconds that feel much longer. There's something in the air between them. Admiration? Mutual respect?

Eventually, and as his lawyer looks on, Stuart says, 'Where do I sign?'

* * *

Once the documents are signed, handshakes are exchanged and I show Stuart and Markus to the lifts. I watch as the numbers descend, 27, 26, 25, 24, delaying

Gregory's inevitable wrath. I stole his show and now there'll be some well-earned fireworks.

I take another lift to the twenty-eighth floor and reluctantly walk, contract in hand, to Gregory's office. He's standing by the window, shoulders back, hips slightly forward, calves taut in his tailored trousers. He's braced for war. With a deep breath, I step into my lion's den.

He keeps his back to me but watches me through the window, jaw tense. At first, he doesn't speak. I know how hard he's trying to control his temper. Then he snaps. 'What the hell did you think you were doing?'

I sigh. 'Gregory, it's eleven-thirty, I'm already tired and I have to finalise this deal; can we talk about this later?'

'We'll talk about it now!' His South African twang is stronger than ever.

I consider apologising and walking away but I know I was right. Instead, I fold my arms across my chest and stand tall in my heels. 'Fine. Talk.'

'You had no right jumping in like that.'

'Oh, really, I had no right? I was stopping you from making a bigger mistake than the one-million-pound mistake you were already making! You were about to offer him more, and for what?'

'You could have lost us the deal.'

'And if I had, I wouldn't be sorry. That deal is high risk and my advice to walk away was sound.'

He takes two steps towards me. The sinews of his neck are stretched tight beneath his late-day stubble. *Christ, he's sexy.*

'To succeed in business, you have to take risks.'

I take one step forward.

'I'm not opposed to taking *reasoned* commercial risks, Gregory, but I can't advise a client to take non-sensical risks.'

'*Advise*, Scarlett. Exactly. That's what I pay you to do. I pay you to advise me of the legal risks but it's my decision, *mine*, whether to accept that advice or to take the risk.'

I move another step forward until only inches of air separate us.

'That's where you're wrong. You're not my client. Constant Sources is my client for this gig and I'm here to act in the best interests of the company, not yours, or those of your overly endowed ego.'

He bends until I can feel his hot breath on my face.

'I *am* Constant Sources. I *am* the GJR group. *I* decide who you do or don't work for.'

'No. *I* decide who I work for and if you don't like

the way I work, I'll close this deal and you don't have to hear my legal advice again.'

'Fine.'

'*Fine.*'

I stare into his eyes, heart jackhammering with fury. I won't back down because I'm right. I'll stare and stare into those big. Brown. Captivating eyes.

Like a pouncing South African cat hungry for its prey, his lips are on mine, fast and ferocious. He pulls up my dress and lifts my legs around his waist.

I want him. My mind tells me. My body shows me. My nipples harden, craving his contact. My bud swells, crying out for him to take me.

I ball my fists in his hair as he carries me to the sofa, his mouth continuing his wild attack.

'I'm going to fuck you. Hard. Because you deserve it.' His words are husky, laced with desperation.

'Gregory, I need to complete the deal,' I say through ragged breaths, already knowing I'll relent.

'Not now.' His teeth clamp down on my neck. 'Your client is a dick anyway.'

I pull my head back from his. 'Too true,' I say, with a smug grin.

He sinks me back against the sofa and forces my legs further apart as he moves between them. He sits back, leaving me bereft, then stretches the thin lace of my knickers with both hands until he can puncture the material with his thumbs and he tears it away from my aching sex.

He leans down, roughly retaking my mouth, twisting his tongue with mine, pulling my lip harshly in his teeth as he cups my breasts through my dress. My hips rise to push against his erection, forcing a growl from his chest. He moves his hand from my breast to thrust two fingers into me, teasing my swollen insides.

'Gregory.' His name leaves my mouth on a pant. His fingers withdraw, then they're in my mouth and I suck my own wetness from him.

He moves quickly, sitting back on his heels and freeing his hard shaft from his trousers and boxers. 'Turn over.' His words are dripping in sex.

I do as I'm told, turning to kneel on all fours, bracing my body with my hands on the arm of the sofa. With one foot on the floor, one knee on the sofa, he rams himself deep inside me, making me cry out. With his hands on my hips, he holds himself buried inside me.

'Please, Gregory.'

'Please what?'

'Fuck me.'

He moves out and in slowly, then quicker and

faster again, until he's rousing me to the brink of a powerful orgasm. He keeps one hand on my hips, bracing himself and making sure he can crash into me, hard, like he promised. The other hand moves to my clit and sends my pulsing muscles into spasm as he swirls with his finger and continues to drive into me from behind.

'Jesus!' he barks.

His hoarse voice is the final push I need. As his rhythms speed up, back and front, he shows me who's boss.

Both hands move back to my hips and with two more gruelling thrusts, he releases into me.

10

My phone rings for the second time in as many minutes. Amanda's face dances across the screen to her designated Sabrina Carpenter ringtone.

'It's holidaaaaaay tiiime,' she screams through the handset.

'I'll be two minutes. I need to finish something.'

'What are you doing? Give it to a trainee or something.'

'I'm finalising a plan to register the international intellectual property portfolio of—'

'Urgh, forget it, I don't care. Just hurry up!'

'I'd be much quicker if you left me alone.' I giggle despite myself. 'Is Gregory with you?'

'No, it's just Ed and me; we're in the car outside. The driver's pissed, too. Says he's on double yellows.'

I look skyward. 'Jackson wouldn't behave like that.'

'But Jackson is on holidaaaaaay!'

I grin, because not only is Jackson on holiday, he's in St Lucia, preparing for his wedding to my favourite woman, friend and stand-in mum. 'Okay. I'm coming. Two minutes. But where is Greg—'

The line goes dead.

I drink the last mouthful of latte from the take-away cup on my desk and click send on my email of instructions to the associate I've asked to manage our foreign counsel whilst I'm away. Despite being tired from my all-nighter, I smile as my computer shuts down for two whole weeks. Two whole weeks of a dev-astatingly sexy CEO.

I wanted so much to go home with him after our showdown on the sofa in his office but I had Kenneth drop me back at Saunders, knowing I'd be leaving from here to go direct to the airport. It's been a long night but the plan to register the intellectual property rights in *Black Diamonds* is set in Europe, China, the US and Australia, then the rest of the world. Once that's done, Gregory and Constant Sources can develop the game and keep it on the market, or they can box it, but one thing's for sure, his company profits will be safe now and, on reflection and after a good tension-busting shag, maybe seven hundred and fifty thousand wasn't too high a price for the benefits Constant Sources could reap. *Not that I'll be letting Mr Arrogant know that.*

I fasten the button of my damson blazer over my dress and pull on my grey mac, releasing my hair across my shoulders. It's soft and a little wavy after the rush job I made of showering and drying my hair in the firm's facilities a couple of hours ago but at least I'm clean.

Not having packed myself or watched my suitcase being lugged into a car to go to the airport is making me slightly anxious. I don't know how Gregory delegates all these things. I really hope Amy didn't forget anything. A little flutter of excitement comes over me. Lots of people who love Sandy and Jackson in one place to witness their marriage. *Eek!*

Before I leave, I hand a manuscript amended document to Margaret in the secretary's station.

'Aren't you supposed to be at the airport by now?'

I glance at my watch: 9.17.

'Seventeen minutes ago. This is the last thing. Please would you make these changes then save the document to the Constant Sources file and email it to Hugh? He'll be managing things whilst I'm away but if you get the faintest scent that he's in over his head, please call me. I'll have my phone—'

'Scarlett, go, now!'

'Okay, I'm going. But call me if—'

'I'm not calling you, Scarlett. Go!'

* * *

A black stretch-limousine, freshly polished for the occasion, waits outside the revolving doors. A grouchy-looking, muscular man who's making a really poor show of wearing a black suit, white shirt and black tie steps out of the driver side.

'Miss Heath,' he grumbles with a dip of his head.

'Hi, erm?'

'Scott.'

'Nice to meet you, Scott. Sorry for the delay. Where's Kenneth?'

Scott moves to the back door of the limousine. 'He's driving Mr Ryans to the airport.'

'Gregory isn't coming with us?'

'No.'

Feeling like I've exhausted Scott's desire to converse, I take a deep breath and prepare myself for the giddiness inside the car.

'Finallyyyyyy!' Amanda leaps from the limousine

and wraps her arms tightly around my neck. 'Hurry up and get inside; I'll get hives from being too close to the office.'

Amanda looks a million dollars, as ever. Her long, flowing, striped maxi seems out of place for the beginning of February in England but less so than the oversized floppy hat that she repositions on her head as she sits back into the black leather of the limo.

'Here,' she says, shuffling a weekend bag my way. 'I think it's stuff for you to change into on the plane.' I peek inside the bag to see material in summer colours and Harrods tags poking through tissue paper.

Julia and Lucas, my knights in Jimmy Choos.

Williams drops a kiss to my cheek as he hands me a glass of champagne. 'Not a replacement for sleep but you could probably use this.'

'Pol Roger,' I confirm after the first sip. 'Where's Gregory?'

'He had things to do. Work, I think he said. He didn't really give me any details.'

'That sounds like Gregory.'

Williams gulps his fizz as if each mouthful isn't worth a small fortune. 'You know what he's like. He's as bad as you at switching off.'

I'd retort with a quip but I know he's right. Gregory and I were, in some respects, cut from the same cloth.

We drive past the Royal Courts of Justice, along Strand, then Fleet Street and out towards London City Airport. By the time my glass of champagne has settled on my empty stomach and tired head, I finally start to relax.

Amanda holds out her empty glass for Williams to fill with sparkling elderflower water. 'Right, so tell me the plan.'

I lean my head back against the seat as Williams appeases her.

'We're flying out at ten-thirty. It'll take about nine hours to get to St Lucia.'

'Whoa, whoa, whoa, at ten-thirty? We're going to be late! If I miss this holiday, I swear I'll—'

'Relax,' says Williams. 'You can't really be late for a private jet.'

'A what?' Amanda's jaw hangs loose, her emerald eyes wide.

Williams and I share a laugh.

'Are we really going on a private jet?'

'Gregory doesn't take commercial flights,' Williams explains.

'Holy shit! Ha! Right, so we get to St Lucia today, late afternoon St Lucia time?'

Williams nods.

'Girls' night tonight, then the wedding is tomorrow

and we're all staying at the resort where Sandy and Jackson are now?'

I suspect Williams nods again but I'm resting my eyes.

'Then we have twelve days of St Lucia beach time. Fabulous!'

'Not exactly. We have one day on St Lucia after the wedding, then we're taking the jet to St Maarten.'

'Right. What's St Maarten?'

'Another island.'

'Is it nice?'

'Of course.'

'Why are we going there?'

'Because that's where the yacht is.'

'The what?'

'Gregory's yacht. It's anchored at St Maarten.'

'Holy shit! We're going on a yacht? Ha!'

We've just passed Canary Wharf and I'm struggling to stay awake when Scott's mobile rings and Gregory's voice comes over the limo speakers.

'Mr Ryans.'

'Scott, I'm at the airport and you aren't here.'

'We're on our way, Mr Ryans. We're coming past Blackwall station now.'

'Why are you late? Is there traffic?'

'No, sir. Miss... er... We had a delay before we left the city.'

'Make time.'

And then he's gone but my stomach is still turning like a seashell wind chime in a gale.

We finally pull onto the airport tarmac and Amanda bursts from the car before Scott can make it to the passenger door. Williams gestures for me to go next.

There he is. At the door of the GJR jet. Beige chinos hugging firm thighs, crisp white shirt unbuttoned by two. And when he sees me, his mouth twists into a knicker-melting smile.

Lord have mercy because I know I'm going to sin.

Amanda bounces up the steps, plants a fleeting and less than heartfelt kiss on Gregory's cheek, then runs inside the plane. Though they still don't see eye to eye, I'm sure the jet is easing her pain.

Scott hands over control of the luggage to a member of the jet crew, the same crew I met on our amazing night at the opera in Rome. I force from my mind thoughts of the day that followed, the pain of discovering Gregory's betrayal in sending me away.

Williams shakes Gregory's hand and says something that makes them both laugh. Then, unusually, the pair share what can only be described as a man hug – shoulders barging, fists thumping backs.

Meanwhile, my synapses have forgot how to send basic commands to my limbs.

'Have a nice holiday, Miss Heath,' Scott says, coming back to the limousine.

I should probably check for drool. 'Thanks, Scott.'

The engines roar to life, dragging my attention to the jet then back to the man who owns it, as he mouths, 'Get here.'

And when I reach him, all I can manage is, 'Hi.'

'Hi.'

I gaze into his eyes, tiredness heightening my hormones that are already raging. He presses his lips to my brow, then rests them on the soft tip of my nose. I breathe in his warm, familiar scent, then he lifts my chin with his index finger and places his lips on mine. I mould to the shape of his body as he pulls me into him, and though my heart is racing, I melt into his kiss.

'Get a room!' Amanda chimes.

Gregory steps back and drops his forehead to mine, muttering, 'We could have another murder charge on our hands if I have to spend two weeks in that woman's company.'

'Stow your Glock for a fortnight, Ryans.'

As soon as the captain announces we're at cruising altitude, we unfasten our seatbelts and the others make their way to three tall stools that are rooted to the floor around a small bar.

'Virgin Mary, sir?' the steward asks Gregory.

'Actually, Michael, let's make an exception to the rule. Somewhere in the world, it's after lunch already.'

'Bloody Mary, sir?'

'Sounds good.' Then he turns to me. 'Scarlett, Bloody Mary?'

'Not for me, thank you. I'm going to change into something more comfortable and I'm sorry to be a pooper but I really need to take a nap.'

'Noooo! Scarlett, it's holidaaaay tiiiime! These next two weeks, I task you to drink whenever I can't.' Amanda squees whilst patting her rounding tummy fondly.

'Amanda, if we're all going to get through this trip in harmony, you need to calm down,' I tell her.

'I'm just trying to make the most of my last child-free holiday.'

'By behaving like a child,' Gregory grumbles.

'All right, you two, play nice,' Williams says, pulling Amanda to his side as he perches his long, athletic legs onto a stool.

I shake my head. 'I'll be back.'

'There's sleepwear on your pillow, baby.'

My pillow? 'Naturally, I have my own pillow on your private jet.'

'High and fast,' he says with a smirk.

'I'm beginning to think that's your trademark, Mr Ryans.'

'Speaking of my intellectual property rights...'

I rush to him and nip his lips shut with my fingers. 'Please. I've been dealing with your intellectual property all night. Not now.' I drop a quick kiss to his cheek – smooth like he's recently shaved – and make my way through the curtains into the section of the jet that hosts four beds, each with its own set of red curtains to match the carpet.

On the last of the four, I find a black silk night shirt. Casting my blazer on the opposite bed, I close my eyes and creak my neck, then flip my long hair across one shoulder, struggling to locate the zip at the back of my dress. A strong arm wraps around my stomach, two luscious, full lips meet the naked flesh of my neck, and my zip is drawn teasingly down my back. I could sleep for an eternity but my mind still jumps immediately to lascivious thoughts of the man pressed against me and rolling his hardening length against my arse.

'I wanted to tuck you in,' he whispers into my ear.

'Tuck me in, or tuck into me?'

I feel his lips curl as he nibbles my lobe. 'The latter.' His mouth moves to my shoulder blade as he pushes my dress down my arms, letting it hang on my hips. 'But I'll be kind.' His tongue traces a lazy line up my vertebrae. 'I'll let you lay back and think of Scotland.'

'England. Lay back and think of England,' I say with a giggle.

'I love that sound. Never stop making that sound for me.'

'I'm going to have to.' I turn and press my chest into his, smirking. 'If you intend to take me on this jet, I'll need to be quiet.'

He drops his head to one side. 'Why, Miss Heath, if I didn't know better, I'd say the thought of getting caught turns you on.' As he moves his hand under my dress, pushing my thong aside and leisurely stroking my slick entrance, he says, 'In fact, I'd have to say it *definitely* turns you on.'

A muffled groan escapes me as he pushes his fingers into me, bending them, sweeping my sensitive wall.

'I'm going to make this quick, baby, then I'm going to let you sleep.'

'You're so thoughtful, Ryans.'

He tugs my lower back, pulling me against him, and grinds his pelvis as his fingers mirror the action against my insides. 'Thoughtful would be letting you sleep.'

I move my hand between us and cup his solid package over his chinos. 'No. That would be very *un*thoughtful.'

He pushes my dress to the floor, his eyes black and wild with hunger. Then he lifts my thighs to his hips and lays me back on the single bed: arse, back, head. I lick my lips with desire as he unbuttons his belt and chinos and slips out of his loafers. He crawls between my legs and pulls the curtain closed across the bed, feigning privacy. There's something about him being too eager to even take off his clothes, something about the fact we could be heard or caught out at any time, and there's *definitely* something about entering the Mile High Club on my boyfriend's jet.

11

Standing in the French doors of the balcony to Sandy's five-star suite, the warm afternoon Caribbean breeze blows in the stylist-perfected waves of my hair, kissing my skin where it's exposed in my purple dress.

Gregory surprised me but almost floored Sandy and Jackson by hiring the entire resort for the thirty-guest wedding.

The perfect white sand of the resort's private beach has been transformed into a most picturesque wedding set-up. Gregory's mum stepped in to make sure everything was just so and I have to hand it to her, everything looks perfect. From the four-post altar, strewn with white chiffon and decorated in all shades of white, purple and violet flowers, to the pillar bouquets lining the walkway. From the wooden chairs adorned with white satin cushions, to the woven beige flooring that creates an aisle. It's no less than Sandy deserves.

The door to the master bedroom opens and Sandy makes her way into the lounge. Her black hair has been partially pinned up with white flowers and her make-up professionally done.

'Are you ready for your dress, Mrs Jackson-to-be?' I ask.

She inhales sharply and slowly pushes an exhale through pursed lips.

I take hold of her hands. 'Sandy, this is you and Jackson. Forget everybody else.'

She nods tightly in a way that makes me want to hold her and stroke her hair the way she would reassure me as a child.

'Let's get that dress on.'

'I'm here, I'm here.' Amanda shuffles in a dress identical to mine but for hers being strapless and mine having thin straps that cross behind my back and meet the dress midway down my spine.

She hangs the wedding dress on a doorframe and unzips the bag, revealing Sandy's three-quarter-length, ivory dress. Amanda unbuttons the back of it and we lift the material carefully over Sandy's up-reached arms. Once she's fastened in, I help her into a lace shrug.

'One more thing.' I take a velvet box from the dressing-table drawer. 'Go ahead, open it.'

Tentatively, she peels back the lid to reveal a thin, platinum chain with a small diamond drop and matching earrings.

'They're actually your something borrowed. They're on loan. For now.' I turn her away from me to face a floor-length mirror and fasten the necklace around her soft mocha skin. 'Then they'll be a gift. A thank you for letting me do you the honour of giving you away. But I'll buy them when we get home. I don't think that's cheating, do you?'

Her eyes glaze. 'You really did grow into a very kind and special woman. Your dad would be so proud of you.'

'That's because of the woman who raised me.' I wrap my arms tightly around her waist and press my cheek against hers.

'Oh, Jesus, the pregnant lady can't cope with this.' Amanda wafts a tissue in the air theatrically. 'I'm going to head down and give you two a few minutes together. You're going to knock him dead, Sandy; you're stunning.' She pecks Sandy on the cheek and gives her a quick squeeze at the shoulders. 'And you look a million dollars,' she says, when she pulls the same move on me. 'I'll see you out there.'

'I'm glad we have a moment alone,' Sandy says when the door shuts behind Amanda. 'I want to tell you that I'm glad you and Gregory have worked things out. He makes you happy, that's plain to see, and let me tell you, that man adores every bone in your body, like you deserve.'

'Sandy—'

'Let me finish. I've watched you grow up to be a beautiful, clever, wonderful woman and I'm pleased now that we both have someone new to share things with and look forward to a new chapter with. Seeing you happy has been my goal for more than twenty years and I'm ready to let someone who deserves you take over that job. And you need to do the same for me, do you hear? I have Geoffrey to worry about me now. You need to have your own life and stop worrying about other people.'

'Sandy—'

She holds up a finger. 'A-ah, I'm not done. I know why you want to give me the money from your dad's house. It's because you're worried about what I'll do next. But look outside, Scarlett; I'm going to be *just* fine. And, I have a little news.'

I raise my brows.

'Geoffrey and me, we've decided we're going to try to adopt a baby.'

'What? Sandy, that's, oh my gosh, that's wonderful news.' I forget her hair, make-up and dress, and throw my arms around her.

She chuckles a hearty, chest-wobbling, Sandy laugh. 'You've always worried that I missed out. Well, I've never thought that. But Geoffrey and I would like to share a little someone together and we know we're far from spring chickens but we think we could make a little boy or girl a good home.'

My eyes fill as I tell her, 'Me, too. I'm not sure this day could get any better.'

'We'll see,' she says, holding my face in her palms.

I add the finishing touch to her outfit – white, crystal decorated, low-heeled Mary Janes – whilst she pops in her something-borrowed earrings.

'Ready?' I ask.

'Let's do it.'

'You look incredible.' It's true. In fact, she's never looked more beautiful.

We link our arms, each of us holding a lilac bouquet. The staff at the hotel have formed two lines and clap as we step out onto the wooden path across the white sand to the aisle. A steel band begins to play behind the small gathering of guests, now standing in rows, fifteen on each side of the aisle, enough to shield the groom and his best man from sight as we take the final steps towards Sandy's new life.

The band grows louder and for the first time today, I see the man I love. Gregory turns in his pale-grey suit and white shirt, open two buttons at the top, just the way he wears his shirts. A silk pocket handkerchief matching the colour of my dress rests in his jacket and that hair I like to tug is slicked back as he stands with his hands held together behind him. Jackson keeps his eyes on the female registrar, not looking at his bride until she arrives by his side. I hug Sandy, take her bouquet and move to where I can enjoy the view of her, ecstatically happy. Gregory shakes Jackson's hand, kisses Sandy on her cheek, and moves to a position opposite mine by Jackson's side.

The ceremony is beautiful. More than once, I look out over the glistening sea and think there's nowhere else I'd rather be. Definitely more than once, my eyes are drawn to the most mesmerising man I've ever known. And whilst I try to keep the thought at bay, more than once, I wonder how happy my dad would be to witness Sandy in love, getting married and about to bring up a child of her own.

*** *** ***

Dinner is served alfresco on the hotel veranda with all guests seated in a square, Sandy and Jackson central and blissfully happy. The whole event is luxurious – exquisite seafood, fine champagne, wonderful music – yet all very intimate and charming, all very much Sandy and Jackson.

Gregory's mum looks wonderful in a damson, floor-length dress. She's gone matchy-matchy with Gregory's stepfather, Lawrence, teaming his cream linen suit with a pink shirt.

We return to the table for speeches and toasts. I delight in Jackson's rare public displays of affection for Sandy, and through Gregory's easy-mannered speech for his bodyguard and close friend. Even Amanda rolls her eyes because I catch her smiling and laughing in all the right places as Gregory speaks.

He'll win you over, Amanda Darling, just you wait and see.

There's a break after the speeches to give the evening entertainment a chance to set up. The steel band strikes up again as the guests spread out around white rattan furniture on the beach.

'Can I take you for a stroll?' Gregory asks, holding out his hand.

He's taken off his blazer and now looks out-standing in just grey trousers, resting invitingly on his hips and across his pert arse. The combination of his thin, white shirt and champagne makes me think of where else I'd prefer to be with this man than on a public stroll.

Brushing it off, I slip my hand into his.

We amble barefoot and hand in hand along a de-serted section of the beach until the sound of music is replaced with only the gentle swooshing of waves and synthetic lights are replaced by the late setting sun. For once, there's no work, no crazed biological father drama, no Alzheimer's, no probate issues or trying to sell my childhood home; it's just us and the vastness of the Caribbean Sea.

As we pause to soak it in, a light wind causes my hair to tickle my bare back and a contented shiver kisses my body. Gregory stands behind me, wrapping me in his arms as we watch the gentle crash of the waves on the shoreline.

'Thank you for today, Gregory. This whole thing is wonderful. What you've done for Sandy and Jackson, flying everyone out here, paying for the wedding. You're amazing.'

He takes my hands to the small of his back, twisting me and pulling me to him. 'It's not just for them, Scarlett. I know how much you wanted Sandy to have the wedding she dreamed of.' He brushes my hair from my cheek and I lean into his palm as he speaks. 'You've saved my life, in more ways than one.' The sincerity in his gaze is magnetic. He's changed so much since we first met, at least with me. 'I feel reborn with you. Like I get a second chance to live and have everything I want.' He pecks my nose. '*Need*. And I want you to have everything you want, too.'

'I already have everything.'

'If there's ever anything that you want, just tell me. I mean, do you even want to work? You don't need to and I would never think any less of you. I'd happily have you as my plaything at home.'

'And let them call me your gold-digging girlfriend in the next *Times Rich List*?'

He doesn't laugh.

'I enjoy my job, Gregory. Being a lawyer is part of me and it's part of the person you fell in love with. I want her to stick around for you.'

'I had a feeling you'd say that,' he says with a mischievous grin.

'Why are you looking like that?' I pout, playfully raising one brow.

'I have two questions to ask you.'

My heart flutters in my chest. 'Go on.'

'Well, we make a good team, you and me. And I don't give your firm legal work, not really; I give *you* legal work.'

My heart rate returns to normal and I internally curse. *Of course he wasn't going to ask you* that.

'Are you listening?'

'Mm, yes, of course. We make a good team. Like Jekyll and Hyde.'

His lips curve. 'Something like that. So, I was thinking, why don't you move in-house? Come and work for me at GJR as my head legal advisor?'

'Work for you?'

'Ja.' He laughs nervously, his eyes searching for an answer.

I step back and nibble my bottom lip, turning slowly on the spot, the hem of my dress floating up from my thighs. 'That could be trouble.'

He looks to the sea across my shoulder and it's his turn to bite his bottom lip as his hands move to his trouser pockets, uncommonly vulnerable. 'Ja.'

'It would mean you'd have to start listening to me.'

'I can do that.' He looks up from his feet and releases his lip from his teeth.

'And I'd need benefits. *Good* benefits. Financial and...'

'And?'

I blush, running my tongue across my lip. 'And good physical benefits.'

His nerves are replaced with his exquisite half-smile. 'That can be arranged.'

I waft a hand flippantly through the air. 'Oh, what the hell, Neil hates me anyway.'

'So you'll do it?'

I pause for a second, then laugh. 'Yes. I'll do it.'

'She'll do it!' He picks me up under my arms and turns me in a fast full circle then sets me back down in front of him.

'Gregory, you don't owe me anything, please remember that.'

'God, you're amazing.' He takes a deep breath in then kisses me. My body instantly yields, instinctively curving into his. I wrap my fingers around his neck and pull him towards me.

'Wait, wait.' He removes my hands and places them by my sides. 'My second question.'

Panting, bereft and confused, I shrug. 'What was the second question?'

His chest visibly expands beneath his shirt, then he exhales, a long, tense breath out, and reaches his big palm to my cheek. 'It amazes me every day that you know everything about me. You know my worst. And you're still here.'

I feel my eyes widen. My lungs slowly emptying.

'You're the most beautiful, brave and true woman I've ever met. More than that, you're the best person I know.'

My stomach starts doing summersaults.

'You were wrong when you told me I couldn't see what was standing right in front of me. I've always known. I knew from the second I first laid eyes on you in my boardroom.' He sighs on his exhale. 'But I was afraid. Afraid of what I could feel, what that would mean, and afraid to believe that you could love me back.'

He lowers his hand from my cheek but his big, brown gems wrap around my soul, making my heart rate soar. 'All my life, I've searched for a reason why I'm still here. A purpose. After everything I've put you through, by some miracle, you're still standing in front of me, utterly spellbinding. I know, in this moment, that *you* are the reason I exist, Scarlett.'

Tears cast a haze across my eyes that I will to disperse so I can see him clearly.

'*You* are my reason. My angel. My light. My everything. I'd like you to let me show you that for the rest of our lives and after.'

A silent tear trails my cheek. 'That's quite a speech.'

'I mean every word.'

He takes a step back then drops to one knee, taking my left hand in his. My other hand moves to my heart in a bid to stop it exploding from my chest when I see the glaze over his eyes.

'Scarlett Heath, please do me the greatest honour. Please say you'll be mine forever.'

I wish I could speak but words, breath, running blood, a beating heart, all have escaped me and I stare helplessly at this perfect man.

He reaches into his trouser pocket and presents me with a ludicrously lavish ring. A large, clear princess cut diamond rests in the middle of two entwined rows of diamonds, one white, one black.

Finally, an almost inaudible whisper escapes me. His eyes widen, his brows rise. 'Yes,' I say louder. 'Yes. Yes. Yes.'

He pushes the extravagant ring onto my finger and pulls me into his arms as he stands, twirling us round in the sand until my head is physically and metaphorically spinning. When he sets me down, he finally kisses me, his fiancée.

'I really hope they're happy tears,' he says.

'I love you to Pluto and back, Gregory Ryans.'

'Isn't it *to the moon and back*?'

'You're really going to comment on *me* muddling a saying?'

'I guess not. Get here.'

I leap up into his arms and wrap my legs tightly around his waist, holding the face of and gazing down at the man I'm going to spend the rest of my life with. 'The ring is beautiful. Are they black diamonds?'

'Yes. They represent your dark streak.' He smirks with a wicked glint in his eye, then whispers, 'Aurora.'

* * *

Two hours later, we've waved Sandy and Jackson off to Barbados for another Gregory treat and I can finally have what I've wanted since the beach: Gregory Ryans, my fiancé, all to myself.

He opens the door to the large, minimalist penthouse suite: cream walls and carpet, oak furniture, white sofas and soft furnishings. I open the French doors to both balconies off the lounge, causing the white chiffon curtains to blow gently into the room. Gregory calls for more champagne. He's had the hotel stock Pol Rodger 2002 and requests a bottle with two glasses and ice.

'Set it up in the lounge,' he says, before hanging up the phone and finding me.

He attacks my mouth, his hand pulling my hair roughly at my neck. He bends me back, my pelvis pushing into his already angry length. He's been waiting for this, too. My chest rises, pushing my breasts against him, the pressure making me moan into him. He groans deep in his throat and grinds his hips against me, his teeth finding my neck.

'You've agreed to be mine.' His words are a hoarse whisper in my ear. 'Completely.'

'Yes,' I say, breathless.

He slides his hand down my back, groping my arse over my dress. His fingers work under the silk and brush the satin thong between my cheeks. He picks up my thigh, bending my leg over his hip. 'You. Are. Mine.'

I open my eyes to find two hooded, black irises fixed on me. 'Yours.'

'Tonight, I'm going to take you every way.'

He claims my lip in his teeth, tugging possessively. He lifts my other leg to his hips, then carries me to the master bedroom, past the four-post teak bed, into the large en suite. He lowers me to the vanity unit around the white porcelain sink then moves both hands to my hair, pulling me to his mouth. He grinds hard against me. Then leaves me squirming with need as he flicks on the walk-in shower.

God, he's hot.

He stalks towards me, unbuttoning his white shirt and releasing the tails from his trousers. I lick my lips, hungry to feel his toned, virile body on me, over me, in me.

'I've had to watch you all day, looking like that, thinking about what I wanted to do to you, not knowing if you'd say yes.'

'That must have been tough for you,' I tease, as he lets his shirt fall down his arms to the floor.

'You have no idea.' He pushes my legs apart and roughly lifts my arse to the edge of the unit, grinding against my cleft.

'I think I've missed dark Gregory.'

'Oh, he's still in here, baby. And he wants to fuck you. He wants to *own* you all night.'

I push up from the unit, rolling myself against his crotch. 'I'd like that.'

My head darts to the door when I hear a noise. He grasps my chin in his hand and turns my head back to him. 'It's room service.'

Straightening, I push a hand between us, rubbing his erection over his trousers. Leaning forward, I bite his pec and revel in the rumbling growl from his chest. 'She wants it rough,' he says, tugging my hair, lifting my face to look at him.

'She does.'

'Game on, Miss Heath.'

He draws down the zip at the side of my dress and pulls it over my head as steam begins to fill the room. As fast as the dress hits the white floor tiles, my nipple is in his mouth. The noise he makes as he pulls it through his teeth makes the pain and the swirl of his tongue that follows an even sweeter sensation. My back arches towards him as he performs the same trick on my other breast.

Lifting me with one hand, he yanks my thong down my thighs then follows with his tongue the line of the satin to my ankles. He takes off my shoes then rises, pulling me to him again. His lips meet my neck, then my collarbone, as his hands work my breasts.

'Take off my trousers.'

I unbuckle then unbutton him and push down his boxers and trousers, freeing him.

He rolls his hard dick against my swollen sex. 'This is what you do to me.'

He lifts me and takes us into the thick steam, setting me down under the shower's hot spray. I move a leg between his and rub against him as his tongue attacks mine, turning, licking, tasting. Then he moves to my breast, biting the nipple, sucking the most sensitive skin, drawing blood to the surface.

Wild, carnal possession that has me writhing against him.

Bending, he hooks my legs over his shoulders and I yelp as he unexpectedly hoists me up, my back pressed against the white tiles above him, his hands and shoulders holding my thighs up and open, his face at my desperate entrance. I fist my hands in his hair as his tongue strikes a line up my centre and massages my clit.

'Jesus! Gregory!'

He quickens his pace, moving his tongue between seductively circling my clit and dipping into me. From here, I can see everything. Watching him control and devour me pushes me towards a climax. My shoulders roll against the tiles, I yank harder at his hair.

'Gregory, I'm there.'

He doesn't stop; he works relentlessly until my head spins, my insides ignite around him and I scream his name.

Leaning my head back, I slide my legs from his shoulders and he lowers me down, steadying me with his hands on my hips. I drop my head to his chest as he rinses his face under the spray of the shower.

With a bent index finger, he lifts my chin. 'Fuck me with your mouth.'

Gladly.

Keeping my eyes on his, I bend to my knees, my hands gliding over his wet muscles, coming to rest on to his hips. A drop of pre-come escapes his tip and I lap it up, savouring his taste. Sliding my arm between his legs, I move my fingers around his back entrance, then drag them forward along his hard base, his moan spurring me on. I cup his sack, still stroking his base, and delight in his head falling back, showing strained muscles in his neck and chest.

I lick from his base to his tip then turn my tongue around the head, taking another bead of early release. He braces his hands on the tiles in front of him, watching as I wrap my lips around him and take him to the back of my throat in one swift move.

'Christ, Scarlett, what you do to my cock. That mouth.'

He moves one hand to my hair and holds my head still as he moves himself slowly in and out of me, bringing water to my eyes. His thighs tense, his arse cheeks stiffen under my hands, and his rhythm stutters. I tighten my grip, pumping quicker, turning my tongue around his tip and teasing his arse with my free hand.

'Jesus! Fuck! That's so good, baby.'

He comes so much, anyone would think it's been

longer than twenty-four hours since his last release. I swallow every drop he has to offer.

We wrap in towel dressing gowns and I follow his orders, moving to the four-post bed, whilst he retrieves the Pol Rodger from the lounge.

Those black eyes are still unsated. Lucky for me.

I hold out my hand but he puts the ice bucket and two glasses of champagne on the bedside unit. Then tugs my legs so I'm lying flat on the bed and yanks the tie from my gown, freeing my arms as he pushes off the robe, exposing me to him.

'Arms above your head,' he demands.

Everything south of my waist throbs in response, excited, expectant.

He wraps the wool tie twice around my wrists, then around the horizontal frame of the bed.

'I like it when you play kinky,' I tell him.

A fleeting smile curls on one side of his lips. He moves backwards off the bed, my head lifting from the mattress to watch as his robe drops to the floor. I throw my head back on a desperate laugh as he takes his own robe belt and moves to the side of the bed. I watch his effervescent champagne fill his mouth and slide down his throat, enjoying the strong rise and fall of his Adam's apple as he swallows.

Gregory and champagne. A truly delectable combination.

His knees part my legs roughly then he leans forward and lifts my head so he can tie his wool belt across my eyes. His weight leaves the bed and I hear him moving around the room, opening and closing a drawer, then The Daysleepers' 'The Secret Place' drowns out all other noise. My sight and sound senses are completely gone, my ability to touch constrained. I worm restlessly in the bed.

Taking me by surprise, the bite of ice moves along my bottom lip and his weight moves over me, not touching my skin. The ice moves down my sternum, my abdomen, down to the top of my sex. My hips rise and the ice travels back up my body. It's gone. Then back, circling the end of my breast in time to the slow, heady sound filling my ears. My lips part; my mouth dries. The ice travels my skin, goosebumps prickling over my limbs, and circles my other breast, the cold stinging the tip.

My breathing becomes heavy. I try to find him with my legs and fail. *Where are you?*

The ice is gone and his weight moves off the mattress. I open my eyes beneath the belt and find only blackness. The track clicks over to Radiohead's 'Everything in its Right Place.' I tug my arms; they're still restrained. The not knowing, the suspense, has me writhing and aching to have him.

His weight is back, resting either side of my head. Champagne bubbles trickle into my mouth and I swallow, yearning for more. Wet, warmed brut is released in a line down my chest, my abdomen, my navel.

My hips jerk as effervescence caresses my clit and falls between my labia. His hands finally touch me, forcing my legs apart before his mouth sucks and his tongue laps up champagne from my pulsing centre.

He drinks alcohol from my belly button and licks a line up my chest. His hands grab my breasts and he grinds his hard cock against me.

This. This is what I've signed up to for the rest of my life.

He lifts my hips and crashes into me on a bark that I hear over the music. He takes me hard, just as he promised, and holds me up on *that* angle as he hammers into me. His thumb rubs my clit, circling with the music. The assault on my senses and the force of him reaching the end of me send a rippling orgasm through my body. My hands fist around the wool belt as my mind fogs with images of his naked body kneeling between my legs.

He doesn't let me come down; he flips me onto my

front and pulls up my hips so I'm on my knees, hands down on the mattress, arse exposed.

'I said every part of you.' His words are drenched in desire and I want nothing more than to sate him.

His knees part mine and he presses his huge shaft between my arse cheeks, making sure I feel him there. He pushes two fingers into my drenched sex and draws the moisture back to my arse.

'You need to relax.'

I nod, gripping the belt at my wrists, and my legs drop further apart.

I've never done this. But I want it.

'Good girl.'

He reaches out and I hear him click open a lid. I gasp as cold gel touches my hole. He moves it around, preparing me. I'm nervous, anxious. But the feel of his fingers, slick through the lube, dipping inside me, it has me rolling my hips, shocked by how much I want him to claim this part of me.

He parts my cheeks wider and pushes gently, until his tip is just inside. I feel myself stretching and realise he's started to move again. It's strange but... okay.

'Relax, baby.'

I breathe out the air I've been holding as he eases himself into me.

'Fuck, that's tight.'

It hurts at first and I don't know if I like it. But the pain passes and I'm more acutely aware of him than ever before. The shape and size of his length. I groan, surprised by the pleasure I feel. His fingers move back to my sex, his thumb to my tight knot, torturing my body, assaulting me as he moves himself, sliding until he's fully inside.

In a way I couldn't have imagined, I feel like I belong to him. Like he's taken something I've never shared or wanted to share with anyone else. Only him.

I push my hips back, wanting more of the new kind of pleasure. The physical and the emotional. He moves slowly in and out of me, his fingers and cock working together in time to the music, sending my head into a trip.

His cock thickens and his rhythm builds slowly, his moves taking me to a crescendo. 'Not yet,' he growls. My erratic breaths come thick and fast as he increases his pace. 'Fuck, Scarlett. I'm there, baby.'

I scream his name into the mattress and shatter. The biggest orgasm I've ever had rips through my body, my limbs weightless, my pelvis bucking, my head in a frenzy. He yanks my hips back and continues to crash into me until his release comes and I feel each spurt, my greedy muscles flexing in response.

He pulls out slowly, an alien feeling I don't enjoy,

and collapses us both on the mattress. His hands move immediately to my wrists, releasing me, then he takes the belt from my eyes. With one arm around my waist, he rolls us onto his back, nuzzling my neck, kissing my skin gently.

'I can't believe I get this forever.'

I wrap my arms around his and interlace our fingers. I can't speak but I can make him feel how much I adore him. Any way. Every way. Always.

12

Gregory pulls us into the port in a rental Porsche. An unnecessary extravagance to get from the airstrip in St Maarten to the harbour but I guess when money is no object...

'I can't wait to see the boat,' Amanda squeals, jumping out of the car. 'Which one's yours?' She glances at Gregory then scans the host of white and blue boats docked in the Marina.

Gregory rolls his eyes and I dig an elbow into his ribs. 'None of those.'

A port official comes to talk to him and is soon replaced by a man maybe in his late twenties or early thirties: cute tan, ruffled, dirty-blond hair, handsome. His black, knee-length shorts and black

T-shirt tell me he's probably crew. He shakes Gregory's hand.

'Nice to see you again, sir,' he says with a North American twang.

Gregory nods. 'Is she ready?'

'Sure is.'

'And is the tender ready?'

'Ready and waiting, sir. We'll get you out there and I'll come back for the luggage. Rick will wait with it on the dock.' He inclines his head in the direction of the wooden jetty. In turn, Gregory flicks his head at Amanda, Williams and me.

'I guess that means come hither,' Amanda jibes.

Ignoring her, I happily swish my way to Gregory's side in my sundress.

'Carl, this is Scarlett Heath.'

'Miss Heath, pleasure to meet you.'

'Scarlett, please.'

Carl eyes Gregory, then me, and smiles. *Guess I'll be staying Miss Heath, then.*

'And congratulations.'

'Thank you.' I blush, taken back by his openness when I hadn't realised Gregory had told anyone our news yet. 'So, you'll be keeping us above water for the next ten days?' I ask, swiftly moving on.

'Whilst you're on the yacht, that's the idea.'

'Then I best keep you onside.'

Gregory guides me along the jetty with a protective hand on the small of my back – whether he's protecting me from the water or the handsome crew, I'm not sure.

Carl helps me into the small tender boat and introduces me to Bryony, a sun-kissed and quite striking woman about my age who's wearing the same crew uniform.

I roll my eyes at Gregory over the rim of my shades – of course the entire crew is flawless.

There's a ghost of a smile around his mouth and I know those goddamn eyes will be twinkling with arrogance behind his lenses as he takes a seat alongside me. He rolls back the sleeves of his shirt and lazily drapes an arm across the rim of the boat behind my back.

'I can't tell you how much it turns me on that you're jealous.'

Scowling at the truth of those words, I glance sheepishly at Williams and Amanda, but she's too giddy looking around at the boat and Williams is chatting to Bryony.

Gregory asks Carl about the weather and the expected sea conditions for the coming days as Bryony backs us away from the pier and turns the boat so we're facing out to sea, her glossy hair blowing in the wind.

We break out of the harbour and pick up speed so water crashes against the front screen and spray reaches my bare arms, cooling my skin under the hot Caribbean sun. We head out beyond a huge cruise liner and a yacht, anchored alone, comes into view, gleaming on top of the turquoise sea.

My jaw literally drops as I switch my eyes between the super-yacht and Gregory. 'You. Are. Fucking. Kidding. Me.'

He chuckles, as does Williams. Amanda almost pees her pants.

'I've told you to mind your fucking language when you're not in the bedroom.'

I pull down my shades to peer at him. 'Gregory. Come the *fuck* on. *That's* your yacht?'

A supercilious grin draws on his face. 'Working hard has a few perks.'

'Ho-ly shit!' Amanda eventually says, each syllable laboured.

Williams wraps his arm around her ribs, pulling her tenderly onto his lap. 'Our baby is going to come out preceding everything with "holy".' He kisses her temple and I want to coo. He's definitely the Bingley to

Gregory's Darcy. Light to dark. Easy to intentionally difficult.

'I have a surprise for you,' my dark and difficult man says.

Bryony slows the boat to a stop, still twenty metres or so from the yacht. Carl speaks to someone through a radio. Then a man appears on the deck of the yacht, near the bow. A blue banner hangs over the brim of the yacht. Gregory takes my hand in his, then nods to Carl, who gives the okay to whoever is on the other end of the radio.

The banner is rolled up slowly and for the second time, my jaw hangs loose as I read the name of the yacht.

S. R. Aurora

My eyes glaze but I still manage to tell him, 'Presumptuous, wouldn't you say?'

He liquefies me with his stunning half-smile and I throw my arms around his neck. 'Thank you. It's incredible.'

Scarlett Ryans, Aurora.

'Oh, for God's sake. I really want to hate you,' Amanda says, swiping away a tear.

I feel Gregory's chest move as he chuckles in my hold.

Bryony and Carl expertly position us adjacent to eight white steps. At the top, another six crew members wait to greet us, all dressed in the same uniform. Bryony asks if Amanda and I would like to be shown around the ship, which of course we do, and I realise as she talks excitedly in her Bajan accent about the three-hundred-foot yacht and all its features, I really quite like her.

She walks us around the bottom deck where there's an eight-seater dining table, two rattan sofas, two matching rattan chairs and four matching sun loungers. The main salon has a fully stocked bar and multiple television screens. There's another dining table and more seating.

The hot afternoon sun beats on my face as I tilt my head and tie my hair back into a ponytail. I open my eyes to a speedboat flying across the sea, two bikini-clad girls waving vigorously in the back as water crashes over the front of the boat. Amanda lifts on to her toes in her gladiator sandals and waves back.

'Miss Heath, Miss Darling, my name is Bertie and I handle all the food and beverages on the yacht.'

The chef meets us out on deck – also dressed all in black, albeit in kitchen attire. He's a tall, red-haired man with pale, freckled skin and, unsurprisingly, the kind of green eyes a woman could dive right into. 'Can I interest you in a fruit punch?'

'Is it virgin?' Amanda asks.

'Absolutely.'

A glowing smile pulls on her lips as she takes the pink-orange juice from Bertie's tray.

'It's delicious, Bertie,' I say. 'Is it your recipe?'

'Sure is. Wait 'til you see what I can do with a bottle of Disaronno and Tequilla Blanco.'

'I'm looking forward to it already.'

Amanda sighs and drains her virgin drink, depositing the empty glass back on Bertie's tray.

'Another?' he asks.

She shakes her head, clearly sulking.

'D'you guys want to continue the tour?' Bryony asks, gesturing to the stairs, one set going down, the other leading up to the top deck.

'Please.'

'Let's go up first.'

We meet the captain, who shows us a heap of gadgets and levers around the steering wheel and the view from the top deck is amazing. Endless, sparkling sea merging into clear, blue sky. I hold onto the metal rail and look out to the horizon, wondering whether I've ever felt more complete in my life. Holding up my hand, I watch the rock on my finger twinkle under the sun's rays. Forever.

And speak of the devil...

I see him standing at the bow, hands in the pockets of his shorts and looking out. All mine. I never knew I was possessive before now.

At the sound of my bare feet on the deck, he turns, welcoming me into his arms. 'Have fun?'

I slip my arms around his waist. 'I did. I like your boat.'

'*Our* boat. It does have your name on it.'

Pulling back, I smile up at him. 'Yes, it does. I like that something is ours. But maybe next time, we could share something like a case of wine. A yacht seems a tad extreme. We're in prenup territory.'

His happy mood dissolves in a nano-second. 'Prenups are for people who intend to break, Scarlett. Nothing is going to break us. Do you hear me? I won't let it. Everything I have will be yours. *Everything.*' He takes my hand and places it across his chest. 'You already have the one thing I thought I'd never give away. If you break it, I don't think I'll survive.'

'That makes two of us.'

He drowns me in a slow, tender kiss.

'Sir, a drink for sail away?'

Gregory keeps me tucked to his side as we accept champagne from Bertie.

'Pol Rodger Sir Winston Churchill 2002, like you asked.'

'Thank you, Bertie.'

'Would you like lunch when we're asail, sir?'

Gregory nods. 'Yes, thank you.'

'After lunch, I'd like to talk you quickly through the plans for *Black Diamonds*,' I say. 'As in the game, not the stones on my finger.'

'All right. Not too long, though; I want you to have a break. You need one.'

'Yes, *sir*.'

Williams crosses the deck to us, his free arm loosely resting on Amanda's shoulder. 'All right, you two, a toast. To finally getting your shit together.'

'Heartfelt, Williams, thanks,' I tell him, smirking as we clink glasses.

Bertie serves up chicken Caesar salad and cool Semillon-Sauvignon. We eat in the shade, a welcome break from the stifling heat. Everything seems right somehow. Williams and Amanda are happy. Gregory and Amanda have gone forty-five minutes without a jibe passing between them. My perfect man is eating with his left hand as his right strokes the fourth finger of my left.

Yet, I have the same lingering feeling I've had since Katrina Martin showed up in Dubai. This is just a hiatus. Somewhere, she'll be thinking up her next move.

'All right, lady. Shall we talk about *Black Diamonds*?'

'Oh, hell, I'm off if you're talking work.' Amanda is out of her seat quicker than she'd hit Harrods in a flash sale.

'Mind if I hang around?' Williams asks.

'Not at all.' Gregory pushes his seat back from the table, his elbow resting on the red tablecloth, his index finger and thumb pinching his chin.

'I just want to bring you up to date with the plan. I get that you want to take *Black Diamonds* off the market to protect the *Jail Run* profits but just buying the game doesn't stop somebody else from coming out with a replica or the actual game if they somehow got their hands on the source code. Now, it can be tricky to register intellectual property in gaming software, particularly app-based games. Well, I don't need to tell you that; look at the hit *Jail Run* is taking thanks to *Black Diamonds* being a similar concept. *But* we do need to get you some registered intellectual property rights to give us a starter for ten if someone tries to rip off the game. Otherwise, you're right back to paying seven hundred and

fifty thousand and employing a new software de-
veloper.'

'I have a feeling he'll come good,' Gregory says,
more to Williams than me.

'I agree,' I admit. 'But the point is valid.'

'And accepted.'

'Good. Now, I'm not an intellectual property spe-
cialist but I can obviously hold my own. I've pulled
together a plan for due diligence and, loosely, registration of an intellectual property portfolio but that part
is pretty fluid, depending on what the due diligence
throws up. Of course, *most* people would have done
that due diligence before putting down an obscene
about of money for a game.'

'It wouldn't be the most costly mistake we've ever
made if it doesn't pay off, Scarlett. We stand to lose a
lot more if we do nothing.'

I hold a palm in the air. 'Let's not go over old ground.'

'You started—'

'You were saying, Scarlett?' Williams interjects,
adjusting his glasses.

Gregory scowls. 'Go on.'

I take a sip of wine and sit back into my chair. 'Halt
me if I'm teaching my grandmother to suck eggs at any
point. I won't fill you with stuff you don't need to know.

Suffice to say, there are various forms of intellectual property rights: copyright, trademarks, design rights, for example. We can register them all to an extent based on what I've seen of the game.'

'I thought copyright was an automatic right?' Williams asks.

'Mm, well, it is. Stuart was a one-man band and from what I know, he wasn't operating through a company. So yes, copyright vests in him as the creator. But that's the case under English law. In some jurisdictions, copyright has to be registered, same for trademarks and design rights. And that's part of the due-diligence jigsaw. I'm sure it's all fine but we need to confirm that Stuart does actually hold the copyright and other rights in the game. Once we confirm that and assuming we do, we look to registration. I've already got a junior looking into Stuart's ownership.'

'And what's the registration plan?'

'It varies from country to country. If everything goes to plan, we'll start registering what we can. My suggestion, unless you object, is that we start with China and Europe. Then we move to the US and Australia. Then the rest of the world, to the extent appropriate.'

Gregory rubs his chin. 'Why do we stage it?'

'Cost, resource. The applications take time. I need support from local counsel.'

'Staged is acceptable but I want the US in the first round with China and Europe. Gaming is too big in the US to delay.'

'I can amend that. Anything else?'

'What can go wrong?' Williams asks.

I scoff. 'There's a seven hundred and fifty thousand pound question. The main risks are, one: that someone already has a knock-off in the making. They could have reverse-engineered the source code or be at work creating identical concepts. Characters and branding, for example. I guess we have to cross our fingers it hasn't been on the market long enough for someone to try. The second big risk is that we don't have the power to register. In other words, if Stuart's ownership of the game, and therefore Constant Sources' ownership of the game, is somehow questionable.'

'How could that happen?' Gregory asks.

'Either Stuart never held the rights to the game in the first place, or he had them and licensed or sold them in such a way that Constant Sources could never have acquired them.'

'And the other risks?' Gregory presses.

'We could stumble on something in a particular

jurisdiction. Say, I don't know, *elements* of *Black Diamonds* have already been registered. But we'll cross that bridge if we come to it. First step is to check Stuart's authority to sell to Constant Sources. Second step is to set out what rights we need to register in the various jurisdictions. I've already put the feelers out with local counsel.'

'How much is this going to cost me: tens of or hundreds of?'

'All being well, tens of.'

Gregory nods and takes a sip from his freshly topped-up wine. 'Fine.'

'You don't want to know how many tens of?'

'If we're not talking hundreds, that's micro detail. I'm a macro man.'

'When I work for you, I'll be taking much tighter control of your legal spend, Ryans.'

'Someone probably should,' he says with humour in his voice.

'Okay. If we're done. I'm going to get changed and join Amanda.' I ruffle his hair and drop a kiss to his scalp.

* * *

The master bedroom looks exactly as I would have imagined the master bedroom of a yacht to look. There's something about it that smells, looks and feels luxurious and at sea all at once. The furniture – trims round the mirrors, chairs, feet of the sofa, coffee table – is all mahogany and cream.

Stepping out of the bathtub-shower, I wrap a towel around me and draw *I Love You* with a heart in the steam on the mirror above the sink unit. Then I go rummaging through the stash of bikinis that Julia and Lucas have picked out for me, choosing a shimmering red bandeau. Thankfully, it fits perfectly. It's classy and, well, hot. But... I close my eyes so I can't see myself. I can't go out there half-naked. *Christ, Williams is a client. There are eight crew.* I'm not uncomfortable in my skin but that's a lot of people who don't need to see my semi-naked body.

Shaking my head fast, I blow a dry raspberry with my lips. *Suck it up, Scarlett.*

On the deck, Amanda is sprawled on her back, head tilted, chin to the sky. Williams is also on a lounger reading a hardback, bare chested, legs pulled up, a full glass of wine on a small rattan table next to him. And my CEO is at the bow of the yacht, torso bare and looking so damn delicious, I can't help thinking about those muscles moving against my body. He hangs up his phone when he notices me walking the deck towards him.

Over the low hum of music, I catch his words: 'Get here.'

Dropping my book and floppy hat to a sun lounger, I go to him. He yanks me the last foot by the small of my back, pulling me against his pelvis.

'If you intend to wear that, you better get in that water. Right. Now.'

Biting my bottom lip, I push my hips forward, adding pressure to the reason he needs to cool off. 'Looks like you have a bit of a problem, handsome.'

'You think it's funny that you've made my dick solid in swim shorts?'

'Not funny.' I push my hips a little further and he brushes his lips across mine, growling into my mouth. 'Sexy as hell.'

'Water. Now.'

I squeal as he lifts me from my feet, leaving my flip-flops behind, and propels us off the side of the boat. He holds me to him, my back, my head. He doesn't let go as we crash into the water. We kick up, both breaking the surface with a deep inhale. Then we laugh. I pause for just a beat to hear him, then start up again.

'What the hell? Are you two okay?' Amanda screams over the side of the yacht.

I hold up a hand to say we're fine as Gregory locks my legs around his waist and keeps us both afloat.

'Did that cool your raging cock, *sir*?'

'Watch those expletives, girlie. And no. It made my thunder cock angrier.'

'Thunder cock?' I raise an eyebrow with a giggle.

'I want to fuck you. Now. In the sea. I can't get enough of you.'

Sighing, I lean back in his arms, my head grazing the water. 'Gregory, I'm going to be your wife. I need you to stop objectifying me. When we're married, I think we should have a routine. Maybe sex on Saturdays. I need to know you respect me for me, not my body.'

'Sex on Saturdays?'

'Okay, Saturday and maybe once on a Sunday morning. It's important that we have boundaries.'

'Scarlett, I respect you. And I would like to help you with your self-esteem issues. Really, I would. But I think the best way for me to do that would be to make you understand how desperate I am to come inside you. All the fucking time. And how I love to hear you call out my name when I drive you to orgasm. How your insides squeeze my cock.'

I shuffle in his arms as my body responds to his words. Wanton.

'And the way you shove those wonderful breasts in my face when I make you hot for me in the sea.'

My eyes fly open as he bites my plump flesh through my bikini.

'I'm going to fuck your tits later and I'm going to come all over this fine chest. And when I do, you can think to yourself, *I deserve that for winding up my man on the top deck.*'

I giggle but it's short-lived as his fingers move into my bikini bottoms then into my sex.

I glance up to the yacht, satisfied that no one is paying us any attention. 'This could be tricky,' I tell him.

'You might have to do the work, gorgeous.'

'Gladly.' I roll my hips and nip his lip.

His kiss takes me by surprise, long, slow, like he's cherishing every second. I close my eyes and savour the feeling. Absorbed in him. His touch, his words, his tongue, the feeling of rightness between my thighs. We move slowly, discreetly, the sun beating down around us, the sea ripples glistening. He holds me, moaning, brushing his lips against mine in a way that leaves no space for me to doubt his love. The thought flips my stomach because his actions reflect my own mind. An overwhelming sense of love, complete physical and emotional love, emulates through me. I lean forward and bite his shoulder to prevent my body from externally erupting as my climax comes. He drops his head to my neck, biting and groaning quietly as he fills me with his physical desire.

'This is perfect,' I mumble into his shoulder.

He strokes my hair and hums against my neck, then drops his lips to my cheek. 'You're beautiful when you're happy.' His eyes change, a switch that's completely ordinary for Gregory but a move that I don't want to see in our paradise. 'I want to always make you happy.'

Shifting slightly, I meet his eyes. 'What is it?'

He shakes his head.

'Oh no, Gregory Ryans, don't you dare. That's the same look you had when you were on the phone just before. What is it?'

'Baby, nothing to worry about.'

I sit up and try to unravel my body from his but he holds my legs around his waist.

'Please don't keep things from me. I thought we got past this. Everything that's gone wrong with us is because you've kept things from me. If we're going to be a team, Gregory, you have to share things with me.

That's what the big rock is supposed to mean, isn't it? That you want us to be a team?'

'Now that you mention it, where is the big rock?'

'It's in the safe; I didn't want to wear it to frolic in the sea with you.'

'That's what we're doing, baby: frolicking?'

'Stop changing the subject.'

Any semblance of playfulness disappears.

'Fine. Don't tell me. Clearly, that ring doesn't mean as much as I hoped.' I kick back from him and start a front crawl to the boat.

'Hey.' He pulls my left hand back before I can lift it over my head. 'What have I told you about that attitude?' He drags me back to his waist.

'Tell me.'

He sighs. 'I'm fixing it.'

'That's not an answer.'

'One of the tabloids has found out about my case.'

My brow furrows. 'Your non-case. It's over; you weren't charged. Am I missing the point?'

He drops his forehead to mine and paddles so we turn in a circle. 'I paid off most of the broadsheets and big corporate papers at the time. Sydney in PR thought that someone might have talked, given the level of sudden media attention.'

'So this is a regional?'

'Yes, a regional tabloid, which means I don't have a settlement in place restricting what they print.'

'So you're going to have to pay them off?' Guilt kicks me in the gut as I speak. Another reality check. I put him in this situation. He's paying for my actions. 'Gregory, I'd like to fix this. Before you jump in and say no, I'll have the money from the house in a couple of weeks. You've paid enough. This was my doing. Let me fix it.'

He cups my face in his hands. 'Baby, you didn't bring this on us. I did. And I would never let you pay for my past. But you're amazing for wanting to.'

'There's no I in team, right? I think we can call it *our* mistake and *our* past now. I want all of you, Gregory: past, present and future. And let me tell you something else: I'd do it again. I'd do anything for you. Even go Dutch on paying off the tabloids.'

'How did I find you?'

'You were supposed to.'

He smiles as he hooks his hands under my thighs and propels me out of the water, squealing. He's laughing when I surface, rubbing hair and salt water from my eyes.

'You're going to pay for that.'

13

'We'll see you on the aeroplane beach around five or six?' I ask, dropping a kiss to Gregory through the window of the rental Porsche.

'By the aeroplane beach, you realise you mean Maho Beach?'

I scowl. 'Did you understand what I meant? Then don't be an arsehole.'

He chuckles as Williams climbs into the passenger seat.

'Are you sure you don't want me to come with you?'

'It's just a catch up with a business acquaintance, not deal specific. Go. Enjoy your day with Amanda. I'll see you later. Be careful.'

'What could possibly go wrong?' I ask, pulling down my shades to wink over the frame.

'Have fun in your business meeting boys, we'll just be, you know, shopping, sunbathing.' Amanda waves a hand in a way I know will grate on Gregory's nerves.

'You be careful with my little man in the sun,' Williams calls.

'*She* and I will be just fine. Aunty Scar will look after us.' She wraps an arm around my shoulder.

Legal jargon, I know. Baby stuff? I'm clueless.

'Just the three of us, then,' I tell her, hugging her back.

Gregory and Williams dropped us on the French side of the island. Shopping is number one on the agenda, followed by a binge on French pastries, then Aeroplane or Maho or whatever beach for sunbathing and plane spotting.

We wander the quiet, clean, Parisian-feel streets, dipping in and out of boutiques, more for air con than shopping and much sooner than her usual stamina would give in, she puffs, 'Can we eat and get a cool drink?'

We find a cute bakery and feast on a basket of pastries: almond, cinnamon and raisin, all butter, chocolate.

'It's nice to have some time just us,' I say, rubbing flakes from my fingers.

'Sure is. I can't believe you're engaged!'

'Pretty crazy, isn't it? You pregnant, me engaged.'

'When did we grow up?'

'You and Williams seem to be doing well.'

She nods but purses her lips. 'We're good in that we agree we want to be together. And he already loves bubba. My pops has started to hate him less about the whole baby, unwed, will he or won't he stay thing.'

'But.'

'But he won't touch me, Scarlett. He says he doesn't want to hurt the baby but I'm like a raging bag of pissed-off hormones twenty-four seven and all I want him to do is give me a bloody good seeing to. Lord knows he can.' She pats her tummy and I can't help but giggle.

'Have you told him?'

'Yes. No. I've tried. I don't... We're not... What if it's not about the baby? What if it's me and he doesn't find me attractive? I'm bloating. I'm irritable. Whoever said this pregnancy malarkey makes you feel wonderful was either a man or talking complete bollocks.'

I practically snort my orange juice. My amusement is short-lived when I realise that my best friend in the whole world, confident, strong, gorgeous Amanda, is doubting herself. 'Amanda, you've got to be kidding. Williams has had eyes for you since that first night in the bar. He's absolutely into you. Have you thought that maybe this is just a big change for you both and he's scared?'

'But that doesn't mean he can't have sex.'

I laugh again and Amanda chuckles with me, her hands resting on her mini-bump. 'Maybe you could try to be non-pregnant Amanda, too?'

'What's that supposed to mean?'

'Nothing bad. Just, I think it's possible you're playing up some because you're scared, too. If you just had an honest conversation with him, didn't try to be tough and didn't try to mask how you're feeling, he might open up.'

She swipes up the cinnamon and raisin swirl and takes an enormous bite. 'You're right.'

'It's okay to be nervous.'

She stuffs the last of the swirl in her mouth. 'How come you got so sensible?'

'I've always been sensible. You just used to call it boring.'

'I wouldn't call you boring now. At it all night, shagging in the sea.'

'Shh.' If I wasn't already flushed by the humidity, her words would do the job.

'Oh, please, I'm impressed. Give Gregory credit where it's due, the man's an animal. I've never been taken all night like—'

'Christ, all right! I didn't think you could hear.'

'Couldn't hear you screaming the yacht into submission?'

I bite my lip but I'm laughing, too. 'I'm sorry. And I didn't think you knew we did the *thing* in the sea.'

She leans forward and takes my orange juice, finishing it. 'I didn't, until you just said you did. It's hardly helping my hormone situation knowing you two are at it like rabbits.'

Shaking my head, I stand. 'I'm paying the bill and you should try booking into a hotel.'

'That's actually not a bad idea. At least I'd get some sleep.'

* * *

'Here good?' I ask for the fifth time, losing the will to live after trudging the length of Maho Beach.

Amanda eventually drops her bag and declares, 'Here's great.'

I see exactly why when I follow her gaze to an incoming bartender, whose board shorts sit on long thighs, and whose biceps are firm and exposed in his

Billabong vest – *very* Amanda. She juts out a hip and plants a hand on it as she waits for him to come our way.

'Ladies. Can I set you up on a bed and get you some drinks?'

Amanda unties and shakes her long hair down her back. *Jesus, she really is horny.*

'Yes, please,' I blurt. 'We'll take two loungers with a parasol and my friend will have a sparkling water. Because she's *pregnant*. With someone else's baby.'

'Killjoy,' she mutters.

'I'm Jake.' The guy holds out his hand and Amanda's pout fades away. 'Nice to meet you. Let's get you set up on these beds.'

He pulls two white loungers closer together, lays a bed cushion on each, then takes our beach towels when we hand them to him and drapes them across the beds.

'The beds are twenty-five dollars and you get five free drinks. One sparkling water and what can I get for you, ah...'

'Scarlett. I'll take a something fizzy and zero, whatever you have.'

'My arse you will!' Amanda springs up from her already horizontal position on her lounger. 'I'll be damned if I'm going to sit here forced to drink sparkling water and you're going to drink a bloody diet *pop* when there's no need.'

'Rum punch?' Jake asks, his eyebrow raised.

'Looks like it.'

I peel off my dress to a nautical striped bandeau bikini and lie back with a contented sigh.

'It feels good to lie down,' Amanda says, turning to face me. 'I've felt like I've been on the boat all morning. Kind of dizzy drunk without the hangover.'

'It is nice, isn't it?' The question is rhetorical. Of course it's nice; it's thirty degrees and we're out of work. I'm lounging with my best friend, people-watching. Tens, maybe even hundreds, of people line the beach, waiting for the show of aeroplanes flying just feet from our heads to land on the airstrip right behind the beach. And I'm getting married. Not just getting married but getting married to a freaking billionaire who truly, genuinely loves me back.

There are things lingering, things that make me uneasy. Katrina Martin being number one. Tabloids that shouldn't be interested in Gregory now that the case is old news, two. There's some unfinished business, for sure, but things are changing, I think. He told me about the tabloids and not *months* after it happened, only *hours*. He's trying to let me in. Hopefully, in time, it will all become a distant memory. His nightmares will stop and the pain of his past will get easier.

'Don't tell him or anything, Scarlett, but the CEO is starting to grow on me. I like how happy he makes you.'

Jake returns with a punch that looks more rum than juice but I take the brownish-reddish-orangey drink from him and sip through the straw. 'Jesus Christ! Is there *any* juice in there?'

He plonks onto the bottom of my lounger and hands Amanda her water. 'Orange, cranberry and pineapple. It's like a fine wine; it takes three sips. Trust me.'

I scowl across my plastic cup as I take another sip.

'I've only just met you.'

'But...'

I stare at the now half-full cup. 'Well, I guess it is quite fruity after a few sips.'

'That's my kind of woman. I'll fetch another.'

I don't argue. I'm parched, it's fruity, and with the combination of sun and only having had pastries for lunch, it's really making my head pleasantly fluttery.

Punch two down, Jake heads back over with a virgin piña colada for Amanda and punch three for me. 'All right, ladies, this is it. There's a 747 headed in. Do you see it over there in the distance?'

The faint lights of the plane twinkle in the clear, blue sky, inbound for the beach.

'This is the plane all you tourists flock for. She's the most powerful and the biggest to land on the strip. Do you have a camera?'

I nod, sipping my rum-laced juice or juice-laced rum. Whichever.

'If you stand right there, you'll get a great picture. If you stand in the middle of the beach, you can really feel the force of the engines but it can get pretty dangerous, bowls people right back into the sea. I've seen it carry sunbeds and pushchairs into the water, so, ah, given your current physical state...' he gestures to Amanda's torso, receiving a huffy exhale in return, '... I'd suggest you keep your distance.'

'Why do the planes get so close if it's that dangerous?' Amanda asks.

'Well, there are warning signs all over the beach. See on the railings back there? But the runway is short for the size of planes coming in.' He points to the airfield abutting the beach. 'The pilots have to land right on the start line to make sure they stop before the end. That means the planes have to come in low to touch down and you never really appreciate how fast they're falling when you're inside but you'll see now. Here she comes.'

We sit upright on our loungers, our legs straddling the sides of the bed. I finally let go of my punch, turning the plastic cup in the sand until it stands unaided. Then I take out my camera and brace myself as the 747 comes drifting in.

'Holy shit!' Amanda says, pulling down her shades to the tip of her nose, her eyes following the belly of the plane.

Holding up my phone, I snap away at the aeroplane until my head is leaning back to look up at the giant metal bird. Jake wasn't lying; people daring enough to stand in the middle of the beach, directly under the plane's path, are clinging onto the railings. Hats fly, hair blows back, a young girl loses her grip and her footing.

'Wow, that's incredible.'

'Told ya,' Jake says with a smug smile. 'Another?'

I shake my head fast. 'No. I really shouldn't; these three have already gone to my head.'

'They should,' he laughs. 'They're free-poured measures.'

'Urgh, if I wasn't pregnant, I'd—'

'Oh, God, enough already. Bring me another please, Jake.'

'On it,' he laughs.

After four virgin drinks for the pregnant lady and

four free-poured, rocket-fuel rum punches for me, we find ourselves in the warm sea. Amanda twirls herself away from me, bending her legs to a sitting position. 'Tell me you're not.' I hold a hand over my mouth but my tipsy giggle escapes regardless. 'You're taking a pee, aren't you?'

She chuckles. 'Well, I am now you've made me laugh.'

'You're gross.'

'I'm more sanitary than going in those toilets with kids' dribble on the floor and dirty door handles.'

Shaking my head, I flip onto my back and move my legs in upside-down breast stroke, the sun beating on my face. 'Amanda, I'm booze-crazed.'

She chuckles and bumps into me, her body in the same pose as mine. 'I know.'

I can't remember the last time I was drunk and not throwing up outside a club, making a mess of my relationship with Gregory, and embarrassing myself in floods of tears. The thought of being drunk-happy makes me all kinds of fuzzy inside.

Amanda heads back to our loungers and the beach is emptying. And I close my eyes, turning in circles, feeling the water move between my fingers, and remembering how my dad would dance with me in our lounge as I stood on his toes. I remember the times

Gregory has twirled me, held me close as we've danced. Our perfect moment on top of Primrose Hill. Just us. Our own world.

I have a feeling I'm never going to look at a sunset, the blue sky, the topaz sea the same way again as I'm looking at it right now.

'I'm alive,' I whisper to myself as I stop and watch the sun slowly descend.

It's a presence. A charge. I know he's here. I can feel him. Turning to Amanda on her lounger, I find Williams sitting on the edge of her bed, massaging her feet in his lap. And my angel, sitting up, straddling my lounger with a bottle of beer in his hand, watching me with a smile.

'You drunk, baby?' he asks with a smirk as I stroll towards him.

I don't know what the right answer is to his question. It's not like it's a difficult question. Words just don't seem to be fitting together right. Instead, I shrug.

That'll have to do. Leaning forward to put my empty cup on the lounger, I stagger, then turn around to look for whatever it was that knocked me off balance. Whatever it was is gone now.

'All right, gorgeous. I think you've had enough fruit juice for one day.'

Bending my knees, I fall to the lounger between

Gregory's spread legs because I need to make him understand. 'The juice s'really good here, Ryans. Yoush try it.'

He leans back on his elbows – playful looks good on him. I slip between his legs and become even more liquid as he runs his fingertips down my arms, as if he has no idea he's even doing whilst we all talk, like four friends, just hanging out. As if this life I'm in isn't completely crazy.

* * *

When we're back at the yacht, Carl helps Amanda first, then offers me a hand and practically pulls me onto the first deck. *Our* yacht. *S. R. Aurora.* I like the sound of that. *Scarlett Ryans.*

'Rum punch?' Carl asks.

'A little too much rum punch,' Gregory replies.

'Bertie was set to serve dinner at eight-thirty, sir; would you like it sooner?'

'Maybe something to snack on would be good and water, lots of water.'

I lean into Carl and pat his chest with both palms. 'He's so bossy, Carl. So, so bossy.'

'Baby, I'm going to change. Are you coming with me?'

'Nope. *Nada. Nein.* No. *Niente.*'

'*Niente* means nothing, baby.'

'Yess'know, Gregory.' I roll my eyes and shake my head. 'I'm going to sit up there and have some water.'

Amanda pats Gregory on the arm, fond and touching. She nestles into a rattan chair and pulls her knees underneath her.

'Let's dance,' I say. 'We should dance.'

'All right. What do you want to dance to?'

I wiggle my hips as I move towards her on the chair, swirling a finger just in front of her nose. 'I think you know.'

'"Mr Brightside"!'

'Carl, can you—'

It's not obvious whether he's laughing at or with me but I don't care because The Killers' 'Mr Brightside', my university party piece, comes over the speakers of the yacht as we slowly back out of the harbour into the ocean.

As the guitar kicks in, I walk backwards to the bow and Amanda struts towards me in time to the music, her lips pursed like a rock star. The beat drops. The voices. Bass. Drums. Amanda screams, running towards me.

We hold hands, jumping, shouting the lyrics.

Hell, I forgot how much fun we used to have.

Amanda stands in the verse, fanning herself as she moves to a lounger and sips cool water. I'm sweating, I'm hyper and I'm on top of the world.

Air guitar.

Head down, one leg bent and bouncing, I play that damned air guitar like a wild thing. I jump, my feet kicking out beneath me, my arms punching the air above my head.

Then I see him. Arms folded. Watching me.

I stop for a second and consider how insanely drunk I must look to him.

Then I think, *fuck it!*

I jump again to the final chorus and repeat my dress-removal action as a massive smirk pulls on his lips and Williams joins Amanda in hysterics.

'Scarlett, come away from the edge,' Gregory shouts over the music.

I check the position of my feet, then challenging him, I shuffle back towards the edge.

'Scarlett.'

'Oh, Gregory, she's fine. Bloody hell.'

He scowls at Amanda and starts walking towards me.

'Scarlett, I won't tell you again.'

I shuffle my feet back further. 'What will you do

about it?' He speeds up when my heels hang over the edge. 'Will you spank me, Ryans?'

He darts towards me, knocking me off balance and ends up catching me, pulling me into him as I chuckle. 'Baby, flirting with men on the beach, getting drunk without me, you were already in spanking territory.'

I swallow audibly under the intensity of his stare, the heat emanating from his body moves directly to my sex without passing Go.

'For this, you're going to be tied to the bed and you're going to accept my cock until you make me come in that fucking marvellous mouth of yours.'

A sharp breath fills my lungs.

'*Then* I'm going to spank you.'

'I want you so bad right now,' I confess.

'My cock is twitching to be inside you.'

'Give in,' I whisper.

He draws his fingers gently down the side of my face and tucks my sea and wind messed locks behind my ear in that way he does. 'I love seeing you happy.'

'Tha's very fortunate, Ryans, 'cause you make me es'tremely happy.'

'God, I love you, Scarlett.'

His hand moves to my nape and pulls my mouth against his. Like there's no one else in the world, he scoops me up, my legs locking around his waist, my fingers gripping his hair.

'All right, all right, Jesus, you two!' Amanda shouts. 'Put her down.'

'She's horny because Williams won't fuck her,' I whisper against Gregory's lips. 'Says he'll hurt the baby.'

'Not my fucking problem. You need a shower before dinner.'

I mumble my agreement and let him carry me below deck.

14

I wake with a start. I've been dreaming and have a lingering sense of emptiness but I can't piece together the story. Reaching out for my comfort blanket, I find sheets and mattress but no Gregory. The clock on the bedside cabinet tells me it's four fifty-five in the morning. I pull on a short, silk nightdress and go in search of Gregory.

His nightmares are less frequent now but they still have a realness that makes him restless in bed, sometimes yelling out. They still make him retreat and put up his walls.

The yacht must have docked at a new port whilst we were sleeping. We're tied up at the back of the harbour, the spot closest to the ocean. The bay is full of smaller boats and flanked on either side by cliffs. Moonlight bounces off the gently rocking waves. A new place, in darkness, silence, stillness. It could be beautiful but it fills me with an eerie sense of apprehension.

I find him on the main deck, resting on the boat's safety rail. His body is almost silhouetted in the night as he drags one hand back through his untamed bed hair. I think it must have been a bad nightmare but then he speaks, his words short and sharp.

'Give them more. Everyone has a price, Sydney. We've got until twelve your time before they run the story. It's already after nine. Put the money to them now. If they don't accept it, ask what it'll take. One way or another, this is not going to print. Call me back.' As if he senses me, he hangs up on his head of PR. 'Go back to bed, baby.'

'You said you'd paid them off.'

'I never said that. You assumed that.'

'And you didn't think to tell me they wouldn't accept money?'

Back to me, he looks to me across his shoulder, his face haunted under the moon's light. 'Scarlett, I'm fixing it.' His words are subdued, as if he's fed up of fighting. I go to him and wrap my arms around him. He holds a hand over mine on his chest as I lean into his back and gently press my lips to his shoulder. I don't want him to have to fight any more.

When his phone rings again, he answers through speaker phone. A small act that means more to me than he probably realises.

'Did they take it?'

'No, I'm sorry, Gregory.'

'How much do they want?'

'Gregory, I don't think they have a price. They're a small paper. They realise the big guns are tied up in settlement agreements. They think this is too big a story to let go.'

His grip tightens over my hand. 'Stay close. I'll call you back.'

Gregory storms to the front of the boat and I follow, sitting down onto the edge of a rattan lounger, pulling one knee under me. He paces, one hand on his hip.

'Level with me,' I say, not confrontational but certainly authoritative.

He faces me, legs firmly planted, arms folded across his chest.

'They aren't this excited about a self-defence story that'll blow over in a week, so tell me what they've got.'

'I don't want to drag you into this, Scarlett.'

'Too late, Ryans, I'm in it for the long-haul. You've got me.'

'The payoff.' He barely mumbles the word.

I want to freak out. I want to lash out or cry in hysterics. Instead, I sit up straight and draw air into my lungs. 'How? What do they know?'

His shoulders visibly drop a half-inch. 'They're clutching at straws. There's nothing to find.'

'Don't try to make light of this and patronise me. They're not clutching at straws; they think they've got something solid. No small press turns down the money I know you'll be offering if they've got nothing. They wouldn't just make up something like a bribe. So tell me everything. Right now.'

His eyes widen and his brows rise in surprise at my tone. *Yes, Ryans, this is* our *future.*

'I've told you everything there is to tell. The money was in relation to the gun. That's all. It had nothing to do with the murder. The deal was, if there was no murder charge, the gun would disappear.'

'Do you seriously expect me to keep believing this?'

'Yes. Because it's the truth. I've never lied to you, Scarlett, never. There are things I haven't told you in the past but you asked me outright and I told you, that arrangement had nothing to do with the murder charge.'

'So if the charge had gone ahead...' My body shudders. 'You know what, I don't want to think about that. What concerns me more is how convenient it is that one of the few papers that could print something on this has wound up with the information. Don't you think that's strange? Who knows about the bribe? Who made the deal?'

'Me, Jackson, Barnes and his contact at the CPS.'

'That's it?'

'John Harrison would be an idiot if he couldn't work it out.'

Holy shit. 'And I thought lawyers were supposed to have integrity.' Then I snort, thinking about the irony of that statement. I killed a man and lied about it. I know about a bribe and I'm hiding it.

'They can't talk, Scarlett. Jackson and Barnes aren't even a concern but the others have too much at stake. They'd implicate themselves.'

'Well, someone thinks you bribed a government official, Gregory. It's an imprisonable offence for Christ's sake, you don't just—' It hits me like lightning, burning through my body, turning my stomach. 'Katrina Martin.'

He nods slowly, resolute. 'I agree.'

'I knew she wouldn't go away. She's got a vendetta and she won't back down. She's not that kind of woman.' Dropping my head into my hands, I roll my fingertips over my temples, trying to make sense of everything, trying to get my head straight.

He bends to his hunkers and peels my hands away from my face. 'Baby, please, don't let this drag us down. No more. I'll fight the world for you but don't let this keep coming back.'

In this moment, his exterior might be strong but I know that's not how he's feeling inside. He needs me as much as I need him.

'They won't find a bribe, baby. Katrina Martin has nothing concrete. There's no trail. There are no more people involved than those who absolutely had to be. She's got a hunch, that's all. The paper will investigate and eventually, they'll come up empty.'

'That's not the point though, is it? That's not even your biggest concern.'

He closes his eyes and covers my hands in his. 'No.'

'You don't want them to dig into your past.'

'It makes me look weak, Scarlett, and if that doesn't ruin my reputation, the fact that people will draw their own conclusions about my motive for killing my father will do it. But it's more than just me.'

'You don't want them to find Elsa.'

He shakes his head, opening his eyes. 'She doesn't deserve it. And it would break my mother. I need you to trust me. I'll fix this. If we panic, we tell the world we've got something to hide.'

'I'm so sorry, Gregory. This is all my fault.' Tears roll warm down my cheeks as a knife twists in my chest.

'You saved me, Scarlett. Please don't be sorry about that. I never will be.'

He drops to his knees and pulls me into his chest, squeezing me against his warm, bare flesh.

'What are we going to do?'

'Right now, I'm going to lay you down and make love to you.'

There are ten things we should be doing instead. The working day is beginning in England. But he needs this. We both need it. Just us, nothing else.

'As long as we're good,' he mumbles into my neck. 'I love you.'

His kiss is deep, full and passionate. His tongue flecks against mine, then licks the inside of my lip as he lifts me from the lounger, grabbing the cushion, and carries me to the bow of the yacht. He throws the cushion on the deck then lowers us down, my back pressed to the bed cushion.

He hovers over me, his muscles displayed to their

greatest advantage, tense above me. 'I need us to be okay,' he whispers against my lips.

'We are.'

The way we make love is urgent, desperate, yet silent in the darkness of the harbour.

After, his fingers move lazily across my back until my muscles have settled and my breathing returned to normal. Then he crawls over me and rolls us onto his back. I shiver when his lips press against my temple.

'You're cold.'

'I don't care.'

He pecks my temple again. 'I do.'

'I just want to lie with you.'

'I know, baby. Me too. But I need to deal with the paper. Then we can spend all day in bed if you like.'

Just like that, the reality of the situation sets quickly back in.

'I need to speak to Barnes and Jackson.'

I nod.

'Scarlett, I don't want to involve you in this. I can go to someone else. But—'

'You need an injunction.'

'Yes,' he almost exhales.

'Okay. I'll go get my laptop. Get Sydney to send me everything she has. I'll call Richard; he's the partner at Saunders who deals with this kind of thing. I'll brief him and get him on the case. It'll cost you because it's a rush job.'

'Money is no object.'

* * *

Thirty minutes later, we debrief each other. Richard is filing for an interim injunction to stop the tabloid going to print and is confident it'll be granted given the lack of foundation to the paper's argument and the attack it represents to Gregory's reputation. It'll take a few hours so it's a waiting game for now. Gregory has told Jackson what he needs to know to keep him in the loop but doesn't want to pull him away from his honeymoon. Katrina Martin is in London and Barnes has put the wheels in motion to suspend her on the basis she's investigating a closed case without consent and she's suspected to have leaked confidential details.

'You know this is going to make her more determined, Gregory. She's looking for blood and if she thinks this will make her name, she won't stop until she gets it.'

'Hey. Enough. We've done everything we can. Forget her. She's nobody and she's going to come up short at every angle.'

'How can you be so sure?'

'I've told you before, my world is different to yours. Can we leave it at that?'

I nod. 'I think you should get Sydney on the case of putting out some good PR for you. Corporate social responsibility projects, that kind of thing.'

'She's already looking at what CSR projects we have coming up. There's a charity gala on Thursday in the week we get home. We'll go and make our presence known.'

'Actually, that leads me nicely onto my other idea.'

He furrows his brows. I really don't want to cheapen what we have but as I turn the diamonds around my finger, brilliant sparkling gems entwined with a streak of darkness, I know it's the right thing to do.

'I think you should publicise the engagement.'

His eyes betray his anger.

'It makes you look human, Gregory. Someone can love you. This whole thing could still leak. You're one of the wealthiest men in the world; I just think showing people that someone can love you looks—'

'Don't you dare!' His words are a bark that howls across the emptiness of the harbour. 'Don't you dare turn the way I feel for you into a PR stunt, Scarlett. Don't ever do that!'

'I just think—'

'No!' He pulls his knee onto the lounger so we're facing each other. 'You're the only good thing in my life. I want the world to know you're mine and it will, but I'm not bringing what we have into this shit. It's worth more than this. So much more.'

'All right. I'm sorry.' I hold his cheek in my palm.

He turns to kiss my skin.

'CSR it is.'

'There's nothing we can do for a while. Let's get some sleep.'

'Can we stay out here?' I look up to the sky, the stars clearing as the blackness turns to grey. 'I like it.'

'I'm happy wherever you are.'

'Where is that, incidentally?'

'St Bart's, baby.'

We take two lounger cushions and lie on the front of the deck. He pulls my body into him – my back to his chest, his knees behind mine – and lays a thick blanket over us.

'You smell of you,' he says, nuzzling into my neck and drawing my hair back across my shoulder. I drift into a peaceful sleep, pushing away lingering thoughts of darkness and the stress we'll have to deal with when we wake again.

15

The sun is beating down on my face. In our brief sleep, I've wormed my way onto Gregory's chest, one hand on his bare pec, one leg wrapped across his. He holds me to him with an arm draped over my shoulder, his hand resting in my hair.

There's clattering and chiming coming from the dining area, followed by the sound of hushed voices. Gregory strokes my hair and presses his lips to my head. Without opening my eyes, I snuggle harder into his chest.

'I prefer waking up with you,' I mumble.

'Me, too, gorgeous. Come on, Bertie's setting up breakfast.'

I groan at first and cling to him. Then the curtain

of blissful contentedness lifts. 'Shit, what time is it?' I sit bolt upright, the blanket around us falling to my waist. 'I need to speak to Richard about the injunction.'

'You need to get dressed before you do anything else.'

I look down over my skimpy nightdress. 'Yes. I do.' Pulling the blanket around me, I leave Gregory in only his lounge bottoms. I can't resist a quick peek at him lying in the sun, arms stretched up behind his head. The epitome of man. In the process, I almost crash into Bertie.

'Morning, Miss Heath,' he says, attempting to disguise a smirk.

'Morning, Bertie.'

'Welcome to St Bart's,' Carl chimes through a bite of banana from the main salon.

'Good morning, Carl.'

'Hey, Scarlett, did you sleep well?' Bryony is laughing and I look back to see my man laughing, too. Someone might as well write S. E. X. across my brow in lipstick. 'Good morning everyone,' I say, only mildly amused as I wave a hand lazily in the air and head to our room.

When I make it back on deck wearing slightly more clothes, Williams and Amanda are at the breakfast table. She's leaning into his side and there's a sparkle in her eyes across the table full of fruit, breads, meats, cheeses and pastries.

I guess I'm not the only one who had a good night.

Gregory is on his phone, pacing the front of the deck in smart navy shorts and a plain white T-shirt, shades in place, hair wet from the shower. I open my laptop and boot it to life.

'You're working?' Amanda asks.

'Something came up this morning. Sorry to have this on the table over breakfast.'

Williams holds up a hand as if to say, *Don't worry.* 'Everything okay?'

I glance back at Gregory as I take a seat and refrain from saying, *Obviously not.* 'A London tabloid got wind of the case.'

'The murder?' Amanda asks, sitting forward and grabbing a slice of wholemeal toast.

I scowl at her flippancy from behind Bryony, who's pouring me a cup of coffee.

'He's settling with them?' Williams asks.

I shake my head and sip the soothing, rich coffee. 'They're going to print.'

'A local tabloid and they won't settle? What do they have?'

I set my cup on the table and type my password

into my laptop. 'They think Gregory bribed the police, or the CPS.'

The sound of Williams saying, 'And they think they have sound intel,' is drowned out by Amanda's shouting.

'Bloody hell, Scarlett!' She's out of her seat. 'Bribes now? Christ, you could lose your job over an association with bribes. Your whole *career*. Your *life*.'

There are things I miss about the old me. How uncomplicated and honest my life was. There are other things I'm glad have changed. Like the strength I've found in my own convictions. The way I won't be a pushover to keep people happy. And something I've learned from Gregory: the ability to take control of a situation, to move at *my* pace.

I retrieve my coffee cup from the table and sip as Amanda stands in front of me.

'At some point, Amanda, you're going to realise that he *is* part of my life. A very big and important part of it.'

Her mouth opens and closes without sound, hands moving to her hips.

'I appreciate what you're saying, and I know you're being a good friend, I do. But you don't know everything about the situation and...' I hate lying to my best friend but I have to, '...he didn't bribe anyone. Money breeds enemies and Gregory has amassed a few. That's all you need to know.'

'Christ, you even sound like him.'

I rise abruptly from my seat to face her, acutely aware that all movement on the yacht has stopped. 'I don't take that as an insult.' My words have much more strength than my eyes, which are pleading for her to trust me, to be my best friend.

This is more than a squabble over her stealing my clean towel, or taking my hair clips from my desk, or me letting her down for drinks after the office. But I can't be the one to back down. Not this time.

'What do you need me to do?' she eventually asks.

Williams exhales and movement starts up again on the yacht.

'Richard is filing for an interim injunction. He might even have it now.' I check my watch. Nine-fifteen here, afternoon in London.

'After that, he'll need to make a case to force them into settlement.' She snaps into work mode but flashes me a fleeting conciliatory smile.

'Exactly. Sydney, Gregory's PR manager, has been sending through details all morning. I need to call Richard for an update. If you could start pulling together a case summary.'

'Got it.'

'He'll need to know the details and background. I can help you with that.'

She bites her toast, takes a mouthful of tea then holds out her hands, bending and flexing her fingers as a request for me to hand over the laptop.

* * *

By eleven-thirty, Richard has confirmed that the interim injunction has been granted and he's putting together a strong case for further action, not really with the intention of pursuing a trial but to use as leverage to get the paper to settle. The settlement agreement will be so tight, they'll have to drop any leads remotely connected to the case. The way things are looking, Richard is confident that will happen, particularly with the amount of money Gregory is willing to stump up to keep the press away from Elsa.

Gregory joins us around the dining table and I give him the update. He's relieved, that much is a true reaction, but I know the way he holds himself, the shades of his irises, the tone of his voice. This is just another hurdle he's had to climb. He's tired and I find myself wondering how he's carried the weight of so much darkness for so many years.

I rub the dull ache beneath my breastbone and lay a hand on his thigh. My want to protect him is overwhelming. I want this to end forever but the feeling of restlessness in the back of my mind is increasing. Something tells me Katrina Martin is not going away. *That* night isn't going away and until they both do, Gregory will never be free of his past. We'll never be free of Kevin Pearson.

'Thank you both,' Gregory says to Amanda and me.

Pressure mounts behind my eyes.

'Amanda, would you come for a drink with me? Soft, of course. A short walk around the harbour? I'd like to talk to you.'

If she's taken aback, she doesn't show it. Maybe she feels like it's time to put some feelings to bed, too, but the lump in my throat is one of gratefulness. Grateful to Gregory for reaching out and trying to make yet another thing right. His life on paper looks like the dream, but he must be exhausted by it.

'Sure.'

Williams and Gregory have an unspoken exchange, in that way they do. Williams's soft eyes tell me he's also thankful for Gregory taking the high ground.

'We'll be back soon,' Gregory says, pressing his lips

to my temple. 'Hydrate, I've got a surprise for you this afternoon.'

In all the sex and legal battles, I think I've forgotten my hangover long enough to be sober.

As soon as Gregory and Amanda are off the boat, I take off my glasses and cover my face with my hands, pulling my knees into my chest on the chair.

'Hey, hey, what's this about?' Williams moves quickly to replace Gregory on the chair next to me and wraps an arm around my shoulder.

'Nothing.' I try to stifle my tears but one escapes. 'It's nothing. I just need to take a breath.'

'Talk to me, Scarlett.'

I sniff and turn on a fake smile for Williams.

Another silent drop escapes and rolls down my cheek just thinking about what to say. 'I love him so much, all of him. I love him so much, it makes everything ache. And the one thing I want to give him, I can't. I'd do anything for him, anything in my power, I'd do it.'

'I think you've already proved that, don't you?'

I snap my head round to look up at him. *He knows.*

'He didn't tell me. Nobody told me, until I just saw your reaction.'

All I can do is stare at him, my tears suspended.

'I know enough about the case to know things

didn't add up. I don't know the detail and I don't need to. All I'll say is this, what you did for him is more than anyone has ever done for him. He loved you before that but now, he'll never let anything come between you. Ring or no ring, you two are unbreakable.'

My next breath blows out my cheeks. He knows and I think it's a relief. Someone to talk to who knows Gregory and me. Who won't judge us. 'I thought that was it. I stupidly thought that with his father out of the picture, Gregory could be free. But it just keeps coming back to haunt him and it's killing me to think that I might have made things worse.'

Williams tugs me into his side. 'Scarlett, he's already changing. He is changed and you're the reason. I've been his friend for twenty years and I've never seen him so happy. Give him more time. There are a lot of years of hurt that he's never shared with anyone and he needs to get past them but he's doing it, trust me. You gave him that chance.'

'Oh, crap, you're going to be a super daddy,' I say, nudging into him and drying my cheeks again.

'I hope so.'

'Are you nervous?'

'Nervous doesn't cover it. Petrified is more apt,' he says, shaking his head.

'You'll be amazing. I know it.'

'All right, let's get you some fruit and water to replace those tears. You heard him...' He leans across the table for flavoured water and pours me a glass. Mimicking his friend's accent, he states, 'You need to hydrate.'

My amusement is short-lived though, because I realise now that Williams knows the truth... 'Amanda doesn't know, does she, about...?'

He hands me the full glass. 'It's not my story to tell.'

I nod. 'Thank you.'

As I'm finishing my second glass of flavoured water and a plate of watermelon, Gregory gives Amanda a hand back onto the yacht. She pats his shoulder and says something that makes him shake his head with a smirk.

Williams and I watch them, waiting for a clue, but they apparently won't be giving any insight. Hiding my no doubt red and puffy eyes behind my sunglasses, I say, 'I've hydrated.'

Gregory bites into a piece of watermelon. 'Good.'

'Can I know what we're doing now?'

'I'm taking you diving.' His wide, youthful grin makes my lips turn in response.

'Diving how? Like off the boat?'

He chuckles. 'Scuba diving. Wet suits, regs, tanks.'

'I can't just *dive*. I've never done it before.' As I say it, I'm already giddy about the idea.

'That's the point, baby; I want you to experience it. With me.'

'But won't I need lessons?'

'Ja. I'll teach you.' His playful South African twang thickens, making my stomach jump.

'You'll teach me how to dive?'

'You only need to know the basics.'

'How many times have you been diving? I'll be breathing through a tank. I don't think it's—'

He places two fingers over my pout. 'I'm a qualified instructor. So's Williams, and he'll be with us.'

'You're a dive instructor?' I ask through his fingers. 'When on earth did you have time to become a dive instructor?'

'In case you haven't noticed, angel, I own a yacht that anchors in the Caribbean.'

'All right smart-arse. When do we start?'

'Right now.' His eyes are beaming as he inclines his head in the direction of the harbour. I see Carl loading six tanks and bags of equipment onto a speed-boat with purpose-made holders for the tanks. I stand to get a better look.

Two strong arms wrap around my waist and a chin rests on top of my head. 'Excited, beautiful?'

'Ha. Damn right I am.'

* * *

Carl manoeuvres the dive boat into a small bay where we're the only people in sight. A small cove of golden sand, flanked by rocks, is decorated with pebbles and shells where waves are rolling gently to make white fluffy clouds on the shoreline.

Gregory stands on the front of the boat in only a pair of board shorts, his tanned skin enhancing the muscles of his already striking body. He drops anchor and gives Carl a thumbs up, then stands, legs spread for balance, with a smug half-smile as I stare, unashamedly delighting in his splendour.

'Like what you see, baby?'

'Always.'

He jumps down to the small deck space, taking off his shades to show me the playful sheen of his eyes. Happy and carefree, at least for a while, in his board shorts with dark hair messed up from sea water, he looks his age.

'You can stay in your bikini for now; we'll be

shallow and the water's warm. We'll put you in your gear on shore and go over the basics.'

'Hmm, and there was me thinking I'd mastered the basics.'

'Let's hope you're as good at the dive basics as you are at the other basics,' he says with a wink that makes me chuckle.

Williams makes his way ashore with two dive tanks and Carl follows with two sets of everything else. Gregory jumps into the water then holds his hands to lower me. When we reach the sand, he talks me through the equipment and very briefly how to set it up, whilst Williams and Carl catch some rays on the beach.

When Gregory feels I've sufficiently listened, repeated back to him and absorbed everything he has to say, and I've managed not to laugh at his patronising method of teaching for more than five entire minutes, he helps me into the BCD jacket. He talks me through strapping myself in with the belt around the waist and harness-type straps over the shoulders, all the while holding onto the tank and breathing apparatus attached to the inflatable jacket, taking the weight for me.

'These things weigh a tonne,' I say, bending forward slightly to ease the weight of four metal blocks attached to my waist by a coarse, thick material belt.

'They won't feel too bad in the water. Ready?'

'Yep.'

'All right, it'll feel heavy when I let go of the tank. Head into the water and kneel. I'll bring your fins.'

'Okay. Let's do it.'

He releases the tank and I fall back, slapstick style. 'Holy shit, that's heavy.'

Gregory catches me with a hearty laugh.

'Don't tell me you're ready if you're not. Ready?'

I blow out. 'Yep. Ready now.'

'Okay, go on,' he laughs.

On our knees, just below the surface, Gregory teaches me how to breathe through my own regulator and switch mine with his spare if I get in trouble. That thought scares me. He shows me how to clear my mask and retrieve my regulator if it falls out of my mouth.

'Don't worry, I'll be with you. I won't let anything happen to you.'

'I know you won't.'

When we're back on the boat, Carl drives us to a stick poking out of the waves, which is apparently a marker for a dive site.

'I was out here with Bryony last week and we saw four turtles,' Carl tells me.

'Turtles?' I turn to Gregory. 'Seriously?'

He nods with a delectable smile.

'Oh my gosh, I've only ever seen them in Attenborough documentaries.'

Gregory hands me a short wetsuit. 'Put this on.'

'Aren't you wearing one?'

'I'll be fine in shorts. You might find the water cold down there, especially your first time. It'll make the weights more comfortable on your hips, too. Dunk the suit in the water first; it's easier to get in when it's wet.'

'I've no doubt it is,' I say with a mischievous wink.

When I'm suited up, he makes me recite the prewater kit checks he taught me but he does the work. 'Big willies really are fun,' I tell him. 'BCD. Weights. Releases. Air and final check.'

He helps me sit onto the rim of the boat, then fixes himself up and when I hear an almighty splash, I find both him and Williams and Gregory surfacing from under the water.

'What on earth? How do I do that?'

'Fully inflate your BCD. Good girl.'

'Don't *good girl* me.'

'Christ. Come on then, *big* girl, put your hand over

your mouthpiece and your mask. Now cross your legs and—'

When I surface, Gregory and Williams are on my side of the boat. Gregory removes his mouthpiece to speak. 'Okay, you need to deflate your BCD and sink down. Don't forget to go slow and equalise your ears like I showed you. If your ears hurt, kick back up just a little and try again.'

My heart starts beating fast but I deflate my BCD and sink just like he taught me. Williams is there hovering just above the ocean bed and once I've managed to stabilise my buoyancy, he signals to ask if I'm okay then for me to follow him and as I do, I notice Gregory slide in line beside me.

It takes me a minute or two to adjust to being in the water, trying to remember everything I learned and swim and float at the same time. Gregory stays right by my side the whole time and signals to ask if I'm okay. My breaths come thick and fast, many more bubbles rising from my regulator than the number coming from Williams and Gregory combined. Gregory rolls onto his back and looks me in the eye, reassuring me and making me feel safe. My breathing calms and when he's satisfied, he drifts back to my side. He takes my hand, rolling his thumb across my knuckles, guiding me along with him.

Now. Calm. Safe. I start to appreciate this new, colourful, exquisite underworld. We move over corals, pinks, purples, blues. Gregory points out an enormous aqua and purple giant clam that snaps shut when we move close. Small, orange, weed-type things, beautiful and bright, like jelly, are just like I've seen on TV. Gregory leaves me briefly to swim to the mini bushes and points out a fish that looks just like Nemo.

I hear a ting and I'm surprised by how easily I can manoeuvre to look at Williams tapping his tank with a piece of metal. He places one hand over the other, fingers bent, interlaced and pointing to the seabed, and he turns his thumbs in circles. Gregory moves quickly at the signal I don't recognise and, taking my hand, he glides us towards the spot Williams is watching. A huge, beautiful green turtle moves its arms elegantly up and down and drifts through the water. The sight is so profound, the bubbles from my regulator stop until Gregory taps my back.

The most important rule is to breathe, Scarlett; you mustn't hold your breath underwater.

I nod and take a breath that makes me rise in the water so Gregory has to take my hand quickly and pull me back to his level, where I continue watching the turtle and follow behind as it swims away from us. When it eventually moves into the distance, I'm so giddy, I roll in the water, amazed at the feeling of complete weightlessness. Freedom. So far removed from the real world. And I get to share my technicolour heaven with the man of my dreams.

His eyes are beaming when he swims alongside me.

I point to my eye, then my heart, then right at him.

16

Yesterday, Richard confirmed that the tabloid has agreed to settle. DI Barnes confirmed that Trina has been suspended on suspicion of releasing a conspiracy theory to the press. We're one week into our holiday and since their talk, Gregory and Amanda are getting along, possibly even enjoying each other's company. Yet, I wake to find myself alone in bed for the third time in five nights and I wish I knew how to help him. I've been doing what I know, what *we* know, helping him forget. But the effect wears off. It doesn't stop the next nightmare from coming.

'Come to bed,' I whisper into his naked back, running my hands down his shoulders.

He's leaning over the rail of the yacht holding a

crystal glass of liquor, most likely Scotch. 'I'll be back shortly. You go get some sleep.'

I lie in bed, tossing and turning, wishing he would come back to me. As tiredness takes over my thoughts, a sense of uneasiness fills my mind. I might think my own worries about Katrina Martin were irrational if I didn't know the same thoughts were keeping Gregory up every night and sending him back to his dark, closed world.

* * *

I stretch in the brightness of our bedroom, sunlight beaming in through the small window and reflecting off the bright walls. I've managed to sleep until after ten; that's practically unheard of. The disrupted previous nights have obviously taken their toll.

After a shower, I dirty back up with an application of suntan lotion, then pull on one of several pairs of light denim shorts Julia and Lucas packed for me. Pairing the shorts with a white vest over a shimmering silver-grey bikini, I head out to the deck.

Bertie has left plates of food from breakfast on the table, covered by linen napkins. I pour a coffee and take it with a slice of fresh bread and jam to the sun loungers where Amanda is laid out with the latest edition of her favourite magazine.

I settle onto the lounger next to her. 'Morning.'

'Hey. What do you think of this?' She opens a double spread of pages to me and I'm confronted by images of ten vintage designer prams. 'I'm thinking of going old chic. I think Baby would like it.'

'I like them. Erm, why do you have a baby magazine hidden inside *Vogue*?'

'Meh, Ed keeps telling me to calm down but it's exciting. I have so many ideas for clothes, the nursery. Oh gosh, there are some amazing Christening ideas in here, too. I mean, I think we should be married before the Christening, it doesn't seem right otherwise, but there's no harm in future-proofing. And, of course, we still need to think about a house for us all.'

'A house? Wouldn't you stay in Williams's place?'

'Ongoing discussion. Ed has a two bed but I think we need a house. A home for Baby.'

'Wow, Amanda, I don't say this to be shitty, really I don't.'

'But you think I need to calm down, too?'

'I, no, not calm down, it's cute that you're so excited. Just, maybe remember that Williams might need a little more time to come round.'

'I know. Bloody men. That's why I'm hiding the

mag. In my defence, he didn't need time to knock me up.'

I splutter through my mouthful of coffee. 'Fair point. I'm sure you remind him often enough. Where are they anyway?'

She points loosely in the direction of the sea, completely disinterested.

Taking my coffee to the side of the deck, I watch both men blazing across the water on swanky-looking jet skis, wearing board shorts, bare chests and huge grins. They power straight towards each other, so fast, my shoulders rise to my ears the closer they get and I hold my breath when they're just metres apart, practically exhaling the words, 'Holy shit!' when they both turn right at the last minute.

I watch them for twenty minutes or so before Gregory notices me and rides back towards the boat.

'Get here,' he shouts, as he pulls the jet ski up to the steps at the back of the yacht.

Carl fixes me into a blue life jacket.

'How come I have to wear one of these and you don't?'

'Because you're small and delicate and you've never ridden a jet ski before... and I love you.'

Grinning, I hold out my hand for him to help me

onto the back of his man toy. 'You win.' Tucking into his back, I wrap my hands tightly around his waist.

'Hold on, baby, I'm going to take you for the ride of your life.'

He skids across the water and sets off in a straight line, turning slightly into the rolling sea. I bounce in my seat, holding onto him tighter with each wave. Water sprays in my face so I can hardly see but adrenalin has me screaming in delight.

'I want to drive!' I shout over the roar of the engine and the crashing of water.

'What?'

'I want to give you the ride of *your* life, handsome.'

He throws his head back with a laugh but slows the jet ski to a stop. He unclips the plastic spiral wire that's attached to his shorts. 'All right, climb around me and attach this to your jacket.'

'What is it?'

'It's a safety wire. If you come off, the wire unclips and kills the engine.'

'Am I going to come off?'

'If you drive like a *girl*, you might.'

I laugh hard from my abdomen. 'I'll show you how a *girl* drives.'

I twist the handle bar right back and we shoot off

across the water, crashing over waves and landing with a thud.

'Scarlett, slow down, you're insane.'

'High and fast, baby!' I shout, enjoying the feel of his chest chugging against my back and his arms wrapped tightly around me.

I turn us into corners, lifting us out of our seats, water blazing into my face. *God, this is fun!*

Eventually, I slow us down in the middle of the sea and enjoy his arms roaming across my stomach. 'I don't ever want to go home.'

'Me neither, baby.'

I lean back into him with a heavy sigh. 'I wish it could be just us, like this, always.'

'But you know what, I'm looking forward to going home. To *our* home and having you all to myself, in our bed, on our sofa, on our desk, in our shower.'

'You've been thinking about this.'

'Every minute of every day.' He presses his lips to my forehead. 'Three more days until I can tie you to our bed and fuck you until you're begging me to stop.'

'I'm not sure that'll ever happen.'

* * *

Around lunchtime, Richard emails a scan of the settlement agreement signed on behalf of the tabloid. I run off a copy in Gregory's small on-boat office and have him sign before scanning the executed version back to Richard to file.

'Would you like wine with lunch today?' Bryony asks when the four of us take our seats and wait for Bertie's legendary fish stew.

'Bring a bottle of Pol Rodger first, Bryony,' Gregory says.

With full glasses – well, Amanda's one third full – Amanda and Williams eye Gregory, waiting for a clue as to why we're drinking champagne. There's no speech to toast, no acknowledgement of what I know Gregory is feeling. He tips his glass subtly in my direction.

We fended off this attack and we'll fend off every other attack that comes our way. Together.

Gregory takes hold of my hand on top of the table and strokes my knuckles. The conversation is lively and Gregory and I are as involved as the others but beneath the table, my foot slips lazily over the skin of his exposed calf. He doesn't react, which I see as a challenge I'd like to conquer.

Sipping the cool champagne, I slide my foot higher, over the seam of his beige shorts. A challenge.

But still no reaction. As he speaks, I work my toes higher still and halt over his crotch. He stops talking and shuffles slightly, pushing back against my instep.

'Wouldn't you agree, Scarlett?' Williams asks.

'Ah, yes, yep, sure.'

'What do you agree with, Scarlett?' Gregory asks, his head angled to one side, a delicious half-smile, cocky and sexy as hell, drawn on his lips.

I jab my foot gently into his package. 'What Williams said.'

Williams continues to talk and Amanda jumps in to protest against whatever his line of argument is. I increase the pressure of my toes over Gregory's growing bulge.

'Here we go, guys. No shellfish in this one for you,' Bryony says, putting a large, white bowl in front of Amanda. She places a regular bowl, with shellfish, in front of me and Bertie places two similar bowls in front of Williams and Gregory.

I rub the ball of my foot across Gregory's crotch one last time before he reaches down, squeezing my toes until I yelp and bang my knee off the underside of the table. He glares at me, shaking his head, as Williams tries to stop a smirk pulling on his lips.

Maybe I wasn't as subtle as I thought.

The stew is fantastic, delicious poached white fish,

langoustine, crab and clams in a rich tomato and onion sauce, just the faintest taste of nutmeg coming through. It's too good to leave but I stay away from the bread, as does Gregory. We're both hungry, but not for bread.

Amanda takes my attention as Bryony clears our empty bowls. 'I'm thinking of cutting my hair. Going for a sophisticated bob. What do you think?'

From the corner of my eye, I see Gregory and Williams have one of their unspoken conversations. 'Are you sure? I love your hair the way it is. You've always had long hair.'

Williams takes Amanda's hand across the table. 'Why don't you let me show you around the island?' he asks, making me look to the instigator of that idea and finding two mischievous browns staring back at me.

'Sure. You two want to come?'

'Oh, no, we're good. You guys enjoy,' I say, not moving my hazel-greens from my dazzling man.

When they're gone, Gregory's lust-filled eyes are drinking me in. He pushes his chair back from the table. 'Get here.'

I go to him, straddling him in his chair.

'You want to make me hard, baby?'

'Rock hard,' I whisper.

'Tell me why.'

I fist my hands in his hair and hover my lips over his. 'Because I want you inside me. I want you to drive me wild the way I know you can.'

He slides his hands under my yellow sundress and cups my bare arse then yanks me forward onto his hips. 'Do you know how much I love to see your face, desperate for me? How incredible you feel around my dick?' He lifts his pelvis, letting me feel his erection, the coarse material of his shorts rubbing against my tender skin. 'Are you already wet for me, baby? Tell me how much you want my cock inside you.'

I dip my tongue into his mouth and draw it across the underside of his lip. 'I want you inside me. I want you to fuck me. Rough.'

'You're going to be screaming my name, baby.'

I grind my hips in response to his husky voice and he pulls me to him, kissing me harshly, the way I want him to take me.

'Make me scream your name,' I whisper.

He stands from the chair, taking me with him, and carries me below deck. He kicks the bedroom door shut behind us then shoves my back against the wall, pressing his stiff crotch against me.

'Feel how hard you make me. I want to come inside you. But first I want to come all over here.'

With his body pinning my waist to the wall, he pulls my strapless dress to my waist, exposing my breasts. He licks my nipple and moans as he bites the soft flesh, stretching it in his teeth. He offers two fingers to my mouth.

'Suck.'

I run my tongue from the base to the tip of his fingers then wrap my mouth around them. He withdraws his fingers and just as quickly, pushes them inside my welcoming sex.

'So fucking wet.'

'God, I want you. Now.'

He pulls me back from the wall and sits me onto the edge of the bed. He takes off his white T-shirt and I run my hands over his chest before moving to the button and zip of his shorts. He lifts my dress over my head. 'You've driven me insane for the last hour, knowing you had nothing on under that.'

'Mission accomplished.' I wanted to make him crazy. Crazy enough that he'd give me the kind of sex I can take home with me and remember when we're fighting off whatever threat is next, whoever tries to break us next.

'Take these off,' he says, gesturing to his shorts.

First, I reach inside his tight white boxers and cup

his hard-on until his head rolls back. Then I free him and indulge in the sight of him, a work of art.

He grabs my ankles. 'Lie back.' He plants my feet flat on the edge of the bed then kneels between my thighs.

His tongue teases my clit, drawing my hips from the bed.

'Oh, God, Gregory.'

He sucks, drawing blood into the sensitive bud, making me beg for more. He works his tongue masterfully down, tasting the inside of my hole, working around the edge then back up to my clit. I'm building fast.

'Not yet,' he says, standing and taking my hands to sit me up. 'Suck me.'

I moan as I wrap my lips straight around the end of his cock, taking him by surprise. I work his base with my hand and draw my mouth up and down his angry shaft, eager to see him climax.

'You know exactly what to do to me.'

His words make me work him harder, encouraging the first drop of pre-ejaculate, lapping it up.

'Scarlett, take me there. I want to come all over your tits.'

I wrap a fist around the base of him and tug up and down as I swirl his end, flicking my tongue across his spot, swallowing another drop of pre-come.

'Come for me, Gregory. I want you to come.'

He pulls out of me and nudges my shoulder. I lie back and watch him, towering over me, taking over with his own hand. 'You're so fucking beautiful, Scarlett. I could watch you all day, hot for me.'

'Come for me,' I beg.

He pumps harder, faster. His hips move forward, the muscles in his neck strain. 'Fuck.' He leans forward, resting one knee on the edge of the bed and with another thrust of his fist, he comes across my chest. 'Scarlett.' My name rolls off his tongue as he leans over me, pressing his chest against mine, smothering his pleasure between us.

I roll my hips up against him impatiently. Then he's back on his knees, licking my clit.

'Gregory! Please.'

'Please, what?'

'Make me orgasm.'

He thrusts his fingers inside me as he sucks my clit. 'I fucking love you, Scarlett Heath.' His words are hot against my bare flesh, and they're unravelling me. As his fingers curl and sweep my insides, I cry his name and explode around him. I throw my arms above my head, relishing in the sensation, my insides pulsing. Then he grabs my hips, pulling me back to the edge of the bed and thrusts inside me almost instantaneously. My body responds, rousing again, one long, continuing, thrilling orgasm as he hammers into me, so deep it hurts. An addictive pain. 'Gregory! Harder.' He flips me by the waist then pulls my hips so I'm standing on the tips of my toes, my hands leaning down to the bed, completely exposing myself to him. He re-enters me on a growl and thrusts over and over until my unrelenting orgasm has me bunching the bedsheets in my fists and I come again, my muscles clamping around his cock. He slaps my arse cheek as my body gives up and drives the feeling higher until I smother my face in the duvet and scream.

'Get on the bed.'

I crawl onto the bed and wait for my next instruction.

'On your back, leaning off the side. Hands on the floor.'

I shuffle back until my arms and head are leaning back off the bed, my legs bent and wide, accepting whatever he has to give.

He leans over me, dragging his hand down my sticky chest and abdomen. 'You look seriously fucking hot like this.'

His fingers move inside me, his tongue moving back to my clit.

'Gregory. No more. I can't.'

'Take it, baby, I know you want it.'

His fingers move lazily in and out of me as he sucks my clit and another round of pleasure has my limbs in spasm.

'My turn.' He moves over me, pushing his hard shaft into me. He raises my hips, the angle shifting him deeper into me.

He pounds into me, keeping my body suspended in a state of ecstasy.

'One more, baby, come with me. Let me feel you.' His words add to the blood rushing to my head, clouding my mind, making me trip on the feel of him. He drives in and out, his muscles strained, his breathing erratic.

'Gregory! I'm coming.'

He thrusts once, twice, and barking expletives, he fills me with warm lust.

He pulls me up and folds me in his arms. 'Thank you,' I manage through panted breaths. 'For giving me something to remember.'

17

'Scarlett, these just came for you.'

Margaret enters my office, taking me away from my daydream of Gregory making love to me on the sand of a Caribbean bay, moonlight illuminating every curve and edge of his perfect face.

Margaret smiles, the soft pink of her lipstick matching the shade of her blouse. 'They're very beautiful,' she says, inhaling the scent of the dozen red roses she's holding.

She places the flowers on my desk and I take the small, red envelope, already knowing who they're from.

I miss seeing you all day every day.

X

'Thanks, Margaret.'

'Can I ask how it went with Neil?'

I move the flowers in their water-filled box to the ledge of my window then adjust my purple chiffon blouse, tucking it into my black pencil skirt.

'It was awful. He wasn't even angry; he was just really disappointed. He thinks I should take some time, mull it over some more.'

'Do you want to?'

I look down at the card in my hand and smile. *If I work with him, I get to see him every day.* 'No.'

'Then you have your answer.' She drops a hand to my shoulder. 'Neil Wallace will just have to accept that you're leaving. He's just panicking about who'll fill your shoes when you're gone. We'll miss you around here.'

I don't tell her that even those few words are making me feel worse about my decision to leave Saunders. She makes a discreet exit when Amanda charges into my office with two lattes and a large bar of chocolate.

'Are you blowing your week's caffeine allowance?' I ask.

'First day back is a bitch; the doctors can go screw

themselves. I know my baby and I know my baby needs coffee and chocolate. Here.'

I chuckle as I accept the latte and Amanda slumps into the seat opposite my desk, unravelling the foil from the sweat treat.

'You know, last time we did this, you threw up in my bin and we realised you were pregnant.'

'Don't worry, I have no intention of repeating the trick. This bad boy is staying firmly in my stomach.' She wraps her mouth around two large squares of chocolate. 'That's sooooo good.'

I snap off a square and let it melt in my mouth. 'I don't think even chocolate is going to help me today. I have major post-travel blues.'

'Mm, speaking of blues, is Neil spewing about you leaving?'

'He's far from thrilled.'

'Is he making you work your notice?'

'No. As soon as he realised I was going to GJR, he changed his tune. He wants me to hand over Mr Ghurair's deal and I won't pick back up the stuff I handed to others before we went away but the rest of my work was Gregory's anyway, so I'll take it with me.'

'Who are you handing over the Dubai deal to?'

'You. If you want it? I think it would be good for you. A big deal before you go off.'

'Sure, I'm in.'

'Well, in that case, I might be out of here next week, maybe even Friday.'

'Holy shit,' she mumbles around another slab of chocolate. 'It'll be the end of an era.'

'And the start of a new one.' I glance at my sparkling diamonds.

'Cheers to that.' She nudges her cardboard coffee cup against mine.

* * *

My phone rings as I'm typing handover notes for Mr Ghurair's final transaction. Gregory's name dances across the screen.

'Hey, you.'

'How's the first day back?' he asks.

'I've had better.'

'Have you handed in your notice?'

'Yep.'

'So when are you coming to join Team Ryans?'

'Actually, if you want me, next week.' I can sense his smile. 'Thank you for the flowers.'

'You're more than welcome, fiancée. Can you come here this afternoon?'

'I guess so. It's not like I need to bank gold stars

here. I'll check on the registration of the *Black Dia-monds* portfolio before I come over.'

'I'll have Anya order lunch. Sushi good?'

'Perfect.'

Scooping up my pile of documents related to *Black Diamonds*, I head to the trainee, Hugh's office. 'Home alone today?' I ask, taking note of the empty desk behind him.

'Charles is in a meeting. How was your break?'

'Too short.'

'Argh, at least you got away. I don't have anything planned until May and I'm already shattered.'

'It'll come around before you know it.'

'I, ah, heard your news. Congratulations. In-house, isn't it?'

'News travels fast. Yes, I'm going in-house for the GJR group, which leads me nicely onto the reason I'm here.'

He pushes his chair back from his desk and twists his pen in the fingers of his right hand. A pose I'm sure he wouldn't adopt if his supervisor were in the room.

'Constant Sources is a GJR subsidiary. How's the registration of the IP in the game coming along?'

'I've been meaning to speak to you about that.'

I raise an eyebrow. 'Sounds like you're going to tell me there's a glitch.'

Hugh leans forward and pulls a few tatty-looking pieces of paper from a disorganised tray on his desk. 'There was a problem in China. Let me see.' He flicks through the messy papers then rummages through the pile in his tray again. 'Here it is. Local counsel in China said there were already registrations for some of the trademarks, including the name *Black Diamonds*, and the copyright, I think. Apparently, the applications were filed hours before we tried to file.'

'Shit, seriously? In the same class? Gaming?'

'Yep.'

'Remind me who we're dealing with in China.'

'Wang Nongfan is handling the applications.'

'Okay and this just happened today?'

'No, let me see.'

I tighten my grip around my documents and tap the grey hardwearing carpet with my foot whilst he flicks through his papers.

'He told me about it Wednesday so I assume it happened then.'

'Wednesday? Hugh, it's Monday. Why am I just hearing about this now?'

'Well, you were on holiday and I tried to chat it through with Richard in the IP team but he was busy working on an injunction so—'

'I know about the injunction but that's not an excuse, Hugh. I told you to contact me if anything went wrong. We've wasted almost a week now.'

'I'm sorry, I didn't think—'

'That's exactly it, Hugh: you didn't *think*. What's the status now?' I fire my words at him, sharp and fast.

He stops playing with his godforsaken pen and sits up straight in his chair, finally looking interested. 'I, ah, Wang Nongfan is waiting for you to get back to him.'

Trying to keep a lid on the fury building inside me, I snap. 'Thanks for doing absolutely nothing in my absence.'

'I'm sorry, Scarlett, I didn't realise it was such a big deal.'

'Hugh, the registration rules in China are first come, first served. This could have a real impact for the client. If somebody else is trying to register our game or a rip off of it, everything the client was trying to protect is undermined. So, yes, it's a big fucking deal.'

His eyes practically pop out of his head. Griping at people and using the F word in the office are two things people aren't used to from old Scarlett.

'I'm sorry,' he says again, heightening my annoyance further.

'You don't need to say sorry to me, Hugh; it's the client you should be apologising to.'

'Should I, do you think I should call the client?'

I all but snarl as I charge out of his office and back to my own.

A call with Wang Nongfan confirms that the registration looks to be for identical entries to the IP we're trying to register in *Black Diamonds*, which means we *can't* register *Black Diamonds* in China, at least not without a fight. What angers me more is that, if I'd been in the office, I wouldn't have allowed it to take over a week to file an application. Being as respectful as possible in the circumstances, I explained this to Wang Nongfan, only to be told the delay was due to Stuart Culliton not providing all the necessary details sooner. Having established the whole frustrating circle of events, my excitement to see Gregory has turned to anxiousness. Whilst my tolerance for incompetence is low, Gregory's is significantly lower. *He's going to take this* really *well.*

* * *

'Mr Ryans is ready for you,' Sue says as I approach the reception desk on the twenty-eighth floor of Gregory's glossy high-rise office tower. Her cheeks flush red, making me cringe inside. I wonder whether she'll have informed the rest of Gregory's staff that I'm not only his lawyer.

'Thank you, Sue,' I say with a soft smile, hoping she'll remember I'm keeping her crush on Gregory a secret in return for her allegiance.

Gregory is on his phone, standing in the window of his large office, his free hand in his pocket. He turns when I click the frosted glass door shut behind me. The flat screens around his room are continually updating with stock exchanges, commodity indices and BBC World News.

'I've read the proposal and I don't like it. He hasn't given me any concrete support for the return. I'm not saying the idea is dead in the water but he needs to rethink and send me a new proposal. As things stand, the answer's no.'

He gestures to the coffee table flanked by two leather sofas, which is covered in plates of sashimi on ice, sushi rolls and Japanese-style salad. I take off my mac and blazer then settle onto a sofa, pouring two cups of hot green tea.

'Chase Mr Cheung for the first cut of the joint venture agreement from Shangzen Tek, too. I'd like to have my lawyer take a look over it ASAP. I don't want him running this down to the wire. If he starts playing games, put him in touch with me directly. No, that won't be necessary; I want to manage this one.'

Gregory makes his way over to me and I hand him a cup of green tea.

'I'm not interested in hearing a pitch from them. If I had an interest in the sector, I'd know who to approach. It's not a good time to invest in the market. Is that everything? All right, let's pick up Thursday. I want an update on all action points. I'll leave you to finish off. Good afternoon, gents.'

He hangs up, drops the phone onto the coffee table, then strokes a hand down my cheek and drops his lips to mine. 'Hey.'

'Sorry I'm late.' I wonder silently when is the best time to broach the *Black Diamonds* registration.

My phone rings inside my handbag. A US number I don't recognise flashes on the screen.

'Scarlett Heath speaking.'

'Scarlett, Malcolm Russell here.'

'Malcolm, hello, how are you?'

'Well. Good. Listen, Scarlett, I'm calling about the US filings for Constant Sources.'

'Great, is everything going okay?'

'No, actually, that's why I'm calling. It looks like we've been beaten to it.'

Shit. 'How so?'

I hear the rustle of papers down the line. 'The trademark *Black Diamonds* and the whole game design were filed on Friday. Even some of the characters have been registered, Scarlett.'

'It's a replica?'

'Hard to say. I'd like to question the creator, ah...'

'Stuart Culliton.' I cast cautious eyes to Gregory, who's waiting for me before starting his lunch, leaning back against the leather with an inquisitive frown. 'I'd want to make sure he hasn't sold or licensed the game. That's if it is definitely his game. By the looks of things, this is either a really great copy, or the actual original.'

'Malcolm, why wasn't it filed until today?'

'We couldn't get the information we needed from Stuart, Scarlett. It didn't come through until Friday, then we had to prepare the applications.'

'That's interesting. Our lawyer in China had the same problem and now the same thing has happened. Okay, let me pick up with Stuart and I'll see where we get to. In the meantime, what are our options?'

'We could fight the true ownership. The fact that Stuart's game is already on the market could help but if it turns litigious, the fact the game is making profit could also go against us if we lose.'

'A claim for loss of opportunity?'

'Right. And if we fight it, we're talking money and locking the game up in litigation for a long time.'

'That might just be our best card.' My mind is jumping down ten different avenues all at once whilst Gregory's eyes are still focused on me, now from his position in the window. 'Constant Sources didn't buy the game to keep it on the market; they bought it to take it *off* the market.'

'It's a possible tactic. Why don't you reach out to Stuart and we can reconnect later today?'

'Great, thanks, Malcolm.'

I hang up and tap the phone against my pursed lips as if the rhythm might help organise my thoughts. Somebody else is ripping off *Black Diamonds*. That's feasible. It was always the weakness and the risk I warned Gregory against. Someone could have reverse-engineered the game and got the code. But if you were trying to rip it off, why not come up with a similar concept? Why go for the exact same game and give it the same name, knowing it would lead to a fight?

I explain everything to Gregory and tell him, 'That's a question we might never know the answer to but what I don't understand is why Stuart has held the information back. It's like he's purposefully stalled the registration.'

'I don't think that's the case, Scarlett; he seems

content here.' Gregory dabs his fingers on a white linen napkin and rests back on the sofa.

I pick up a bowl of spiced seaweed salad and sit back to eat it with my chopsticks, my mind still wandering. 'Do you think he's angry about you buying the game at seven hundred and fifty thousand?'

'I really don't think so. He's onto a good thing here.'

'But if he thought that game was his millionaire ticket?'

'Speak to him, see what you think, but I don't get the impression he's vindictive and I'm generally a good judge of character.'

I swallow and place the bowl back on the coffee table. 'And what about the fact these registration problems have happened in the same order we're trying to register?'

'China then the US? Baby, that's hardly a pattern. It's electronic gaming; they're obvious jurisdictions.' He picks a piece of tuna sashimi with his chopsticks, dunks it in soy sauce then eats it in one mouthful.

'Why aren't you concerned about this, Gregory?'

He dabs the sides of his mouth with a napkin.

'Should I be concerned?'

I sigh. 'Maybe not yet. I guess I'm more irked than

concerned at this stage. If I was here overseeing things, I don't think we'd be in this situation.'

'You're entitled to a holiday, Scarlett.' He stands, drops his used napkin on the coffee table and adjusts his cuffs beneath his blazer so the shirt hangs just slightly lower than his jacket, a Gregory-ism that makes me smile. 'I trust you. You'll sort this.'

'I need to speak to Stuart.'

'Not yet. I want to show you something.' A delicious half-smile makes its way to his lips. I have to blink away libidinous thoughts. 'Come.'

He holds open his office door and I step into the hallway. Adjusting his tie, which was already perfectly central, he leads me down the corridor. We walk side by side, my knuckles grazing but not holding hands in a way that feels unnatural these days.

'We're here,' he says, sounding almost triumphant. I look around the end of the corridor and see nothing, other than a corner desk in the open-plan area opposite the frosted glass office spaces. A short metal nameplate with *Melanie* in black letters rests on one side of the L-shape desk. A similar tag with *Laylla* rests on top of a computer screen on the other.

Smiling at Melanie and Laylla, I whisper, 'What am I supposed to be looking at?'

He turns me away from Melanie and Laylla to face

the door of a frosted glass corner office. I run my eyes over the door and the glass. It takes seconds for my focus to fall on the black letters.

SCARLETT HEATH GENERAL COUNSEL

'I'm getting a corner office? When did you do this?'

He holds open the door to let me into the ridiculously large office, not as big as his own but certainly not small. He lets the door close behind us as I take in my large chrome and glass desk in the window, two flat-screen televisions on the walls, a round table with four leather chairs in one corner and a black two-seater sofa with a matching footstool in the other.

'Like it?' he asks.

'Like it? Are you kidding?'

He gestures to the black leather desk chair. 'Take a seat.'

I do as instructed and spin in my chair to face a bunch of white roses in the window. 'Are these for me?'

'Who else would they be for? Look in the drawer.'

I open the top drawer of a three-drawer chest to one side of the desk and find a rectangular black box.

'Oh my gosh, a Mont Blanc?'

'I'm not having my wife use biros.'

'I don't use biros; I have a nice pen.'

'Well, if you don't want it...'

'Shh, of course I want it, I love it. This is insane though, Gregory; these pens cost a fortune.'

'A perk of being a billionaire,' he says, so incredibly arrogantly that I laugh.

'You had this done when we were away?'

He nods and walks to the window. 'You can always see home, too.'

Standing beside him, I look across the city to the Shard, then I lean up and kiss his cheek. 'I love it.'

* * *

Stuart has a desk in an open-plan techy space on the twenty-third floor. I've had no reason to visit this floor before. Everything feels grey, full of wires and metal, sort of futuristic. There are tens, if not hundreds of computers and machines. The floor is mostly filled with men, heads down, most wearing headphones as they play with source code on various programs or work with small tools on what look like computer and mobile accessories.

I make my way through the computer stations, some machines stacked two or three high, all displaying different screens, and head to the bottom left corner of the floor where Gregory told me to look. Stuart's ears are covered in large, padded black headphones. His eyes are focused intently on a black screen covered in some kind of green code. With his black hair, square jaw and black shirt, I think of Neo and *The Matrix*. The One.

He catches me in his peripheral vision, taking a second to blink and actually look up. *Those eyes.* The same unsettling feeling washes over me as the first time I met him. His eyes are beautiful. Deep brown and too familiar for a boy I've met only twice. They're alluring, magnetic even, yet I don't want to look at them. I rub my arm as goosebumps form on my skin.

'Scarlett, hi,' Stuart says with that strong Zimbabwean accent.

'Stuart, do you have a moment to chat about *Black Diamonds*?'

'Sure,' he says, freeing himself of his headphones and standing from his desk, tapping keys on his keyboard and sending his screen to black. 'There's a coffee area over there.' He points back towards the lift.

I take a seat on a stool set at a high white bench in the small kitchenette area. 'How are you settling in?'

'It's great.' He takes a can of Pepsi from a double-door fridge. 'Want one?'

'No, thank you.'

'You know I was irritated at first; I wanted to just sell the game, make my millions.' He laughs, a warm, soft chuckle. 'Gregory was right, though; *Black Diamonds* wasn't my big break. I'm working on some really exciting stuff and Gregory has the technology to help me do it. Some of the stuff here...' he shakes his head and gulps from his can, '...it's real high quality. Innovative. Tech I've never worked with or even seen before, only heard of. And London's growing on me, too. I've got a more permanent place, finally, after four months of being here.'

'Well, that's great, Stuart. I'm glad you're enjoying it and settling in. But listen, you know I'm trying to register the intellectual property in *Black Diamonds*, don't you?'

'I guess that seems obvious.'

I lean my head to one side. 'Right. So you understand that I'm trying to register the intellectual property you sold to Gregory, to Constant Sources.'

'Sure.'

'That means you don't own it any more.'

'Yes, 'course.'

'Stuart, before you sold the game to Constant Sources, did you try to sell it to anyone else? Did you try to license it to anyone? Did you give anyone access to the source code?'

'I, er, no. Why do you ask that?'

'Well, it looks like someone is trying to register the game, or an identical knock-off, at least, as their own.'

'Scarlett, I swear I never sold the game to anyone. Well, not before Gregory.'

'Could the source code have been reverse-engineered?'

He shrugs. 'It's encrypted but I guess there are ways and means.'

'Did anyone else help you make the game?'

'No. It's mine. Just mine.'

'It's Constant Sources' game now.'

'Sure. I mean it *was* mine.'

I pull the stool closest to mine out from under the bench. 'Sit down here for a second. My lawyers in China and the US said you were slow to get the information to them that they needed to file intellectual property applications. Why?'

'I know, they emailed me a couple of times but I was busy here. When I get into something, it just takes over me; it's like a part of me. I find it difficult to concentrate on other stuff.'

'Stuart, not giving them the information on time has allowed somebody else to file an application before us and that's a big problem.'

'I didn't realise. I'm sorry. But Gregory doesn't want

to use the game anyway, right? He just wants to make sure it's off the market so it doesn't compete with *Jail Run*. So does it matter if someone else filed?'

Is he playing dumb?

'Well, yes, Stuart. There's no point in him taking *Black Diamonds* off the market by buying it from you if someone else puts the game on the market, is there?'

'I get it. So have I messed it up for him?'

Taking a deep breath, I stand from my stool. 'I hope not.'

'Hey, you're engaged?' he asks, clocking the obscene ring on my finger.

'Erm, yes.'

'To Gregory, right?'

'H-how did you know that?'

He shrugs. 'Guess I could just tell by the way you are together.'

Are we that obvious? I think of the one time that Stuart has seen us together. Full business mode in the negotiation meeting. In fact, in business mode and sour with each other.

'You must have good intuition.'

'He's lucky.'

I feel my brows furrow. 'Thanks. Listen, Stuart, it would be helpful if you could be more responsive with the lawyers from now on, okay? And please come and talk to me if you remember anything, anyone who might have approached you to buy or license the game, anyone who might try to pass off the game as their own. You can speak to me any time. I'll be here full-time from Monday; you can pop in to my office whenever you like.'

His smile reaches his eyes, the brown pools shining. 'Thanks, Scarlett. I will do. It's nice to know someone else in London. It can be a bit... ah...'

'Lonely sometimes?'

He shrugs.

'Any time, Stuart, just pop up.'

'Scarlett, can I ask you something?'

'Of course.'

'Is Gregory pissed with me?'

'No. Not yet. Just try to stay on top of your emails, okay?'

He nods and jumps down from his stool.

I watch him leave with a feeling like something just isn't quite right.

* * *

After following up with the lawyers in China and the US and asking Richard to expedite the *Black Diamonds* filings in the UK and Europe, my first day back turned into a long and tiresome one. The last thing I needed was a call from the Real Estate team at my firm to tell me my dad's house sale is set to complete a week on Friday.

I call Sandy as Jackson drives me back to the Shard, having already dropped Gregory home around six. I've arranged for a moving company to take care of the contents of the house but they need me to give them directions: what's staying, what's trash, what's for charity, where boxes should be delivered if they're kept. Sandy agrees to help and I gratefully accept. I can't do it alone. My dad was a hoarder and as much as he pretended he wasn't by putting all of my childhood keepsakes, toys and clothes in the loft, I've always known they're there. The thought of having to go through them now, as if they're nothing, throwing them away or marking them to be delivered to charity, that's hard enough. I couldn't let someone else go through our life and box it up, designate it as useless or 'to be binned'; those are our memories. They're all we have left and the only person who can share that and really understand the piece of my father hidden behind each item is Sandy.

Jackson drops me and heads off to Lara's house to be with Sandy. It's still strange to me sometimes that my only mother figure now lives with and works for my mother-in-law-to-be. *Weird.*

The lift rises to the sixty-fourth floor and dings to announce my destination in the clouds. I'm struck by a chill through my veins when I catch sight of the apartment door ajar. It stops me in my tracks, reminding me of *that* night. My body tenses as someone's fingers grip the side of the door.

Fear cripples my body and threatens to choke me. I'm frozen, trying to think of anything I can use as a weapon and wishing I wasn't alone.

'Scarlett, perfect timing! How are you, peaches? How was your holiday?'

Amy springs from the apartment and envelopes me in her arms as my lungs fill against her silver bubble coat. I hadn't realised how much I'm still affected by this apartment and the events of the night I murdered Kevin Pearson.

'Amy, hi. I'm well, thank you. How are you?'

'Fine. Fine. I have to get home, the hubby is working night shift, but I'm glad I caught you. You'll have to tell me all about the Caribbean next time. I'd love to go. Oh and the engagement. I want to hear all about the one and only time that man will ever be on his knees.' Her words should make me happy but I know that's not the only time Gregory was on his knees. In my head, I see him in Dubai, begging for my forgiveness after telling me about his past. 'Now, hurry up and get inside; I've left you a little something. My way of saying congratulations to you both.'

'Oh, gosh, Amy, you shouldn't have.'

'You don't know what it is yet,' she sings, bouncing forward to hit the button on the wall and keep the lift doors from closing, her blonde ponytail swinging. 'Go on. Go on.'

As she skips into the lift, my heart rate returns to normal.

I close the door behind me in the apartment and ditch my bags on the rosewood flooring, trying to push dark thoughts from my mind. Gregory walks down the staircase into the lounge, rustling a towel over his freshly showered hair, his black T-shirt displaying the muscles of his lean chest above his indigo low-rise jeans. Laid-back Gregory. My heart rate begins to rise again, this time in a good way.

'Hey.' He drops his lips to my brow. 'You look tired.'

I shrug, feeling defeated by my day. 'Just life.'

'Well, *just life*, Amy has gone all out and made us a three-course congratulations meal. She's set the table, too. Do you want to grab a shower first or are you good to go?'

'I'll shower. But do you know what I'd love?'

He wraps his towel around my neck and pulls me towards him. 'What?'

'If we ate on the sofa, watched trash TV and snuggled.'

'If that's what the lady wants, that's what the lady shall have.' He bites the tip of my nose then clips my arse cheeks with his towel so I move upstairs to shower. When I come back down, I'm dressed in a pair of leggings and an oversized white shirt, my damp hair towel-dried. Gregory has shuffled the sofa to be directly facing the large flat screen and lit two candles on the coffee table. Two wine glasses are filled with a chilled white of some variety and two small plates host goat cheese and roasted vegetable salad.

He sits up from his position laid out on the sofa and hands me the remote, which I use to stream one of Amanda's new recs. I sit down and pull my knees up to my chest, resting sideways against Gregory. 'This is exactly the medicine for today.'

He strokes my hair from my brow. 'Rough day?'

'Oh, you know, handed my notice in, found out the registration of my client's new software is going to shit, been told to clear out my dad's home. Regular day I'd say.'

'When do you have to clear out the house?'

'This weekend. Sandy's going to help me.'

'I can help, too.'

I hug my knees tighter as I ask, 'Would you be offended if I asked you not to?'

His jaw rolls and I can see his mind working in overdrive. 'Not if that's what you want.'

I really don't want to get into my dad's things being too personal for a stranger. There's no way of saying that so he'll understand. More than that, I can't tell him about the part of me that doesn't want him there because it doesn't feel right. My dad was murdered and he was alone when he died. That's something I'm still coming to terms with. I've accepted, most days, that helping Gregory take over Pearson's company was at least something I did for the right reasons. But I'm not ready to put side by side my dad's death and the role that the man I love played in my dad being taken before his time.

The way Gregory fusses, shuffling on the sofa, adjusting the volume of the TV and dimming the lights in the room, sipping his wine and handing me my plate without meeting my eye, all tells me he's not okay with the idea. He knows how my mind works, he knows my thoughts, but voicing them won't help either of us. So I accept my plate and remark on the romcom we're watching until Gregory's shoulders relax and he lifts one knee onto the sofa, pulling my feet across his straight leg.

'Are you ready for main?' he asks, taking my empty plate from my lap.

'I can get it. What are we having?'

'No, Amy has left strict instructions as to how I pan fry our duck and heat through her special plum sauce.'

I follow him to the breakfast bar with our wine glasses. 'What makes it so special?'

After discarding our plates in the dishwasher, he shrugs. 'Amy made it?' he says with a short laugh. *He's back.*

We eat duck then Amy's Special Chocolate Orange Cheesecake: special because Amy made it. I'm stuffed to the point of waddling by the time we're done. 'I can't remember when I last ate like that,' I say, placing my empty dessert plate on the coffee table then leaning back to hold my triplet belly. 'I feel like a female Bruce Bogtrotter.'

'Bruce who now?'

'Bogtrotter. From *Matilda*. You have seen *Matilda*? Come on!'

Leaning across him, I grab his phone from the opposite arm of the sofa and google Bruce, chocolate cake all around his mouth, a sadistic grin on his face.

Gregory takes the phone from me and holds it next to my face. 'Jesus, you're right. Such a likeness. You're just a chubby boy trapped in a skinny-lady body.'

'Hey,' I protest, slapping his arm with a giggle. 'You just ate what I did.'

'Yes, and I'm about six inches taller than you and twice as wide as you. Plus, I fill up from my nose.'

'Huh?'

He scrunches his face. 'I fill up from my nose.'

'Does that really make sense to you?'

'Sure. You fill your nose first, so your stomach doesn't get as full.'

'Poor baby. It's toes. You fill up from your toes.'

He leans his head to one side, turning the words in his mind. 'Maybe that makes more sense.'

We watch the rest of the movie curled around each other on the sofa, my feet tucked between his legs, his arm wrapped around my waist. Sometime later, I feel him lift me from the sofa and carry me to bed.

18

I watch my feet as I step out of the lift. My black heels click on the marble tiles of the sixty-fourth floor of the Shard. I fasten the belt of my black mac tighter around my waist for comfort. My body shivers, wet from standing at my dad's graveside as he was lowered into the ground and cold from the air and eerie silence of the vestibule.

In my hand, I carry a white rose. I watch as my fingers and the rose reach out to the door of the apartment. Ajar. Blackness creeping out through the small gap.

I don't want to go inside. I'm afraid.

My legs keep moving without conscious instruction. The door creaks as I step inside. Blue floor lighting dimly glows on the rosewood under my feet. The open lounge is otherwise dark, illuminated only by the moon and the lights of the city beyond the windows.

He's here.

The top of his head sits two inches above the back of the black leather chair as he faces the silent streets of London.

The white rose falls from my hand and bounces on the ground as if time in the world has been slowed, almost to stillness.

'You came alone.' Kevin Pearson's voice is low and husky. 'You love him that much. You'd give your life for his.'

'What do you want?'

He revolves in the chair until he's facing me, his black suit jacket open, his white shirt unbuttoned by three. As the moon's light catches his face, I see it's not Kevin Pearson at all. It's his body, his eyes. But the face is Stuart Culliton.

'You can't save him, Scarlett.'

He raises a hand, pointing a Glock straight ahead. Only it's not aimed at me. Gregory is beside me, holding me to one side with an outstretched arm, ready to take the bullet.

The safety clicks off.

'No. No. Nooooo...'

Pushing away his arm, I dive across Gregory's body as the force of the metal leaving the barrel of the Glock thuds and echoes in the open space.

A searing pain burns through my abdomen before I crash against the cold wood floor.

'Gregory!'

'Shh, baby, I'm here. I'm here.' He sits up in bed and takes control of my shaking shoulders. 'Jesus, you're crying. Come here.'

I know the nightmare is over. He's here. He's alive. But I still check my body for a wound before I relax into his chest and sob, letting him take me back to the mattress in his embrace.

He holds me, kissing my forehead, stroking my hair and the skin of my back until my breathing calms, then he slips back into sleep. I fight it. Afraid. I can't give myself over. I won't let it come back. I can't see that again.

I don't want to be here, in this apartment, any more.

As the black sky shifts to charcoal behind the bedroom blind, I slip out of Gregory's hold and downstairs to the gym.

* * *

Jackson warily pushes open the gym door and I stop pounding the bag with a combination of gloved punches and sidekicks.

'Everything all right?'

Hugging the bag and rolling my wet forehead across the short sleeve of my aqua Climacool top, I let him answer his own question, my mouth open only to drag air into my lungs.

It must be five-thirty. Jackson tends to come into the gym whilst Gregory goes out to road run. He fits in his own workout before he acts as Gregory's PT.

'Want to talk, or want to kick the shit out of that thing together?'

'The latter,' I say, pulling back from the bag.

'All right, give me a right hook, left uppercut, right jab, then do the same starting on the left.'

Grunting through each move, I hit the bag six times.

'Through it, Scarlett. Don't hit the bag, punch through it, like I've told you.'

Repeating the sequence, I elongate each of my moves and feel a damn sight better for the beating I'm giving the bag as Jackson holds it from behind.

Jackson casts his attention over my shoulder and nods twice towards the door as I hammer through the next sequence, finishing with a kick that rocks him back on his feet.

'You're getting stronger, kid. Want a break?'

I nod but don't move from the spot. Instead, exhausted by my workout and lack of sleep, I slump down to my bum next to the bag and drop my face into my boxing gloves, pressing tears back into my eyes. 'I just want it all to go away, Jackson.'

Jackson being Jackson, he doesn't say much but I know he understands exactly what I'm talking about. I wanted Gregory's past to stop haunting him. Now it haunts me. The constant feeling of distrusting people – Trina, Stuart – unable to get past that fatal night. The worry that Katrina Martin is out there and, suspended or not, she'll be digging.

I clear out of the gym before Gregory gets back from his run. I shower, pin up my hair and dress in record time, then head out before Gregory's even finished his session with Jackson. I text him that I agreed to meet Amanda for breakfast before work. A lie I feel guilty about but a lie that will make him feel better than the truth. I just need to be alone. Away from the apartment where I killed a man. Where I'm scared of Amy stepping out of the damn door. Away from the bed that's home to my nightmares. And as much as it breaks my heart to admit it to myself, away from the man who brought it all upon me.

I can't shake this feeling that something just isn't right but if you asked me what that thing is, I wouldn't know.

It was my choice. All of this. That's what I'm reminding myself as I ride a black cab to work. I could have walked away when I knew the takeover was hostile. I didn't. I wanted to save the little boy from my dreams. Retribution for the scars on my perfect man. And eventually, revenge for the only two men I've ever loved.

At Blackfriars, I head for a seriously necessary hit of caffeine.

'Now there's a lady who looks like she needs a latte,' the barista who thinks he's being nice says, handing me the double-shot latte.

'You have no idea.' I thank him and accept a paper bag containing an almond croissant.

'Holy hell!' I turn smack into Gregory's chest, still covered in a light-grey, sweat-drenched hoody.

'Amanda stand you up?'

I don't know what to say so I say nothing at all. Instead, I stare into the eyes I saw in my sleep and shudder.

'Americano,' he says across my shoulder. Then he looks back at me. 'Sit.'

After retrieving his Americano, he pulls up a seat opposite me across a small wood table for two in the otherwise empty café. He takes my croissant from the bag and tears off a chunk for himself then pushes it on top of the bag towards me. 'Eat.'

I tear the croissant into pieces but push them around the paper bag, preferring instead to sip my latte.

'Scarlett, I need you to talk to me.'

'That's rich,' I snipe.

'I can see what's happening to you and I won't let it. I won't let you fall into darkness. Not you. Not ever.'

'I'm not. I just— I had a nightmare and I... I couldn't be there any more. I needed to get out.'

'Do you want to leave? Will it help? I can buy us somewhere else. Sell the apartment. We could go to the farm for a few weeks or stay in a hotel in the city. I'll do whatever it takes to make things right for you.'

'None of that's necessary. I'm fine, generally, I just... can't stop thinking that the payoff could come back to haunt us. And this thing with *Black Diamonds* and Stuart is on my mind. Then I— It sounds ridiculous, but Amy came out of the apartment last night, and the door was ajar and it just, I don't know. I thought I was better than I am. Maybe it's the stress of yesterday, that's all, and my dream last night was just... messed up... it got to me. But I'm fine.'

'I want to ask you something. Don't be offended.'

I nod uncertainly.

'Would you like to see someone? A therapist?'

And tell them what, exactly? 'It was a nightmare. You know better than I do that nightmares happen.' *Yes, I can play you at your own game.* 'You retreat. It took you months to talk to me about anything. I'm just taking a morning. Is that too much to ask?'

His eyes soften with a pity that could break my heart. After everything he's been through, I'm the one behaving like the world owes me a favour. Shaking my head at myself, I move around the table and sit onto his lap, wrapping my arms around his neck and not caring who might see us. 'I'm sorry I left. I'm okay. I promise.' I drop my lips to his.

'You're my reason, Scarlett. My Aurora. As long as we're okay, the world is right.'

'We're okay. I love you.'

* * *

By the time people start filing into the office, I've been over the information foreign counsel have sent me on

Black Diamonds in China and the US. Both adverse registrations have been filed by newly incorporated companies, set up in the respective jurisdictions, and their sole shareholder is a parent company incorporated in France. I google the companies but they show only websites under construction. I email local counsel and ask them to take a look at the corporation documents of the Chinese and US companies to see if there's anything suspect about them but both lawyers confirm the companies look legit.

Why doesn't it feel *legit?* A question I'm unable to answer, therefore I have to trust the judgment of Malcolm and Wang Nongfan.

Amanda pops into my office to say hello and show me a bamboo unisex clothing range for Bump Darling. She leaves on a less than subtle hint that she'd quite like a baby shower.

Luke, my university ex and friend, calls me at eleven to catch up on my holiday and profess his concern that Gregory being engaged makes it less likely he'll be gay, or at least dabble, with Luke.

I arrange a twelve-thirty lunch with Emily, Lawrence's niece, which Amanda gets in on when she stalks my calendar to remind herself of the time of our handover meeting for Mr Ghurair's final deal this afternoon.

By 4 p.m., I've kept myself too busy to think about nightmares.

As I'm thinking I might have done close to enough for today, my desk phone rings.

'Scarlett Heath.'

'Scarlett, Richard here.' The tone of his voice tells me there's a problem. '*Black Diamonds*.'

My heart sinks. 'Someone has beaten us to the registration?'

'Yes. In the EU and the UK. Registrations are already pending. How did you know?'

I breathe out heavily through my nose. 'Call it a hunch. Do you have the applicant details?'

'I do. It's a French company, seems above board from the register. What's strange is that they only filed yesterday. They literally just got there first. Is there a fight going on for ownership of the game?'

'The creator swears it's his and that he hasn't sold or licensed any part of it before the deal with Constant Sources. Do you think it's a copycat or the same game?' I ask.

'Hard to say but I can tell you the concepts look identical and obviously the name is the same.'

I want to believe Stuart, for Gregory's sake, but something tells me this is the game Gregory paid seven hundred and fifty thousand pounds for. The question is, who has the software? How did they get it and why would they try to claim ownership when they surely expect a fight?

* * *

Jackson is waiting outside when I step through the revolving door of my office block at six-thirty. An early finish for me, but then I am about to leave the firm. He steps out of the driver seat of the Mercedes in his usual black suit, white shirt and black tie combo, moving to hold the passenger door open for me. I smile when I see Gregory already in the back seat.

'Thanks, Jackson.'

He nods and closes the door behind me as I slip onto the leather seat next to Gregory, who hangs up his call and drops his phone into his inside pocket. The privacy screen is already rolled up to the roof, shielding us from Jackson or, judging by the look in Gregory's hooded eyes, shielding him from us.

'Get here.' His hand is under my hips, lifting me towards him as the Mercedes eases into rush-hour traffic.

Hitching my dress far enough up my thighs to drop my knees either side of Gregory's legs, I straddle him, sitting back onto his legs.

'Gorgeous,' he says, pulling his hands down the sides of my body. 'I haven't stopped thinking about you today. Now I have a raging dick in my trousers that's dying to be inside you.'

His words speak to my groin and it takes physical and mental strength to focus my attention away from the thought of him entering me, his thick length filling me completely.

But I do kiss him, getting lost in the feel of his warm, wet tongue on mine, the softness of his lips.

'Gregory, I need to talk to you about *Black Diamonds*,' I manage, pulling myself back from him to sit back on his thighs, panting.

He slips his hands under the hem of my dress and they move like silk across the bare skin of my legs above my stockings. With his thumb, he traces a line over my thong, gently parting my labia.

'And I need to talk to you, but unless you mean the black diamonds on your finger, it'll have to wait until after.'

He pushes the satin to one side and dips his thumb just inside my lips, purposefully not touching my clit. Teasing me.

'After what?' I part whisper, part moan.

He finally rolls his thumb across my swollen bud,

dragging a breathy groan from my lungs. His fingers slide easily into my drenched entrance.

'Your first orgasm of the night.'

* * *

'God, I needed that,' he says, pulling my hair down one shoulder, brushing the skin of my neck with his lips. 'I've needed *you* all day.'

I return his touch, nuzzling into his neck as our bodies calm and he starts to retract inside me. 'I really do need to talk to you about *Black Diamonds*,' I mumble against his rich scented skin.

His phone rings and I move to the seat beside him, adjusting my clothes as I go.

'Ryans.' His tone is clipped, maybe even more than his usual CEO abruptness. 'What did you find?' He casts his eyes fleetingly to me. 'Email it to Jackson. Agreed. No, keep monitoring.'

The Mercedes rolls to a stop outside the front entrance to the Shard and the privacy screen separating the front and back of the car winds down. My cheeks flush red as Jackson's profile comes into view. I look anywhere other than the rear-view mirror.

'Scarlett, go inside and call the lift. I need to talk to Jackson.'

'Excuse me?'

'I'll just be a minute. *Please.*'

Gritting my teeth, I climb out of the car.

'Good evening, Miss Heath,' the concierge calls, dipping his head.

'Good evening.'

The lift doors open and I step inside with my laptop in one hand, my frame handbag over my opposite forearm. I press sixty-four and as the doors begin to draw closed, Gregory strides inside. His body is tense, his eyes ablaze. He rides the lift as if I don't even exist, rubbing a hand across his late-day stubble then sliding it, too tightly, down his throat.

When the doors open to his floor, he steps to one side, finally acknowledging my presence, to let me out first. He opens one side of the double doors to the apartment for me to walk in, his black eyes meeting mine as we cross. The lounge smells of something delicious, meaning Amy must have just left.

I place my bags down on the floor and as soon as I stand, Gregory thrusts me back against the wall of the lounge, lifting my hands above my head, holding them still with one hand as his other drags up the side of my body. His mouth assaults mine, fast, rough, his teeth meeting my lips. His body pushes against mine, his pelvis ramming my arse against the wall. His cock hardens as his body touches almost every part of mine.

'You're angry.'

'Yes.' He pulls my lip hard between his teeth then rests his brow on mine, his eyes squeezed shut.

'About what?'

'More than I care to discuss.'

'Tell me.'

He's silent but his exhale is long, hot and heavy against my lips, a wave of heated desire. His hands grab my waist and shoulder, turning me so I'm facing the wall, my palms pressing the plaster above my head. He yanks my hips back an inch so they're pushed up against his crotch, then he pulls down the zip running from my neck to my coccyx and pushes the material apart, exposing my back. His hands roam across my bare skin as his hips turn slowly against my arse. 'My day started with you having a nightmare and running away from me.' His words are thick, deep and masculine. 'It got worse, and right now, I just need you to take me out of my head.' His mouth meets my shoulder, sucking and biting the skin. 'Give me what I need.' He blows air in a line down the nape of my neck then follows the same path with his tongue. 'Give me you. *Please.*'

My head rolls back and drops forward in acqui-
escence.

'Say it.' His hands move inside my dress, around
my waist and up to my breasts, pushing down the cups
of my bra to tweak my nipples.

'Yes.'

It feels like one swift move as he pulls my hands to
my sides and pushes my dress across my shoulders to
the ground. I return my hands to the wall, palms down
above my head, balancing my body as I lift my heeled
feet out of the dress.

His hand grips my hipbone then slips into my
thong which is no doubt drenched from our ride
home. His fingers move over my still sensitive clit then
breach my entrance, pulling my pelvis back against his
erection. 'You're soaked. Still full of me. Do you have
any idea how much of a fucking turn-on that is?'

'Gregory.' His name leaves me on a breathy
whisper.

'What, baby? Tell me why you're saying my name.'

'I want you.'

'Where?'

'Inside me. I want to feel you.'

'Take off your thong.'

I do, bending further back into him to slide the

material down my legs. I lift one leg to step out, then the other. He hooks his hand under my elevated thigh and moves it back, my heel locking around his waist, exposing my sex to him.

'Feel yourself.'

The embarrassment I feel is fleeting. My body is too desperate, too charged and too wanton. I move my hand between my parted lips and realise how wet I am. My fingers glide across my clit. Gregory holds his hand against mine, encouraging my fingers lower then pushing me inside so I can feel our earlier pleasure.

'That's it, baby.'

He removes his suit jacket, casting it to the floor with my dress, then unfastens his trousers, leaving me briefly to take them off and remove his shirt. My entire body is tingling, mounting, as my own incendiary fingers work me higher. His naked body rests against my back, his legs inside mine. He gropes my breasts, pulling me back against his chest.

My legs start to feel weak, trembling as I near the precipice. His hands trace every curve of my body. His rock-hard penis lies in the crease of my arse.

'Gregory, I'm close. I want to come with you inside me.'

He growls as he pushes me forward, my palms

meeting the wall. I'm in my heels but I still rise to the tips of my toes to account for his height. When he's positioned, he teases me, entering just an inch. I drop back onto my heels and he thrusts deep inside me. Delicious. Deadly.

'Gregory, God, Gregory.'

'Keep touching yourself,' he barks.

It's sensitive, too sensitive, my legs could give way, but I do as he says, my hips bucking back into him when my fingers touch my clit. The tips of my fingers find him, thick and wet, entering me tirelessly. The feel of him. Knowing I'm taking all of him. It sends my head into a spiral. He wraps a hand around my waist, holding me to him, stopping my legs from collapsing beneath me. His teeth clamp down on my shoulder.

'Not yet,' he says, groaning into my back.

'I can't wait. I can't.'

'Wait.'

He pulls out, leaving me panting against the wall, my insides on the edge and screaming for more. He grabs my hand from the wall and leads me to the stairs, guiding me to kneel halfway up. Then he kneels on the step below mine and straightens my body against his chest. He pushes my knees further apart and I lean my head back against his shoulder, my sex crying out for him to re-enter, my legs grateful for the relief from standing. Holding my hips, he thrusts up into me, both of us moaning as he slips back into place, my body instantly lifting again. He takes my hand and moves it back to my entrance so we're both feeling him driving into me.

'Gregory. I need to come.'

His lips clamp onto my neck and he sucks my skin hard as his cock sinks deeper. 'Now, baby, together.'

Need. Delight. Relief. I scream his name as he roars expletives and our bodies shudder together, bucking in sync, his arms holding me against him as we climax violently, him deep inside me, my body merging into his.

'Thank you,' he whispers against my neck, holding me to him until our breathing settles.

'Don't ever thank me, Gregory, not for that. I love you.'

'Baby, I love you so much, it's going to be the death of me.'

'Food first or bath first?' I ask as we fumble to our feet at the bottom of the stairs.

'Bath.'

'Okay. I'm sorry to burst your bubble of ignorance, Mr Ryans, but we do actually need to talk about the game.'

* * *

I stand between his legs whilst he adjusts his position, then guides me down into the bubbly water between his thighs. Leaning back against his chest, I hum contentedly as he strokes water up and down my chest.

'*Black Diamonds*, come on then.'

I don't intend the enormous sigh that escapes me before I speak. 'Someone has applications pending in Europe. They pipped us to the post by a matter of hours again.'

'And now you're very concerned.'

I roll over and rest my chin on my hands on his chest. 'Very. Whoever it is, they're following the exact pattern of my registration plan.'

'Four jurisdictions, couldn't it be coincidence?'

I shake my head. 'No. Not now. It's too coincidental that the registrations are so proximate, and the pattern.'

'Surely the pattern is obvious: you dealt with the biggest jurisdictions first.'

'Gregory, you need to start hearing what I'm saying. I think this is purposeful. Now, someone thinks they own this game or they've made an exact replica and want to register their game before we register ours. That way, if there's a fight, they have a solid claim, particularly in jurisdictions where the rule is first to register wins.'

'I sense there's a but.'

'I just can't stop thinking about the order and timing. Gregory, I think someone is doing this maliciously. Either someone, like you say, knows the most obvious pattern of registration, or...'

He pushes himself to sit higher in the bath. 'Or they have *your* plan.'

'That's where I'm getting to. I've spent the day thinking about who it could be and the obvious place to start is people you, or I, or both of us have pissed off.'

He looks up, searching, listing, realising. 'That's a pretty big list.'

'Yes. The people who have access to the plan are Tim and Jean-Paul. Perhaps they're pissed about the way Nick Henshaw was fired?'

'No. The game is to benefit Constant Sources; they wouldn't do it.'

'Nick Henshaw? Would they have given the plan to him?'

'No. Their allegiance doesn't lie with Nick. They wouldn't dare.'

'Well, there's Stuart? There's something about him,

Gregory. And he works in your building, he knows computers; it's not like he couldn't find the plan.'

'Why on earth would he be looking, Scarlett? He works for me now and it was his game. He'd breach the terms of our deal if he did anything like that and I doubt he wants to pay seven hundred and fifty grand back.'

He does have a point.

He reaches out, encouraging me to lie back into his chest. 'It's that woman Stella, from Lara's party and the hunt. She hates me for being with you. She's malicious.'

His chest vibrates against my back as he chuckles. 'Do you really think Stella would get back at you for taking me off the market by entering into an intellectual property battle with you?'

I laugh with him. 'I guess not. There's an obvious person in Trina. I thought about her a lot. I'm waiting for her next move. But what would she know about games and IP?'

'And it's way off the mark in terms of her motivation. She wants to pull the lid off a pan of bribes; stealing or copying a game isn't going to achieve that.'

Now I laugh harder. It's completely inappropriate but his muddled saying in the midst of him being serious is just too damned cute.

'What can possibly be so funny right now?'

'Baby, what you just said was a whole other level of mess. I think you mean *lift* the lid, not *pull* and God knows what a pan of bribes is. For an intelligent man, you—'

His hands move to my hips, his fingers digging in until I squeal. 'Say sorry.'

'I'm sorry.' I giggle. 'Seriously, though, there is one other person. I don't know how he'd know about the game necessarily but he definitely wouldn't need sight of my registration plan to know what I'm thinking.'

'Jack.'

'He was my boss for a long time, Gregory. He might be a sick bastard but he taught me a few things in that time.'

'And me putting him behind bars gives him a damn good reason to want retribution.'

'Yep. I can't piece everything together but he fits the bill of seriously pissed off and knowledgeable about the market and the legals behind everything.'

'All right, lady, you're starting to wrinkle; let's eat.' He pushes me up, standing and climbing out of the bath. The conversation might be over but his own thoughts are just getting started and he needs space to mull it over. I get that. It's how I work, too.

I follow him out of the tub and let him wrap a

white towel around my shoulders after he's tied his own around his waist. 'What did you want to talk about?'

'My mother wants to discuss wedding plans with you. She'd like you to have lunch with her at the weekend.'

'Already? We've only just gotten engaged.'

'Well, she thinks she could pull something together soon, like in a month.'

'A month? That's insane.'

'Hey.' He holds my chin. 'I waited long enough to find you, Scarlett Heath; I don't want to wait any longer to make you mine. Please don't fight me on this.'

I can't resist his plea and my head is really too busy to start fretting about anything else. 'I'll meet with her,' I tell him. But I'm not conceding.

'Good. The other thing is, you need a dress for the charity gala on Thursday.'

'Oh, crap, I forgot about that.'

'I've made an appointment for you with Julia and Lucas tomorrow.'

'Gregory, I don't need another new dress. I can't buy something new every time we go somewhere; I'll be bankrupt.'

'That's fine because I'll be paying, with *our* money,

and on this occasion, you absolutely do need a new dress. It's our first public appearance since the engagement and given the hype surrounding me at the moment, there'll be a lot of eyes. I want you to feel comfortable and a beautiful new dress to match my gorgeous fiancée will help that.'

Whilst I hate to admit it, what he's saying does make sense. I want to look good but not for me: for him. I want him to be proud of me and that's hard enough in a room full of stunning and insanely wealthy women. 'Fine.'

He clears his throat theatrically. 'That's it? That's all the grief you're going to give me?'

'It's a one-off and don't push it, Ryans.'

'Fine. Jackson will pick you up from work at six and take you. I have something to take care of tomorrow.'

'Fine.'

'Fine.'

'Stop trying to have the last word.'

'I'm not trying to have the last word.'

'You just did it again.'

'Didn't.'

He chuckles.

'Did,' I say, stomping my foot like a child.

'Stop it.'

'Okay, I'm done.'

'Fine.'

'Fine.'

'Okay.'

19

I picked everything I knew he'd love on me and for the first time, Julia and Lucas didn't say it looked 'all wrong.' In fact, they said nothing. Julia held her perfectly manicured fingers to her lips and Lucas fanned his face. I took that as meaning I'd achieved my goal. Amanda confirmed as much as she sat on the plush sofa of the style room facing me, sipping a virgin cocktail, compliments of Harrods – or rather compliments of Gregory's account.

'You look fit to be the fiancée of a bazillionaire,' she said with a proud, sort of mothering smile.

Now, Amy helps me into the gown. She lowers the crimson silk base layer over my arms and down my body, being careful not to touch my hair, which has been curled and pinned low at the back of my head, the front swept softly across my brow. As the silk reaches the floor and pools around my high-heeled shoes, Amy adjusts the deep red lace layer over top and fixes the train, the lace overhanging the silk by two or three inches. She fastens the invisible zip, then adjusts the half-inch straps – lace, silk and a white-gold chain entwining across each shoulder.

I'm grateful for her help but missing Sandy. Remembering how she had helped me into the blue gown Gregory bought and had delivered to me the first time we went to an event together. Jumping beans dance in my stomach. It's our coming-out night. There'll be cameras, eyes of jealous women, catty whispers like there always are when I'm seen with Gregory. But tonight, I don't care. I glance down at the rock on my finger. He's mine.

Amy turns me to face the floor-length mirror in the walk-in wardrobe, then moves behind me and hangs a necklace against my chest. Three thin rows of shining diamonds grace my skin above the structured sweetheart finish of the dress. He'll love it.

Amy holds up two long diamond earrings to match the necklace. Once I've secured them myself, she fastens a matching bracelet around my wrist, then Amy hands me a small silk bag.

'Knock 'em dead, peaches.'

I take a deep breath and exhale slowly, watching my shoulders move up and down in the mirror, the dancing beans in my stomach fiercely trying to escape. 'Let's do it.'

I hear Gregory winding up a call. By the time I make it to the staircase, he's standing in the lounge, watching me descend, gown trailing the steps behind me.

I will never get used to how striking this man is.

He has one hand in the pocket of his trousers, holding his dinner jacket back, exposing his black waistcoat. His bow tie sits against a crisp white shirt. His hair is slicked back, making his strong, dark features seem more intense. And he only has eyes for me.

He offers a hand to guide me down the final steps. As his skin meets mine, fireworks burst from my chest, a charge running through my blood, as if it's the first time we've touched.

As I reach the lounge floor and stand, hopelessly lost in him, he raises my fingers to his lips.

'You're going to make my dreams come true when you agree to be mine forever.'

'I'm already yours, Gregory. Every part of me. There's no going back from you.'

'Forever,' he whispers, before pressing his mouth

to mine with a gentle, lingering kiss. 'You're beautiful,' he tells me. 'This dress.' He takes my hand and pushes me away from him, twirling me under his arm.

'I thought you might like it.'

'You were right.' He pulls me back to him, leaning into me. 'And I can't wait to see it on my bedroom floor,' he whispers, causing me to laugh against his chest.

'All set?' Jackson asks, making me aware of his presence in the room.

Gregory winks at me, arrogant and delicious. 'All set.'

* * *

We join queuing cars of guests opposite Hyde Park and Jackson rolls us to the red carpet for our allocated arrival slot.

'Okay?' Gregory asks.

I realise that my grip has tightened on his hand, my fingers digging into his skin. There's an answer to that question but I need to think about what it is and in that thinking time, he leans into me and holds a calming hand to my cheek.

'It's just us, baby, going to dinner. You and me.'

I nod once uncertainly. He takes my left hand and

adjusts my engagement ring so it rests just so on my finger as Jackson opens the back door of the Bentley.

As soon as Gregory climbs out of the Bentley, cameras start to flash. He reaches out for my hand and holds me firmly as he leads us along the red carpet.

'Mr Ryans!'

'Mr Ryans, is it true you're engaged?'

'Mr Ryans, who is she?'

She. I guess that's me and I guess they're surprised that I'm not some model or actress or socialite like most of Gregory's red-carpet dates.

I'd like nothing more than to get away from the invasion but Gregory turns into me. 'Look at me, baby. It's just me. You and me, angel.'

As he stares into my eyes, he gives me that irresistible half-smile and I genuinely smile back in response. Then he takes my left hand and lifts it to his cheek. My muscle memory takes over, moving my thumb across his freshly shaven skin as he rests the tip of his nose to mine, then his lips meet mine and my eyes close, taking me to *our* world.

'Just us,' he whispers.

'You just made me flash my ring, didn't you?'

'Too right. You're mine and I want the world to know that I'm the luckiest man alive.'

With the confidence he gives me, I turn back to the

cameras with a tight smile, his hand still firmly gripping mine.

We're greeted in the hotel lobby by another photographer, who takes a formal shot, then we're each handed a glass of very welcome champagne. The space has been transformed into a swath of colours representing the four charities benefitting from the evening: purple for Transform, a children's abuse charity, pink for Brainy Children, a charity researching brain tumours in children, sky blue for Early Birds, dedicated to premature baby studies, and aquamarine for Dreams, a children's hospice that works in conjunction with the hospital Gregory visits every quarter or so.

'Gregory, old boy.' A man in his late fifties with soft eyes, a healthy tan and a slick head of silver hair heads our way.

Gregory takes the hand offered to him. 'Thomas, are you well?' Then he leans in to kiss Thomas's wife, Norah, on each cheek. 'May I introduce you to Scarlett, my fiancée.'

'Scarlett, Thomas and Norah are heavily involved with Dreams. Norah is the chair of the charity and does a marvellous job.'

'It's a pleasure to meet you both,' I say genuinely, not least because they are two of few seemingly sincere people I've met at events Gregory frequents. 'You must be immensely proud. The place looks superb.'

'I wish I could say that was down to me,' Norah says. 'But I have a wonderful company that I work with every year, me and the chairs of the other charities here tonight anyway. It's they who pull everything together, and for free. The designers have an eye for those finer details.'

'It must be a very rewarding job.'

'It is rewarding, indeed, though it never feels much like a job. You should meet some of the children we get to work with. Wonders of the world. Incredibly courageous.'

The pianist returns from a break and begins to play and for a moment, the room falls quiet but for the hypnotic sound of her music. It's a song I recognise from an album by Yiruma. My dad would listen to his music sometimes after a long day in surgery and when he became very sick, on the bad days when he struggled to leave his room, Sandy or I would put the album on loop. It always soothed him, comforted him and with that, it brought me pleasure, too. I don't realise I'm transfixed until Thomas speaks close to my ear. 'The piece is called "Love Me". Her name is Violet. Wonderful, isn't she?'

'She's played for our annual gala for the last three years,' Norah adds. 'Such a lovely young woman.'

I turn back to them and nod, swallowing the lump in my throat, afraid to speak until the haze over my eyes dissipates. 'It's beautiful,' I eventually say.

'You know, I think she plays for weddings,' Norah says, casting mischievous eyes to Gregory, who rests his hand on the small of my back.

'Excuse us,' Thomas says, taking his wife's hand. 'We'll see you at the table.'

'A delight to meet you,' Norah says.

'Gregory! Darling!' Lara's voice hits us before we see her making her way through the crowd. Gregory's mother is as glamorous as ever in a structured black satin gown, her ears, neck and wrists adorned in pearls.

'How are you, mother?' Gregory asks.

'Oh my beautiful daughter-in-law-to-be, look at you. Absolutely dazzling,' Lara says, ignoring her son in a way that makes me chuckle and tell him in a look, *I guess I'm the apple of her eye now.*

'Hi, Lara, how are you?'

'Better now, better now.'

'Hi, Lawrence,' I say, accepting a kiss on each cheek from Gregory's step-dad and business partner.

As Lara begins excitedly hurling extravagant wedding plans at me, my eyes lock onto a group of three women over her shoulder, whispering, their attention obviously fixed on my left hand until one of them notices me looking. With a tut, an eye roll and one hand on hip, they turn their backs to me. Then I see *her*: Stella. She has a scowl like thunder as she makes her way towards us, practically dragging her very wealthy husband, Jean-Pierre, behind her.

She all but dives on Gregory, wrapping her arms too tightly around him and putting her lips too close to his as she kisses his cheeks.

What a magnificent dick she is.

'Stella, how nice to see you,' I lie, turning her body to me and away from my fiancé to air-kiss her cheeks.

Urgh, I really wish Amanda hadn't decided she was too fat and not pregnant enough looking to face a camera. She'd have a passive-aggressive put-down just perfect for Stella.

As I'm thinking that, Gregory tucks me into his side and nuzzles the hair at my temple.

'Feisty,' he whispers.

Our table is one of three closest to the stage in the room that must seat at least a thousand people. The colours from the reception shine in even brighter swags and swaths throughout the room. The walls have been draped in black curtains and the cheerful shades burst like shooting stars, lights twinkling against the darkness. As Gregory guides me to our table to the continuing sound of Violet, the pianist, playing through large speakers, I can't help thinking back to the children's ward of the hospital.

It was the day after Gregory and I had first made love. Sandy and I visited my dad whilst Gregory went to Paediatrics. Once we'd said goodbye to my dad for the day, we went in search of Gregory, finding a man dressed in a giant lion head and a ward full of giggling children. One of the first moments I knew I was un-equivocally in love with him.

The children loved him, too. He was incredible with them. There wasn't a nurse without a smile as he broke the mould of white-collar CEO. The room is exactly how those children were that day. Sick, some of them dying, the truest darkness of the world. Yet their smiles really were like shining stars, just like the lights glimmering around the room.

We take our seats at a table for which Gregory has paid. We're joined by Lara and Lawrence, Norah and Thomas, Stella and Jean-Pierre, Lawrence's niece Emily and her fiancé Harry, and Gordon and Vivi-enne, a couple I remember from the fateful night of Lara's bonfire party. A night I push quickly from the forefront of my mind.

Once the lights are dimmed, Norah makes her way to the stage to welcome the guests. She speaks about the purpose of the night before inviting up to the stage the chairs of Early Birds, Transformed and Brainy Children. They give frankly shocking and astoundingly moving speeches about their respective charities and give the guests details of a silent auction and various other fundraising things happening throughout the evening.

Norah returns to the microphone with a beaming smile. 'Well, I would like to tell you all a little bit about the fabulous charity, Dreams. But, tonight, we have a very special guest of honour. She is a shooting star. A burning light we should all take inspiration from. Her mum tells me this little girl demanded to stay up beyond her bedtime tonight to come here and tell us how amazing she thinks Dreams is and what the charity has done for her. This brave girl has fought two bouts of leukaemia in her short five years and is currently nearing the end of her third round of treatment. The doctors say she's doing very, very well. Ladies and gentlemen, please welcome to the stage tonight, the star of the evening, Isabella Willows.'

It's the little girl from the hospital. Isabella, Gregory's 'girlfriend', who'd informed me that it was okay for Gregory to have two girlfriends. Her mum helps her navigate the four steps to the stage, pausing on each to take a breath. With each step, I will her frail, tiny legs to win, the lump in my throat and constriction in my chest building with every anxious second. The piano music changes to 'Part of Your World' from *The Little Mermaid* and the whole scene has my eyes full for the second time tonight. In the middle of the stage, Isabella pauses, gathering her breath. She waves to a table and a man who I guess is her dad. He in turn blows her a kiss. Then she looks around the room; those big, bright eyes that melted my heart the first time I saw her are shining, distracting from the dark circles beneath and her hairless head, which is decorated with a white hairband with one big daisy.

When I think I can take no more, she turns to our table and shouts above the piano, 'Gregory!'

He waves but she holds out her hands towards him. His jaw tenses and I can read his mind. His image as a stern, ruthless CEO will be shattered if he goes. If he doesn't, he denies that little girl, standing there with her weak arms outstretched. He debates it for a second then rises from his seat and goes to Isabella, bending to the stage as she wraps her arms around his neck. I have no idea what he says to the little angel but she laughs, the most profound and wonderful sound.

* * *

It was unintentional, but Gregory made sure his public image was angelic tonight. Nothing has leaked about bribes. Yet. But anything is possible whilst Katrina Martin is still lurking and tonight has done no harm to his reputation. That's something his head of PR, Sydney and I agree on as we subtly discuss the situation over an after-dinner coffee.

As I'm talking to Sydney, Francis, the jerk in finance or, more specifically, *private equity*, who Gregory obviously can't stand but doesn't upset due to his willingness to invest in a broad portfolio of business, brings his stunning and much younger wife, Adriana to say hello. From the corner of my eye, I watch Adriana throw her head back, flicking her long, black hair back and forth across her shoulder as she laughs at absolutely nothing.

'Oh Francesco,' she fake laughs. 'You're so baaaaad.'

Francesco. I've never heard of Francis coming from Francesco. I continue my conversation with Sydney until Lara asks me to accompany her to the ladies' room.

'Scarlett, I'm sorry if I was a little intense earlier about the wedding. I'm just excited. He's my only child and—' She stops when she notes the unintentional but – in hindsight – extremely obvious pull back of my head. 'He told you about her.' Her eyes immediately fill and my frosty reaction wanes.

'Elsa. Yes, he did.'

'Scarlett, you have to understand. I wanted to leave—'

I hold a hand up gently to stop her. 'Lara, you don't have to explain anything to me. Will I ever understand how you stayed? Probably not. But that's because I've never been in that situation; I don't know what it was like. All I do know is that it must have been horrific for all three of you.'

She opens her mouth and I will her not to speak. One day, we might have that conversation, but not here, not now.

She raises her lips silently in a look that I think may be the most authentic I've ever seen on her. That front-of-house show she puts on for other people isn't here in this room. She's just a woman, as fallible as everyone else, who went through something horrific. Something neither she nor Gregory have to hide from me any more.

Going to the bathroom in a floor-grazing gown is not the easiest thing I've done in my life. After navigating the going and flushing part, I work at putting my dress back in the right places, twisting, shuffling.

'She's so ordinary. I mean, a lawyer, really?'

'He's just having a final fling before he finds the right woman. And he will, ladies.'

'I bet she's rubbish in bed.'

'I bet she sleeps in pyjamas.'

'Well, I hate to state the obvious, ladies, but she's beautiful and there must be something about her to have landed the bachelor of the century. She's finally taken Gregory Ryans off the market. That's something women in this room have tried and failed to do.'

'Oh, please, no man is ever completely off the market.'

My hand is frozen on the door. Part of me wants to go and put them in their place; part of me thinks they're right. Gregory could have any woman he likes, and maybe he will get bored of me.

'Let me tell you something about my son.' Lara's voice cuts through the catty voices. 'He is a good man. A man of integrity. And that woman you're talking about is the best thing that's ever happened to him. She's worth a thousand of you all. So why don't you take your bitchy tantrums back to your husbands and leave my son to be happy with a genuine and honest, good-hearted woman.'

I hold my fingertips to my mouth, waiting for the toilets to clear.

When I come out from hiding, there's only Lara left, reapplying lipstick in the over-sink mirrors.

'Thank you,' I tell her.

'I meant it,' she says, dropping a hand to my shoulder before she leaves me washing my hands.

As far as mothers-in-law go, maybe she won't turn out too bad.

A man in a suit catches the corner of my eye as I step back out into the corridor.

'Fancy seeing you here.'

Nick Henshaw, the director who tried to take Gregory's company from him after the shooting. The director Gregory forced to resign from Constant Sources. He moves close to me, too close.

I offer him a fleeting glance of disgust before turning my back on him but he slaps the wall above my head, preventing me from walking further. As I turn, he leans towards me, forcing me back against the wall.

'I have nothing to say to you,' I spit.

'That's good. Then you can stand there whilst I tell you a few things.'

His breath smells of alcohol. Hard liquor. His six-foot frame towers over me. His stone-cold grey eyes bore into mine.

'I bet you're surprised to see me here. Of course, you remember our last meeting. You and your boyfriend tried to take everything I'd ever built. Forced me to resign from *my* company. And do you know what that bastard told me when I asked for a fair and reasonable sum to compensate me for my resignation? My resignation, which came about because he fucked up and fucking killed his own fucking daddy.' His words are wet on my face, making me squint and turn my head to one side. 'Do you know? He told me to go fuck myself.' A hollow laugh bellows from the depths of him and he leans closer to my face. 'You two took everything from me. I. Want. It. Back. And guess what, I'm going to take it back, any way I can get it. You see, I'm starting again, 'cause that's the thing you forgot in your clever little plan. I could just start again. Get a new company. Get funding from Francis Benedetti, a man who can see talent and a good thing. And now, my company will bring your man creeping to my door.'

Francis Benedetti? I thought he was a serious investor, not the kind to scrape the barrel for fuck-ups to invest in.

'I wish you and Francis every success, Nick, but the

reality is, you already ran one company to its knees and it was Gregory who had to come and bail you out then. Let's just say I won't be holding my breath.'

I try to move away from him but he slams his free arm to the other side of my head, pinning me to the wall.

'Not so tough when you're on your own, sweetheart, are you?'

'This is what you do now? Try to intimidate women? Perhaps your time would be better spent improving your business acumen.'

My heart is pounding in my chest. I hold his gaze even though there's no denying I'm afraid.

'You think you're so fucking perfect, don't you?' He removes one hand from the wall and swirls a finger in my face, a sadistic grin drawn on his plump lips. 'I know your dirty secrets. Oh, yes, Katrina Martin has told me about your corruption. How you're covering up for your fiancé, how he bought his way out of prison. Bought his way out of prison so he could steal my company out from under me. Yes, I know all about it.'

Katrina told Nick Henshaw? What does she have to do with Nick Henshaw? My head is spinning. In part from the new information but mostly because I need to get out of this situation.

'Let me go,' I snarl, taking advantage of his dropped hand to step away from him.

I get two steps before he pulls my waist and rams me back against the wall, my head crashing against the plaster, fuzzing my vision for a second.

'Don't rush, I haven't said congratulations yet. I'm pleased you two are getting married. Really, I am. You know how I like fucking other people's wives.'

His face is ripped away from mine and slammed back against the opposite side of the corridor as a large vase shatters across the tiled floor. Gregory pins Nick Henshaw by the throat, the sinews of his neck rigid and bulging, his body tall and strong. He's raging and this time, there's no one to stop him. He slams his fist into Nick's face, drawing blood from his nose and eye, then lets his limp body fall to the floor as staff, then guests, teem into the corridor.

I can do nothing but stare in shock.

'Let's go,' Gregory says, tugging my shoulder and moving us quickly down a staircase. He takes his phone from his inside pocket and dials. 'Now. At the back entrance.'

I follow in a daze as he leads us along corridors and eventually out of a back door where Jackson is waiting with the Bentley.

Jackson opens the back door and Gregory holds

me by the shoulders, gently shaking me until I look at him. 'Are you okay?'

I nod, first slowly, then quicker, until my brain starts to function in real time. 'Yes. Yes. I'm fine. Your hand.'

'It's fine,' he snaps, taking it to the rim of the door and encouraging me to climb into the back seat.

I wait for him to open the door and slide in beside me, but he doesn't; he gets into the front passenger seat and before I'm over that subtle gesture, he rolls up the partition between the front and back of the car, blocking me out of his conversation with Jackson.

He just knocked a man's nose across the other side of his face. He got us out of there before the press could show interest. Despite his red and swelling hand, he asked *me* if *I'm* okay. This is what I keep telling myself in an attempt to rationalise my building anger at being isolated in the back of the car like a child as he has a private conversation with Jackson.

It's not the solitary confinement that irritates me most, though; it's the fact he didn't overhear the majority of Nick's venom before landing his fist in Nick's face. Sitting here now, I realise that's because he didn't need to. He already knew.

Jackson parks the Bentley and I'm out of the car

first, slamming the door, heading straight for the basement's lift vestibule.

'Scarlett.' My name is bundled amongst frustration, tiredness and yes, ironically, anger.

He is angry with *me*? *You've got to be kidding.*

I turn quickly, my breaths jagged with rage. My reaction stills him and we stand facing one another, staring, both of us indignant.

'You knew,' I fire. 'You knew he was there tonight and you knew he was in bed with Francis.'

'Yes.'

Jackson moves slowly in the background, feigning interest in nothing on the side of the car.

'Why have you sat chatting with Francis as if it means nothing?'

'Because it doesn't. It's business. He's made an investment. And just in case, I like to keep potential enemies where I can see them.'

As I process that new information, I shake my head, my anger easing marginally now that he's talking. I move into the vestibule, punching the button harder than necessary to call the lift.

My arms are folded across my chest and I glare at Gregory as he and Jackson join me in the lift, Jackson hitting sixty-four.

'And Trina? Did you know she's spoken to Nick? She's obviously digging for dirt. She told him her bribe theory. Except, of course, we know that isn't just a theory, Gregory, don't we?'

As soon as I've said that last part, a pang of guilt strikes my gut. Hacking at old wounds is low and I know it but right now, the guilt is losing out to temper and the question I can't find an answer to. *Why would Katrina Martin go to Nick Henshaw?*

'Yes. I knew.'

'How? Since when? More importantly, why don't *I* know?'

The lift doors open and despite his tense body, Gregory remains still, waiting for me to exit first. I want answers and I won't break the silence until they come.

I expect Jackson to leave and head to his room when we're in the lounge. Instead, he takes three crystal glasses and a decanter of Scotch and brings them to the breakfast bar where Gregory is standing with his hands locked onto the edge of the granite worktop. One hand has white, strained knuckles, whilst the other is red and angry.

Despite my need to see out this argument, I don't want him to suffer for protecting me, so as Jackson pours three glasses of Scotch, I fill a towel with ice from the dispenser on the front of the refrigerator then lay Gregory's hand flat on the worktop and hold the ice against it. I can feel him watching me.

'Sit,' I say, hooking a stool with my free hand and moving it behind him.

He does and takes the glass Jackson offers to him, draining half the Scotch in one.

'After Dubai, I had Trina followed.'

I look at him now, grateful that he's letting me in.

'You were right. She won't give up until she finds something.' He suddenly looks exhausted. 'She was photographed with Nick weeks ago. I didn't tell you because I didn't want you to put two and two together and come up with a thousand explanations. There's been no contact since.'

I would have done that, he's right.

'You still should've told me. If you've had her followed since Dubai, you've known she's a threat all this time and I'm not crazy.'

He says nothing, neither agreeing nor disagreeing. That's my cue to leave. He has some thinking to do and, as he knows they will, the cogs in my head need space to turn. I need to process everything from today and I can't do that around him. I balance the ice on his hand, drain my Scotch, and make my way to the stairs.

'I'm sleeping in the spare room.'

His silence makes my weary limbs heavier as I trudge the staircase in my gown and heels.

20

My father used to say you should never go to bed on an argument. I guess that's true because I've woken even more pissed at Gregory than I was when I fell asleep. Yet, I'm now staring at the muscles of his naked back as he climbs out of bed.

Damn it. I know my body and I know I'll have caved. Whenever he carried me in here from the spare room, I'll have given myself over to him, probably cuddled into his chest and wrapped my legs up in his. Hell, as I watch him move into an arms-raised stretch, I want him, too.

'Good morning, beautiful.'

I scowl my silent response, unsure whether I'm more annoyed with him or myself. On a head shake, he leaves the bedroom and when I hear him bound down the stairs to go out for his five-thirty run, I know the coast is clear for me to head to the gym.

'Still pissed?' Jackson asks me as I pummel the punch bag.

I land a right hook. 'What do you think?'

'I'd say you're getting a lot of power in those arms these days. Let's get your elbows involved.'

Mopping my brow with my forearm, I turn my back on the bag, then holding my gloves together in front of me, I thrust an elbow back and up into the throat of the bag like he taught me.

Katrina Martin and Nick Henshaw. Why? Did she question his motive for resigning from Constant Sources? And Francis. Why would someone in private equity invest in a man who ran one company into the ground and was pushed out of another?

I'm on blow number three with my elbow when the gym door opens and Gregory removes his plugs from his ears, looking damn fine with wet hair, masculinity radiating from him. I pause and watch as he peels off his hoody and reveals his toned, bare chest.

God, help me. I can feel Jackson's silent amusement by my side.

As Gregory moves towards the bag, I take off my gloves. This is the routine. Now Jackson trains Gregory whilst I stretch out and leave to get ready for work. But today, petty though it may be, I throw my gloves so they land on the weight bench at one side of the room, then I barge past Gregory.

'Don't you have anything to say to me? Shout, rant, anything?'

I pause before turning to face him, trying desperately to look only at his face.

'Yes. Actually, I do. I reviewed the draft joint venture agreement with Shangzen Tek yesterday. You need to agree a share option. GJR is bringing more knowledge to the joint venture than Shangzen and both companies are getting equal equity and voting rights. If the JV company makes a profit, I would suggest you have an option to increase GJR's stake, exercisable on the annual accounts of the first and second years in operation.'

'That's it? That's all you have to say?'

'Yep.'

'You don't have anything to say about this?' He holds my engagement ring in the air between his forefinger and thumb.

'I took it off to go on the bag, Gregory. If I'd taken it off because I'm pissed at you, I probably would've thrown it at your head.' I snatch the ring from his fingers and make to leave.

'I'll need you to draft that option into the agreement,' he calls as I open the gym door.

I reply over my shoulder, 'It's already done. Now you need to agree it.'

'Well, I'll do that.'

'Fine.'

'Fine.'

'Fine!'

* * *

I'm eating Amy's expertly round poached eggs on an English muffin, talking to her and drinking coffee. It's impossible to be angry in the company of one of the happiest people in the world and my mood has improved tenfold. As she tells me about her son's rugby game last night, she looks over my shoulder to the staircase.

'Poached eggs, flower?' she asks Gregory when he takes a seat on the stool next to mine.

'Please.'

Amy cracks two eggs into her already hot pan of water, then places a black coffee and a glass of fresh orange in front of Gregory.

'I'm sorry.'

I look up from my plate, almost choking on his

unexpected words. He's wearing a navy suit with a crisp white shirt and sky-blue tie and *Christ* does he smell amazing. Not ending last night the way I thought we would is clearly playing havoc with my hormones.

'The worst thing wasn't what Nick said, Gregory; it was that I wasn't prepared. I didn't know how to react. I couldn't control my reaction because you kept me in the dark. Again.'

'I know. I get it.' He exhales heavily. 'Scarlett, this is my life. I deal with dark and twisted and I deal with it in my way. Let me finish. I've never had anyone living this close to me, who wants to know things about me. I've also never felt the need to protect anyone as insanely as I do you.' He casts an eye to Amy who, less than inconspicuously, leaves us. 'I've told you before, you're everything to me now and I won't let anything happen to you. I won't let anyone hurt you. Sometimes, that might mean keeping things from you but you have to trust that everything I do is in your best interests. Even if I get it wrong sometimes, or you think I do.' He smiles fleetingly. 'I'm always thinking of you.'

'I know that.' And I do. 'But I want us to be a team. Work together. Face challenges together, whatever they may be. You're not alone any more, Gregory.'

He squeezes his eyes shut and raises my palm to his lips. 'Aurora.'

* * *

'Wait.' He pulls me back as I manoeuvre somewhat awkwardly out of the Mercedes in my black pencil skirt. 'I don't want you to find out and think I've been keeping things from you.'

He glances at Jackson in the rear-view mirror then back to me. A look that makes me lift my legs back into the car and pull the door closed.

'I went to see Jack.'

My old boss Jack? The man Gregory forced to confess to sexual assault? *That* Jack? My skin crawls until the tingling grows to a shiver and my shoulders shudder. I should consider myself lucky. All those late nights in the office, the crass jibes, the way he used to look at me like I was his next meal. But Jack never actually touched me. Thanks to Gregory, I never became one of the women he abused.

'When?' I don't need to ask why; I know why. He went to see him to determine whether Jack is behind the trouble with *Black Diamonds*.

'Wednesday.'

I nod. 'And?'

'It's not him, Scarlett, I'm certain of it.'

I nod again, unsure how I feel about that. 'Thank you for telling me.' I lean across the back seat and press my mouth to his. 'It means a lot.'

He strokes my hair behind my ear and pushes the curled ends back across my shoulder. 'Don't overthink, baby; enjoy your last day at the firm. I can't wait until I get to see you all day, every day.'

'I'll be working,' I say with a smile I can't help because I'm really looking forward to working next door to him, too.

'Your boss might give you extended breaks,' he says with a suggestive half-smile and the kinky sparkle in his eye throws my mind back to images of us fucking over his desk.

'I don't know,' I say, pecking his cheek and making my move out of the car. I bend and lean back through the open door. 'I've heard he's a bit of a dick.' I blow him a kiss, leaving him laughing as the door closes.

* * *

It wasn't Jack.

I need to start making my final handover notes and packing up the contents of my desk but before I do, I open my matter file for *Constant Sources (GJR): Black Diamonds.*

'Hey, you.' Amanda appears at my office door. 'Leaving lunch and embarrassing goodbye shenanigans at one.'

'Oh, Amanda, please don't go over the top; I'd rather slope off quietly.'

'And that's why you have a fantabulous best friend to make sure you don't.' She leaves as swiftly as she arrived, calling back, 'I'll collect you at twelve fifty-five. Be ready.'

I start working back through the information I have on the *Black Diamonds* IP registrations. *Nothing.* I scour my documents and notes on the subsidiary companies that filed the registrations. Local counsel said there was nothing suspect about those companies nor the French parent company. I put on my headset and dial each lawyer in turn, asking them to urgently send through the details of the three companies, names of directors, shareholders, constitutional documents.

Ten minutes later, I'm scouring the documents on my screen and I see one common thread.

Francesco Benedetti, Director.

I can hear Adriana's whiney voice chastising her husband. *'Oh, Francesco, you're so baaaaad.'* The man I know as Francis is... Francesco Benedetti?

Typing *Francesco Benedetti* into a search engine gives me a link to Carter's Private Equity House. I remember the name.

Unsettled and feeling like I'm onto something all at once, I click the link to the company's website. The homepage is full of spiel about the PE house's investments. *Latest News. Corporate Social Responsibility.* Then I click *Team*.

There he is. A black and white image with a bio sits under the heading *Francesco Benedetti*. Francis.

Francis is registering Black Diamonds?

Gregory answers almost immediately when I call.

'Ryans.'

'It's Nick Henshaw.' His name tastes vile as it leaves my mouth.

'Scarlett?'

'Francis, Adriana's Francis, is Francesco Benedetti.' I try to slow my pace and keep it together as I explain.

'Yes, one and the same.'

'Last night, when Nick Henshaw told me he'd gone into business with Francis, he said it like a threat.'

'We've been over this.'

'This morning, I had local counsel send the registration documents of the companies behind the *Black Diamonds* registrations, Gregory, and there's one constant. Francis, *Francesco*, is a director of them all.'

'Ja, so what does that mean?' His South-African twang rolls off his tongue like he's relaxed but I know I have his attention.

'Why would Francis try to register *Black Diamonds*? He doesn't have a vendetta against you, you said so. His new business partner on the other hand... Nick isn't listed as a director but I just know, Gregory, from last night, from Nick's knowledge of the gaming industry, it *has* to be him. I don't know what their financial arrangement is but I'm certain Francesco Benedetti and Nick Henshaw are in this together. They're trying to steal *Black Diamonds*.'

He's silent for a second. 'That's not Francis's way. He's out for money but he's not vindictive. He's not into those kinds of battles. His reputation as an investor would be on the line and like you say, he doesn't have an issue with me.'

'So maybe he doesn't know? He could think he's investing in gaming software. Legitimate. Above board. He doesn't need to know Nick's motivation. *Black Diamonds* has only been on the market for a matter of weeks; it's feasible that Nick could own the game and be registering the IP as any new owner would. That could be the story he's told Francis at least.'

Gregory is quiet again, to the point that I start to

wonder if he's still on the line. Eventually, he snarls, 'Fucking bastard.'

* * *

'Ready lady? The only answer to that question is yes, by the way.' Amanda stands, coat on, handbag over her wrist, at the door to my office.

'In that case, yes.'

'You seem distracted,' she says as we walk towards the dim sum restaurant.

'Sorry. I am but I won't be. I'm really looking forward to lunch. Thanks for organising.'

'You're also a terrible liar.'

I know that. 'It's a failing I was born with.'

'Is everything okay? Are you and Gregory okay?'

'Oh, gosh, yes, fine. You remember the game Gregory acquired before St Lucia, and the intellectual property issues?'

'Right, yep. That's still going on?'

I pull open the heavy glass door to the restaurant. 'After you. Yes, it's still going on. Bit of a mess really.'

'That's all? You're sure?'

I laugh internally at Amanda's simplistic view of everything work-related. 'Yes, that's all.'

There are already ten others from my office

seated at benches. We eat far too many dumplings on a long wooden table then I'm presented with spa vouchers for two as a leaving gift. From the look on Amanda's face, I know the identity of my intended guest.

My phone vibrates for the second time in ten minutes and I'm desperate to answer but Amanda has gone to a lot of trouble, so instead, I watch Gregory's name light up the screen before a message comes through.

Can you come here?

After saying my goodbyes and giving my final handover notes for Mr Ghurair's transaction to Amanda, I leave. Jackson comes to my office and carries my box to the Mercedes as I take in the space one last time.

The end of an era. So much has happened in five months and it all started with one pitch. One boardroom. One glance. I roll my engagement ring between my fingers and close the door on old Scarlett Heath.

Daughter. Trainee. Associate. Senior Associate. Legal Director.

By the time I reach the lift, I realise a new door has opened, a new chapter has begun, and a new, stronger version of Scarlett Heath has been born.

* * *

Jackson takes my box, together with my wool coat and dripping-wet dome umbrella, to my new office whilst I head in search of Gregory.

The staff outside his office appear sheepish. As I approach the frosted glass door, Stuart comes out looking like he's just witnessed an unhappy CEO.

'Hi, Stuart.'

Those familiar eyes soften. 'Hi, Scarlett.' His voice betrays his disheartened mood and gives me a small insight into what's waiting behind the door.

Gregory is pacing, the tails of his blazer pushed back by his hands in his pockets, his tie looser than usual at his neck, hair out of place like he's dragged his fingers through it. Even the air in the room is tense.

'Close the door,' he snaps.

I do so, taking steps into the middle of the office.

'You were right,' he says, pausing but facing out to the city. 'It's Nick fucking Henshaw.'

I nod but don't speak.

'Stuart swears he has nothing to do with it. Says he's never heard of Nick or Francis.'

'Do we believe him?'

'He swore on his mother's life. That's not something a man does lightly.'

I venture forward now, taking a seat in the chair opposite Gregory's desk. The black leather is still warm. No doubt Stuart got a thorough dressing-down. Most likely a threat on his life if he so much as thinks about crossing Gregory.

Gregory laughs now, sardonically, and strokes his forefinger and thumb along his jawline, his other hand still resting on his hip. 'He wants a payout.'

I had suspected as much but I let him speak.

'Three fucking million. Three. Fucking. Million. It's nothing to do with the fucking game.'

'He wants money because you forced him to resign.'

'Fucking prick.'

'I had a feeling that would be the case once I re-alised it was him. The way he spoke at the gala, he—'

'Well, fucking marvellous, Scarlett. When the fuck were you going to share that feeling with me?'

I stand abruptly from my chair.

'Attitude check, Ryans. Right the hell now! Or you can stare at my back as I walk out of this office and leave you in the shit.'

He turns from the window and opens his mouth to protest. He doesn't apologise but he does move to sit into his desk chair opposite me, putting us on the same level when I sit, too.

'I've been thinking about it all morning,' I say calmly.

'I'm all ears.' His tone is as tame as I suspect this hungry lion is going to get.

'Stuart created the game. If we believe he isn't involved, he still has certain unregistered intellectual property rights.'

'Does that help us?'

'Absolutely, so long as we can prove it. If Nick's demanding money, it tells me he doesn't really want *Black Diamonds*. If he wanted to set up alone and put a new game on the market, he would; he has the knowledge to do it. He's trying to threaten you that he can use whatever version of *Black Diamonds* he has to eat into your *Jail Run* profits. He'll know that's why *you* wanted *Black Diamonds*.'

'I think I'm following.' Given the speed the words are leaving my mouth, that's nothing short of a miracle. 'He thinks the threat of him having the game on the market is worth three million pounds to me.'

'Right. So let's call his bluff. Let's make it so he doesn't have the threat of taking *his Black Diamonds* to market. Then he has nothing on you.'

Gregory's eyes widen and he sits a little straighter in his chair. 'How do we do that?'

'We fight him. In China, the US, Europe. We make

a case against his registration of the game. We claim ownership. It's not a cheap plan. It will cost you.'

'But it'll be a damn sight cheaper than three million pounds.'

'Precisely.'

He leans back in his chair, his eyes distant as he processes the idea, his fingertips forming a steeple that rests against his chin. 'And whilst you're working on that, I'll take pleasure in letting Francis know exactly who he's getting involved with.'

'He'll pull the funding?'

'I'm almost certain of it.'

21

He's propped up on one arm, his dark hair messed from sleep, a light dusting of stubble coating his chin. The white cotton sheet is wrapped around his waist and between his legs. He's otherwise on display for my own personal viewing.

'This is a nice way to wake up.' My eyes run shamelessly over the perfect sculpture of man, falling on his eager crotch, a sight that heats the blood that travels to the tips of my breasts and between my legs.

'You know what I was thinking? I was thinking I've never met anyone like you.' His fingers trace the side of my body, moving away the sheet so his hand comes to rest on the small of my back. My body reacts, bending closer to his heat.

'I hope that's a good thing.' The sound of my voice betrays my want.

'Mostly,' he says, with that half-smile I adore. 'No one else challenges me the way you do and no one else dares to tell me to check my attitude.'

'What can I say, sometimes, you need an attitude check, Ryans.'

'As do you, Mrs Ryans-to-be, and you're going to get it.'

I moan greedily as he pulls my body against his, letting me feel his intention against my navel. His hand slides to the sphere of my arse, pulling my thigh across his and coming to rest in the crease between my thigh and calf.

'You're right when you say we work better as a team. We do, don't we?'

I assume, on this occasion, he's referring to the fact Francis wants out of his arrangement with Nick Henshaw and local counsel are already on the case of challenging Nick's registration of *Black Diamonds* in the UK and Europe. All of which kills Nick's chances of getting three million pounds out of GJR.

'If I said it, it must be true.' I'm feeling particularly cheeky and ready to play this morning, something that pulls his lips to a smirk, but his eyes are serious.

'I've never had that. This. I've never been part of a

team. I'm always the man in control and with you...
you throw me off balance. Some days, I wonder if I've
dreamt you. As if it's taken me thirty years to realise
what I need and you're a figment of my imagination.
You're beautiful. Smart and strong. You're so perfect,
I'm terrified of waking up and losing you.'

I hold my hand to his cheek and wait for him to
open his eyes. 'I feel the same and I'm not going anywhere, Gregory. You've changed me in so many ways.
You're the anchor in my new world.'

'*Our* new world.'

He drops his mouth to mine and rolls us so my
back is on the mattress, my thighs locked around his
hips, my body rising to make contact with his, desire
turning to a wet, aching need between my legs.

He lowers himself, his weight resting against my
pelvis, his forearms either side of my head, his fingers
gently stroking my hair. 'I love you so much.'

I brush his hair back from his brow and lock my
fingers behind his neck. 'I love you, too.'

He leans down, his tongue dipping into my mouth
and teasing mine, the soft skin of his lips grazing my
own. I drown in his touch, in his love, in him.

* * *

'Sorry to interrupt but can I take a car?' I make my way into the lounge in my skinny jeans and oversized jumper, eating a bagel on the move so that I'm not late for picking up Sandy.

Gregory and Jackson look up from the photographs and documents they're studying on the coffee table. I don't need to look to know that Nick Henshaw will be the star of that storyboard. They're blindly trying to plot their next move, not knowing how Nick will react to the fact his plan imploded. This fight has only just begun. The one saving grace is that Gregory hasn't opted for his usual first port of call and had Jackson bring in extra security. That's something I can take comfort from. He thinks this will be a white-collar war rather than one that requires him to step into the ring.

The men have a silent conversation before Jackson stands and declares, 'I'll take you.'

I hold my hand up whilst I swallow. 'No, thanks, Jackson, I'm good to drive.' I glare at Gregory. 'I know you put me on the insurance; I saw the invoice on your desk. And before you dare to make a remark about my driving capabilities, let me remind you that you've never actually been a passenger in a car with me.'

He rests back against the leather of the sofa. 'Two things.' He holds up one finger like a completely patronising arse as he speaks. 'One, you don't drive often.' He lifts another finger and I'd like to mirror that action, flashing my knuckles in his direction. 'Two, you don't have the first idea about driving one of *my* cars. Jackson will take you.'

Whilst I take his point on the supercar front – the paddle gears, no clutch, the car screaming out to go faster – I don't appreciate his tone.

'Why would you put me on the insurance if I'm never going to be allowed to drive the cars?'

'In case.'

'In case of what? A rally opportunity on South Bank?'

'See. This is what I'm talking about.' He raises his hands and faces Jackson. 'Baby, you drive rally cars in a rally.'

'Quit being a dick and just give me some keys.'

His eyes are bright when he looks back to me. He moves to the small safe in the corner of the lounge and types in his code then throws me a key.

'You can take the Range Rover. It's a normal drive and it's safe. Don't play games. Don't take risks. Don't drive over the speed limit and—'

'Bugger off, Gregory.'

* * *

Sandy and I run from the Range Rover, coats over our heads to shield us from the torrential rain, not stopping until we reach the porch. I have to fiddle with the lock, yanking the door handle towards me as I turn the key. A sign of how infrequently the lock has been turned in the last five months. I push the door past a stack of mail, most of which looks like adverts and trash. I stopped the important mail after my dad died. Sandy helps me scoop up the paper and envelopes into a pile on the dark wood side table in the vestibule.

We stand for a while, looking around what used to be a bright, happy home. It has a strange, musty smell and even with the lights turned on, it feels dark and grey, like the colour has been drained from the furnishings and the paint on the walls. I run my finger along the side table and look at the thick, grey circle that forms on my skin, a symbol of the past.

'I'll put the kettle on,' Sandy says. 'I brought a pack-up and luxury biscuits. It's going to be a long day.'

'I didn't even think of that, thank you. I'll get the boxes from the car.'

* * *

Long day doesn't cover it. *One of the hardest days of my life* might come close. We started downstairs: the lounge, the kitchen, the dining room. The removal men will be packing up and disposing of everything we haven't agreed to keep or leave to the buyers and there weren't many personal items downstairs. I decided not to look at photographs, wrapping them in old newspaper and packing them into a box before memories could form in my head. Sandy started with the opposite approach, wanting to remember and talk, but her smiles were cast in the shadow of tears and it took all my emotional strength to comfort her and drag us both through the godawful morning.

Now we're upstairs and I'm in the doorway of my dad's bedroom, staring at the empty space left by the removal of the special equipment he was given on loan from the National Health Service. The bed, the chair and commode, the drugs cabinet. All gone. In their wake, there's the pungent smell of stale urine, a worn carpet and an overwhelming sense of death. I make my way into the room for one thing: the picture of my dad, Sandy and me at Brighton Pier in '94. We're all smiling, holding candyfloss. My dad drapes his arms around our shoulders. The sun is beaming down on us. He's young, well, happy. It was his favourite photograph of the three of us and he asked for it to be put by his bedside on one of his good days. My throat constricts as I trace his smile with my fingertips and I close my eyes, willing myself to get past this moment for me, for Sandy.

'I love you, Dad,' I whisper, then press my lips to the frame.

The loft is the worst room. It was always going to be. But the reality is worse than the thought of it. My dad kept so many things from my childhood that I'd forgotten even exist. Dolls, bears, drawings, pictures with glitter and wool that Sandy helped me make. School reports, trophies from athletics and dancing, swimming badges. I can't bring myself to throw away these things because I see in each of them the tremendous sense of love my dad had for me. I'm eternally grateful to have had a dad who loved me and protected me.

Sandy talks about the stories behind the things we pack into the boxes and I smile outwardly, sometimes even respond appropriately to her comments, but I don't give myself over to the memories. I hide behind an invisible wall of safety because I'm afraid that when the tears come, they won't stop.

* * *

Sandy holds in her lap a small bag of belongings that she asked to keep as I drive her back to Lara's house. I hardly speak as we make our way, nodding and shaking my head as she talks. This is Sandy's way of coping, talking through it, but I can't help her. I can't get words past the pain in my chest, the ache in my stomach, the stinging sensation behind my eyes.

I love Sandy, possibly more than she'll ever know, but I'm relieved when I turn onto Lara's driveway because once I'm alone, I can break.

'Scarlett, hunny, come inside,' Lara calls from the doorway.

Lara, the wedding. I forgot. I close my eyes, reboot and climb out of the car.

Miranda, another of Lara's staff, brings tea and bitesize cakes which I take, both to calm my rumbling stomach and to comfort me through a conversation I have to endure when all I really want is Gregory.

Lara settles onto one end of a sofa and I sit next to her in a high-backed grandad chair.

'I wanted to show you this,' she says, opening a large leather-back album full of page after page of wedding snippings, drafting notes and sketches. 'I've agreed the date with Gregory. Saturday the sixteenth of March.'

I know from the excitement in her eyes that she

doesn't mean next year. 'Lara, that's only a few weeks away.'

'I know but that's more than enough time. I've planned a lot of events, Scarlett. I will make this the best day of your life.'

It will be but because I'm marrying the man I am 100 per cent besotted with, not because Lara is planning what looks like the wedding of the century. She turns the pages through an extravagant champagne reception in her house, a huge marquee on her lawn. Bridesmaid dresses, sketches for bridal gowns. *Do I get a say in anything?* She talks through the layers of a five-tier cake and the stature of the three hundred and fifty guests, as I work my way through the plate of cakes, washing down the sugar with tea, trying to hold the dams in my eyes just a little longer.

I don't want this. I don't want a big wedding with hundreds of people I don't know. People who don't care about *us*.

I've just cleared out my dad's house, the person who should be giving away his only daughter to the man she loves. My dad should be giving me away knowing that Gregory will take over protecting me, that he'll love me back in every way he can. My father is dead. He won't get to tell me I look beautiful in my ivory dress, whether it's true or not. He won't be able to walk me down the aisle. He died alone, without me, not knowing how much I truly love him. He was murdered because of me.

I need Gregory. I need him to hold me, to tell me everything's going to be okay. To tell me he'll fix this. I need him to reset me and help me find my equilibrium.

I drive through the darkness too fast, craving his touch and his soothing whispers in my ear. I need to forget and he'll know that.

I'm breathless, panicked and lost by the time I get back to the apartment. I open the door and call his name. He isn't here. He isn't here and I need him.

I close the door and push my back against it before my body slides to the ground and my dams break. I clutch my knees to my chest and sob, audible, heart-wrenching tears that I might never be able to stop.

'Baby, Christ, I'm here. I'm here.'

He hooks an arm under my legs and I throw my arms around his neck, fisting the back of his black T-shirt, clinging desperately to the only thing in the world that can earth me. He carries me to the sofa and sits with me in his lap. He lets me cry, stroking my hair, kissing my temple, accepting me falling apart.

'I can't do a big wedding, Gregory. I don't want it. My dad won't be there.'

'Shh, I've got you. You're fine, baby. I'm here.'

When my tears subside and my chest no longer chugs with every breath, I look at his stunning face, not self-conscious about the fact I must look a mess. He strokes my hair with both hands and two big, wide, sympathetic browns read me.

'Gregory.'

He kisses me without me having to tell him what I need, that I just want to get lost in him, have him take me out of my head.

His mouth is gentle at first, then he kisses me urgently, with a fierceness he knows I need, a kiss that has us both breathless. He stands and places me down to sit on the edge of the sofa. He kneels between my legs and when I raise up my arms, he pulls my jumper over my head.

His lips are back on mine, fast and furious, sucking, biting as he unhooks my bra. Our contact is lost momentarily whilst he pulls my bra down my arms.

He pushes my chest so I fall back against the sofa. Then he tugs my legs at the knees, sliding my hips forward. His eyes are heavy, showing his own desire as he unfastens my jeans and pulls them down in one move, casting the denim and my French lace knickers to the floor.

He eyes me now, asking permission.

'Yes. Please.'

He peels his black T-shirt over his head then pushes my legs apart, bending forward to kiss me chastely before moving his head between my legs.

'Gregory. Yes. Oh God, yes.'

He holds his hands against the inside of my thighs, applying pressure as he dips his tongue lavishly in and out of me, then across my swollen bud.

'Is this what you need, baby?' His breath is hot on my sensitive skin.

I can hardly speak. 'Yes.'

'Say it. Tell me what you need.'

'You. I need you.'

He sucks hard on my clit, his groan vibrating against me.

'Please.' I don't even know why the word leaves my mouth but it does.

He pushes his fingers into me and I roll my head against the back of the sofa as my body lifts to a crescendo. His fingers move in circles, my body tensing each time he strokes my wall. My head clouds from my erratic breaths until I think I might pass out. His spare hand moves to my breast, squeezing hard as he sucks my clit again and I come undone.

He stands and pulls off his jeans but when he

crawls between my legs, I put my hands in his hair and lift him towards me.

'Let me taste you.' I stare at his angry cock and lick my lips at the thought of him in my mouth.

He yanks my hips further down the sofa then kneels across me, his shins either side of my hips, his erection level with my mouth. Keeping my eyes on him, I take him in my hands first, working his sack and the base of his shaft.

He pants, his hips rolling forward. 'Let me feel your mouth around me, baby.'

I move my tongue up his length and around the tip. When a low growl leaves his chest, I wrap my mouth around him, sliding down him to meet my hand then drawing back to the tip. I work him until he loses control. His hands drop to the back of the sofa and he moves back and forth, fucking my mouth as I stay still, accepting him, ready for his release. He's close; I can feel him thicken in my mouth and taste his juice. Then he pulls out.

He takes us to the floor, turning me forward on my knees as he does, my hands braced on the sofa. He pushes my thighs further apart and drives into my drenched sex.

'Fuck! That's the best feeling.'

He fucks me: rough, hard, thoroughly.

'Thank you,' I whisper.

22

'Where's Gregory?' Williams asks as we ride the lift to the twenty-eighth floor and my new office.

'Truth or the business lie?'

'Erm, truth?' he says, playfully uncertain.

'Beautifying and pruning this morning.'

Williams chuckles and rolls his eyes but something tells me he has similar appointments and it's not only his perfectly manicured nails.

'Then he has a brunch and I think he's working from home after that.'

'Can't blame him, it's rough being massaged and cleansed.'

The lift pings at twenty-eight and Williams leads

me to my office, as instructed by Gregory, despite the fact I already know where it is.

'You really don't have to babysit me, Williams.'

'Oh, I do. Trust me, it's not worth my life.'

We're both laughing when Williams opens the door to my new office.

'Scarlett!' Sue jumps from behind the desk. 'I was just getting things ready for you.'

Someone has had far too much caffeine.

'Thank you, Sue, the place looks great.' I look around the large, bright space. She's hung my certificates on the walls: undergraduate degree, legal practice course, masters. She's set my Mont Blanc pen neatly to one side of my keyboard.

A large arrangement of two dozen roses decorates the table in the corner of the room. I smile before I open the card.

Welcome to Team Gregory. Have a great first day, baby. xxx

'Scarlett, Sue is your PA now,' Williams says, reclaiming my attention.

'It's a trial,' Sue jumps in, suddenly making apparent why she's so jittery. 'If I do anything you don't like, if you want me to do anything differently, just say so.'

'We've left her role fairly fluid,' Williams explains. 'We thought it would be best if you tell Sue what support you need and what you expect from her.'

'Okay, that sounds sensible. Perhaps we could go for lunch today, Sue – my treat. I'll have had a look around the systems by then and we can discuss how we'll work together. Sound good?'

'Perfect. Excellent. Yes. Wonderful.' She turns to leave the office, her skirt swishing as she moves.

'Step number one is to convince her to drink less coffee,' I tell Williams once Sue is firmly out of earshot. 'Before you go, I'm going to throw Amanda a baby shower. Not yet but I want to get a date in diaries. Could you send me a list of any people from your side who I should invite? I'm thinking afternoon tea at the Savoy.'

'You know her well. Expensive indulgence and an afternoon that revolves around Amanda. She'll love it.' There's no malice in his words, just good humour. 'I'll think about it and drop you a message.'

'Thanks, Williams, and thanks for this morning.'

* * *

My mind wanders far too often to Gregory, as if being in his glass tower somehow makes him ever-present. The jury is definitely out on whether this move is a good idea. What's harder is knowing that he's willing to have me in his office.

Concentrate.

I focus on the latest draft of the joint venture agreement with Shangzen Tek, which Shangzen's lawyer emailed during the night. Between that, first-day IT hiccups, a stream of questions from Amanda in relation to Mr Ghurair, and a two-hour lunch with Sue, I already have a backlog of emails.

I'm sifting through confirmations from external counsel about the progress made in the challenges against Nick Henshaw when there's a tap on my office door.

'Come in.'

Sue appears. 'I'm heading off now. Well, unless you need anything. Then I'm happy to stay.'

I turn to the two walls of windows forming an L-shape around me and realise the winter darkness is already set in and raindrops decorate the glass panes. In the reflection, I see Stuart, now standing in the doorway behind Sue.

'No, I'm good, you head off.'

'Thank you. Oh, and Mr Culliton has come to see

you. Is it okay?' I have to suppress my laugh as Stuart points to himself then the office floor as if to say, *I'm already here.*

'Yes, fine, thank you, Sue. Have a lovely evening and I'll see you tomorrow. Come in, Stuart. Take a seat.'

He sits into one of the chairs opposite mine with his coat and tie in his hand. The top button of his shirt is undone and his hair is ruffled like it's been a long day. 'I just wanted to return the favour,' he says. 'You came to see how I was settling in and it was nice of you.' He shrugs. 'You were one of the few people who made me feel welcome, so I wanted to make sure I did the same for you.' He smiles but his eyes remain a mystery.

'Thank you. That's sweet of you. It's been a long day and I dare say I'll be here for a while yet but I'm getting there. I think I've cracked the systems now.'

He nods and turns his head around the room, his eyes fixing momentarily on the bunch of roses then turning back to me. 'Are they from Gregory?'

'Ah, yes, they are.'

'Do you think he's a good man?' he asks bizarrely.

I feel my brows furrow and there's a wash of realisation on his face.

'He is a good man. The best. He can seem a little uptight at work but give him a chance.'

Stuart nods again, seemingly contemplative. 'Are you working on my game?' He inclines his head to the open file of papers in front of me.

'Er, yes, I am.'

'So did you stop Nick using the game?'

My head snaps up to meet his.

'Gregory told me,' he adds quickly.

He did?

'Yes. We did,' I say, wondering when that conversation took place and hoping Gregory hasn't taken out his temper over the whole thing on Stuart again. He swore on his mother's life he knows nothing about the trouble.

Stuart takes a deep breath and closes his eyes for longer than a blink. 'I didn't mean for any of this to happen, Scarlett.'

'I know. Don't worry. We'll fix it.'

He drags a hand through his hair and slowly rolls his body to stand, looking tired.

'Have you got plans?' I ask, in a bid to improve his mood.

'No,' he snaps, making me regret the effort. 'I don't really know anyone here,' he adds in a softer tone. 'Microwave meal and biltong for one.'

'We'll go out sometime. I can introduce you to some people.'

'Thanks but you're a little old for me, Scarlett.'

My jaw drops open but I'm laughing, happy because finally, he's smiling. 'Get out, right now!'

He pauses at the door and turns back to me. 'Listen, Scarlett, if—' He stares at his feet. 'Have a good night.'

'You, too.'

I dim the lights once Stuart leaves, the glare of my computer screen becoming too much against the darkness surrounding the glass office. It's deathly silent, the entire floor desolate. Perfect for reading and drafting. I didn't realise the door hadn't closed behind Stuart until a dark shadow in my peripheral vision makes me jump and squeal.

'Shit! Paul. You scared the life out of me.'

'Sorry, Scarlett.' He steps into the office in his janitor get-up. He looks bigger than he did just a few weeks ago. He's eating. 'I call in to see Gregory on Mondays, if he's around. Just, you know, to check in. I like him to see I'm on track.'

'It's good to see you,' I say as my heart rate returns to normal. 'How's everything going?'

'Good. Really good. Great, in fact. I feel like I've

been thrown a lifeline, you know, and I'm going to make the most of it.'

'Good for you. Well, Gregory isn't in the office today but I can let him know you called by and you're not slacking.' I throw him a smile.

'On that note, there are floors to be mopped. I guess I'll see you around now you're working here?'

'Sure will.'

I get back to my emails. A two-page rant has dropped into my inbox from Shangzen's lawyer, trying to negotiate what I've already told him is a deal breaker for GJR. I'm immersed in the detail of a reply when my phone rings and this time when I jump, I crash my knee off the underside of my desk. *Damn, that hurt.*

I look at the screen, which is pointless because there aren't any numbers programmed into the phone yet.

'Scarlett Heath.'

'Scarlett, it's Stuart. I left my fob on my desk. Could you come down to the ground floor and let me in?'

'Erm, yes, sure. I'll be down in a minute.'

Urgh, I'll never get anything done.

It's dark and cold waiting for the lift and I wish I'd pulled on my suit jacket, my blouse and skirt doing nothing to fend off the overzealous air conditioning.

As I step into the lift, my phone rings again. This time, I recognise the number as Gregory's but my signal cuts out as the lift doors close. By the time I reach the subdued lighting of the ground floor, I have a message announcing a voicemail.

Stuart is outside on the pavement on the other side of the glass doors, his shoulders hunched in the rain. A black limousine is parked by the curb, which strikes me as odd – not uncommon in London but unusual for this part of the city. My heels click on the marble floor as I wave to Paul, in full mopping mode, and hold my phone to my ear.

'Scarlett.' Gregory's voice sounds panicked on the message. I step into the revolving door. 'Stay at the office. I'm on my way. It's Stuart. He's involved.'

I drop the phone as I come face to face with Stuart.

'I'm sorry,' he says.

I'm yanked backwards.

A hand covers my mouth. Everything goes black.

23

GREGORY

I pull the Lamborghini to a screeching halt outside my office block and fly through the revolving glass door.

'Gregory! Someone took her. They took her!'

'Who? What? Where is she?' I skid to stop in front of Paul.

'I don't know. There was a kid, the new one from the twenty-third floor. He was outside. I think she was going to him. Then another guy pulled her. Put something over her head. They put her in a car and they left.'

My gut falls to the floor, heart racing. There's no air in my lungs.

'Greg!'

Jackson bursts into the building and I've never been so fucking dependent on him for my next move.

'Trina was here. They took Scarlett. Three of them. My guys tailed as far as they could but they lost them. They must have switched cars.'

I bite the knuckles of my clenched fist and fight the anger and grief that's tearing me up. 'Jackson, what the fuck do we do?'

'We go home, kid. We get the team together. We fuckin' find her.'

I rub my hands roughly up and down my face then shake my head. 'No. Now. We have to go now.'

'Greg, we don't know where she is. I know how much you want to lash out. You need to keep your cool.' He's calmer now, trying to rationalise things.

I feel like I'm outside my fucking body, watching myself break down. My eyes are on fire. 'Jackson.' It's all I can say.

'We'll find her.'

I can't lose her. It feels like a bullet cuts through my chest and I ball my fists, screaming out as I punch the door of the lift. I close my eyes and rest my forehead against the cold metal, thumping the side of my fist against the door again.

'Greg, every second we waste, she gets further away.'

I rub my face roughly one more time. 'Bring him,' I growl, pointing to Paul as I charge out of the building and tear away from the curb in the Lamborghini. As I burn through the dark streets, swerving through traffic, ignoring red lights, I look for her, knowing I won't find her. Twice, I fight back the start of crushing tears.

'Scarlett,' I mumble into the empty car.

Jackson must drive like a maniac too because he pulls into the basement right behind me. We ride to my penthouse together. By the time we reach the apartment, Jackson's security team are already there and I've got my head straight enough to listen to Paul.

I roll up the sleeves of my shirt and unfasten another button at the neck, then I crank up the air con. I pace the floor of the lounge as Jackson gets everything he needs out of Paul, vaguely aware of other conversations going on in the room. I know they're doing everything they can and I'm so fucking grateful for Jackson right now.

'He was about Gregory's build. Older. Jeans and a polo. He looked normal,' Paul says.

'Nick Henshaw,' I bite.

Jackson nods. 'The guys are pooling everything we've got on Trina, Stuart and Nick. Ken is looking for any links to places they might've taken her.'

That's the reality. He's said it himself, we've got no

fucking idea where she is. I swear to God, if they touch her. If Nick Henshaw lays a fucking finger on her...

I pick up the first thing I can get my hands on – a crystal decanter – and launch it at the wall with a wail that sounds more like an animal than me. The glass shatters, liquor spraying out across the floor.

There are seven other men in the room and they all turn to look at me.

'Fucking find her!'

'Greg, we need you with us,' Jackson says. 'Get a drink and get your shit together.'

I sit onto the edge of the sofa and drop my head into my hands. *Come on. Take control. Take. Fucking. Control. Put her out of your head. It's a game. One big fucking game. Come to the fucking table.* I drag air through my teeth and do as Jackson says; I take a bottle of Scotch from the kitchen, swig a mouthful to take the edge off and get ready to play the man.

Two of the guys are on the phone; one of them is Ken. One guy in khakis and a black hoody and built like a brick shit house is on a computer with devices and wires all around his space at the dining table, all connected and linked into the monitor. The other two guys are with Jackson and Paul and they're in the lounge now, papers and tablets spread out in front of them.

'Get Barnes,' I say, eyeing Jackson as I approach them. 'If Katrina Martin is involved, she's looking for a story. She wants the bribes. If Scarlett's got any sense, she'll give me up.'

'She won't do that,' Jackson says, and damn that girl, I hope he's wrong but I know he's right.

I nod, not wanting to accept his truth. 'She might not talk.'

Jackson stands from the sofa. 'Or she'll do what she thinks is right, she'll do what you and I both know she'll do.'

'She'll confess.'

Jackson nods now. 'I'll get Barnes in.'

'Get his team, Jackson, not just him.'

'Greg, not the bobbies. That's the wrong move.'

'Jackson.' My words sound defeatist. 'Get them. I don't care about the bribes. I don't care about me. Get everyone we can. I'll take whatever comes. Just find her.'

He slaps my arm. 'All right.'

I'm listening, taking in what the team are doing and trying to think logically. Ken shouts us over to the dining table and starts spreading documents. This is everything we have on Stuart Culliton. He pulls up a still on his computer of Stuart and Trina from tonight. The photograph that one of Jackson's guys emailed to us earlier. A CCTV still taken near my office block that told us Stuart was mixed up with Trina in some way. The image that made me call Scarlett, too late.

The intercom buzzes and I let Jackson deal with it, thinking it'll be Barnes, but when I turn towards the door, Sandy comes hurtling at me, her arms flailing, landing blows on my face, my chest. Christ, I let her. I deserve it. I failed Scarlett. I failed them both.

'You did this,' she cries. 'Ever since she met you. This is your fault. You find my little girl. You find her.'

Jackson moves towards Sandy but I hold up my hand, telling him to stay back, and I wrap my arms around her, pulling her into my chest, accepting two more blows until she relents and breaks down against me. She's the only other person in the world who has any idea how I feel right now.

'I'm sorry. I'm so so sorry,' I whisper. 'I'll find her, Sandy. If it's the last thing I do. I'll give my life to have her back. I won't stop. I'll find her so help me fucking God.'

Lawrence and Williams are here and ask Jackson what they can do. There's so much commotion, I almost didn't notice my mother. Now I do, and she's staring at the image of Stuart and Trina on the computer screen, walking towards it with her hands over her mouth and tears in her eyes.

'What is this?' Her words are barely audible. Then she screams, 'What is this?'

'It's two of the kidnappers,' Jackson says.

I flinch at the use of the word but it's right; that's what's happened. Tonight, the woman I can't live without has been kidnapped.

'Stuart? He—'

I leave Sandy and run to my mother, twisting her by the shoulders, shaking her. 'You know who that is?'

Tears stream her face. 'Yes.'

24

SCARLETT

My eyes struggle to focus. The first thing that hits me is the smell. Damp. Decaying. Then the cold. My clothes are wet. Rain. It was raining. A shiver courses through my body and the shudder brings the low-lit room into sharper focus. Blurred but less so.

My head throbs at the base. I try to touch it but my hands are trapped behind my back. I rattle my fists and feel metal around them. I'm handcuffed to a chair. A metal chair. The kind you'd find in a roadside truck stop.

My feet are bare. My clothes look dirty but intact. The feeling of relief that brings is fleeting. There's a metal table in front of me, secured by bolts to the ground. A chair like the one on which I sit is on the opposite side of the table. A large horizontal mirror hangs on the wall behind it. I turn my head around the room, wincing as my neck rotates. It's a small room. One miniscule, glassless window looks out to the dark sky. There's a lamp on the table giving the low hum of light. Wireless. Battery powered.

This is an interview room. An interview room similar to the room I sat in to give a statement that Saturday night in November. Except there's rising damp here. The corners of the room are wet. Green, yellow and black. The plaster is cracked and peeling off the walls.

The heavy door opens in on the room and my heart rate doubles. I hold my breath.

'We've been waiting for you to come round.'

Katrina Martin.

Oddly, her familiar face settles my pulse a notch she comes to the chair in front of the mirror. She's been watching me from behind the wall.

'Like it?' she asks, sitting in a cheap black suit, legs parted in her flat, scuffed shoes.

There's no badge on her belt and I remember that she's been suspended. Yet a handgun is holstered on her hip.

'Don't fret. It's mostly to let you know how things

are going to go,' she says. 'As long as I get what I need, the gun stays right where it is.'

She looks tired. Worn. Haggard. Much older than her years. Older than she looked just weeks ago in Dubai.

'Not talking? You usually have so much to say.'

My mind is still processing everything, completely drawing a blank after those words left Stuart's lips. *I'm sorry.*

Stuart and Trina?

She stands now, one hand on her hip, the other turning around the room. 'This one is a little run-down. The building's been derelict for a long time. But I thought it would be nice to give you a little taster. Once you give me what I want, you'll be in a much nicer version to make your statement against your boyfriend.'

My throat feels like it's being grated with glass as I speak. 'That's what you want? That's why I'm here?'

She glares at me. Unresponsive.

'You want me to tell you something that isn't true.'

She throws her head back with a deep, menacing laugh that comes from her gut. Then she stops it abruptly, slamming a palm down on the table.

'Except you and I both know that it *is* true, Scarlett.

Don't we?' She brings her forearms to rest on the table between us. Her voice low and sinister as she tells me, 'You know what makes me sick? People like you. People like your boyfriend. Gliding through life, exterminating anything and any*one* who dares to stand in your way. And *men*. Men thinking women are nothing. Using us, hurting us. Not letting us get to where we *fucking* deserve in life.' She leans back with a loud, harsh snort. 'They say they want to put away the bad guys. Think because they have a dick between their legs, they're better than us at doing it. But you know what the truth is? They only want to fight the bad guys if the bad guys don't pay. Bad guys can't be rich. They're the scum of the earth if they don't have money. The dregs of society. If they have money, they *pay* to be good.'

My shoulders ache when I hold my head up but I do because I can't tear my eyes away from her venom. Her hatred. I can't help but wonder what or who made her this way.

'Do you see, Scarlett? Do you see why I have to do this? For us. For women. For the greater good of society. And you can help me. Don't you want that? Don't you want to set right a wrong?'

I lost my hold on what's right and wrong a while ago. All I know now is that there are so many wrongs, the only thing to do is what feels right. She'll never know how much I'd like to go back. To do things differently. But I'm not sorry that bastard is dead. It was right to take him out of this world, to take him away from Gregory and bring him the justice he deserved for everything he ever did. To Gregory. To Lara. To Elsa. To *my* dad. Everything else that's happened has to be right because it sent that man to hell.

'Let me ask you something, Trina. Where do you stand on doing something that may be wrong in the eyes of the law to put right an evil? To correct something that's morally repugnant?'

Her eyes darken and burn into mine. It resonates.

'You think that your plan for the greater good involves putting a man behind bars for serving justice?'

'Justice is what the law is for,' she snarls. 'Justice is why police walk the streets. Justice isn't served by corrupt men.'

'You think kidnapping to uncover a non-existent bribe is serving justice?'

She leans forward and slams the side of her fist against the metal table, the sound echoing in the room. She stands, clashing her metal chair against the mirrored wall. My blood pumps harder as she moves around the table towards me.

She takes her gun from her holster.

Air leaves my lungs.

I stare at the barrel before she raises her hand and crashes the gun across my cheek and temple, sending me and the chair slamming against the concrete floor. My shoulder burns. My head rings.

'You said we weren't going to hurt her.'

Feet. Converse. Combat trousers. I blink, trying to refocus, and watch Trina's scuffed shoes storm out of the room. My breathing is erratic as the new feet move around the table towards me.

He grunts as he lifts both me and the chair back upright. Then Stuart Culliton sits onto the edge of the table, triaging at my head. I can feel myself bleeding before a crimson bead rolls down my cheek.

My body trembles. Shocked. Cold. Terrified.

He rubs his hands harshly across his face and those familiar brown eyes are full of despair when he stops.

'Are you thirsty?'

I feel my brows furrow as I process the absurd question. Of all the things, *that's* what he says. I nod, trying to understand how this boy, who's shown moments of true sweetness, has come to sit before me now, taking a role in my kidnapping, messed up with Katrina Martin.

He reaches for a bottle of water behind him on the table. 'Put your head back.'

I lean back, uncertain, but I open my mouth. He holds my chin as he carefully drips water into my mouth and I look into those eyes again.

'This is not you,' I whisper, not knowing whether he should be helping me, or who is behind that mirror.

He squeezes his eyes shut and when they reopen, they're black. 'You don't know me.' He takes the water and leaves.

* * *

I don't know how long I'm alone. I don't know how long they've had me here. Rain continues to pour outside. The night is still dark. Wind blows in through the open window and whirls freezing-cold air around my body.

'Gregory.' His name carries as a whisper in the room, drowned by the wind. I know he can't hear me. Tears mount behind my eyes. I close my lids to stop them from falling. They're out there, watching me, and they won't see me break. Gregory will be doing everything he can to find me. Jackson will have his team on this. I know it.

I won't give him up. I won't.

But as time passes and I don't stop shivering un-controllably, I wonder whether giving myself up is the only way to end this. Give Katrina Martin more than she bargained for. Give her the win she so desperately wants.

My teeth chatter and my head drops against my chest. My eyes close but I won't sleep. My body wants to shut down but it can't. They're out there.

* * *

The door opens with the sound of metal grinding against concrete, making me raise my head from my chest. Stuart takes off his coat and wraps it around my shoulders, still warm. I could cry out with gratitude but my throat is dry. My entire body aches. Tears don't come. The heat of the coat sifts into my ice-cold skin.

'Would you undo my hands?' I croak.

He stands on the opposite side of the table, consid-ering me with, I think, pity, but he doesn't move.

'Please.'

He doesn't glance back at the mirror, which tells me we're here alone. He moves to my back and unfas-tens the cuffs. I whimper in pain as I move my arms from behind me, my shoulders burning through the change of position. I bite down on my lip, raising my numb arms until I'm able to rub my aching muscles.

'Thank you.'

He moves the chair forward from the wall where Trina left it and takes a seat opposite me. There's nowhere for me to go. I don't have any strength to fight and he knows it. Even if I tried to run, he'd catch me. He rubs his face. He looks young. Helpless and lost.

'Why?'

My question doesn't induce a reply but there's a subtle change in him. Recognition? Regret?

'Why?' I ask again, louder this time.

'It's not about you. It's about him.' Stuart's head is down, his chin angled to the floor. He mumbles as he speaks.

'What did he ever do to you?'

His Zimbabwean twang is thick. 'Men like him. Men who have everything. *He* has everything.'

'Christ, Stuart, she's brainwashing you. You don't know anything about Gregory and the shit he's been through.'

'He worked hard for what he has, right? Don't feed me bull, Scarlett; you're better than that. I know what tough really is. I know what it's like to grow up with nothing. No one.'

'He's dealt with more than you know and he's been nothing but nice to you.'

'He's got a fuckin' funny way of showing it.'

'He took you on.' I run a hand down my throat, trying to ease the pain as I speak. 'That's not something he'd do if he didn't like you, if he didn't see potential in you, if he didn't want to get to know you.'

His body seems to soften and I allow myself to hope that I'm getting through to him.

'We *both* like you, Stuart. This is not you. We can walk out of here together.'

He stands, anger raging from him as he snatches the metal cuffs from the table.

'In front. Please,' I beg.

He cuffs me roughly, yanking my arms forward so they're locked around the leg of the table. I'm alone again and the coat doesn't hold off the cold for long. My muscles shiver and my head is increasingly weary.

Think. Find a way.

He grew up alone. That's what he's talking about. He told us in the first meeting we had with him that he didn't know his parents, that he'd never met them. I laugh internally. *He swore on his mother's life he wasn't involved.* Of course he did. He's never met her.

How could we have missed that?

What else am I missing? What do I know? Trina wants a confession that Gregory and DI Barnes were involved in bribery. Stuart wants what and why? Moreover, how in the hell do they think they're going to get what they want?

25

At some point, I surrender. Whether it's sleep, exhaustion or something else, I don't know, but when my forehead rolls on the cold metal table and my eyes open, the sky is charcoal, not black, and the rain has stopped.

The living nightmare continues. I swallow, trying to soothe my throat, and push myself back, sitting as straight as my cuffed wrists allow, my vertebrae cracking as I rise.

I feel the presence in the room before I see the figure sitting opposite me. His tousled, dirty-blond hair looks dry, messy compared to his slick appearance at Thursday's gala. Steely greys are focused on me. His usually clean-shaven face is sketched with stubble and the remnants of a bruise I suspect Gregory made. He wears a thick, warm, duffel coat, fastened to the neck, making his shoulders look even broader than they are. His hands rest in the pockets of his coat.

'Scarlett, so thrilled you're awake. And, if you don't mind me saying so, looking significantly less smug than usual.'

I stare at the missing piece of the puzzle. Nick Henshaw.

He leans his head to one side. 'Nothing to say for yourself today?'

'Why am I here?'

'Speak up now, Scarlett.'

'Why am I here?' My effort to raise my voice is lost in the gruff of my words.

He stands, moving slowly towards me. 'Well, because you just.' His fist locks around my hair and yanks my head towards him as he grates his words into my ear. 'Keep. Getting. In. My. Way.'

He releases my hair, pushing my head away from him, then pulls his chair around the table so it's next to me, rather than opposite. He straddles the seat, leaning onto the back, his face so close to mine I can feel his hot, liquor-laced breath. 'You're the brains of everything. Aren't you, princess? So good. You excel at so many things, Scarlett.' He taps my nose with the tip of his finger the way he might torment a child. 'Including getting yourself kidnapped.' Now he laughs, rocking back and forth on his chair.

'So you intend to kill me, Nick? Wind up behind bars for life. Is that your plan?'

He laughs harder now, throwing his head back on a chortle then rocking forward, thumping his hand on the metal table and making me jump. 'Ah, she's funny. You kill me. No. I don't intend to kill you, princess. That would be a waste of such a pretty thing.' He twirls a finger in my hair and I lift my shoulder fast, pushing him away. 'Oops. Gutsy. Perhaps I'll change my mind. My new friend – I think you've met her, Katrina Martin? – she tells me anyone can pay their way out of a murder charge these days.'

'If you don't want to kill me, what do you want?'

'Oh, sweetheart, you're just a pawn in a big boys' game. There's something that means a lot more to me than your life. Or Gregory's. Or putting both your bodies into the ground.' He sits upright, drumming his fingertips on the metal frame of his chair. 'The thing is, *you* keep taking it from me. First, you take my company when it was starting to turn a profit again. All those years of putting sweat and blood and money into my company, then you and the mighty CEO try to take that all away from me. Then, you force me to re-sign and I *think* you forgot to write my goodbye hand-shake into that resignation letter, princess, didn't you?'

He stands from his chair and starts to pace the floor behind me. I watch him move in the mirror, my body tense, waiting for a blow.

'My wife left me.' His face contorts in a strange mix of, I think, anger and tears. He swipes the back of his hand under his nose as he snorts. 'She's the only fucking reason I signed your letter. That bastard used her against me and she fucking left me anyway.'

'Maybe you should have thought about that before you fucked someone behind her back,' I snipe.

'Maybe you should have thought about that before you fucked someone behind her back.' He mimics my words like a puppet, then grabs my hair and yanks my head up so I'm staring at the scene in the mirror. 'So fucking clever.' The veins in his neck and temples are fat. His face red with rage.

'Third!' He releases my hair and his reflection holds up three fingers on a sadistic smile. 'Third, you ruin my plan. AGAIN!'

'*Black Diamonds*,' I say, watching him move so his back is leaning against the mirror and he's staring right at me.

'Fucking *Black Diamonds*. I was supposed to get a

payout. The game for three million.' He folds his arms across his chest. 'Poof! Like magic, there you were again, fucking up my plan. First, you convince Gregory not to pay what the game's worth. But he screws up, he offers us an in, lets Stuart take a position on the inside where he can see your next move. And I know the market, so I start registering the game that *I* own. But there you were again.'

Finally, all the pieces fit together. 'This is your new plan. You want a ransom.'

'Ding! Ding! Ding!' He rattles his hands in the air with an enormous fake smile. 'Jackpot! And from where I'm standing, it looks like you can't fuck this one up.'

'I've got to hand it to you, Nick, you've played a good game.'

He takes a theatrical bow. 'Why thank you, although, I already knew that.'

'So call him, tell him where you are, ask him for what you want.'

He smiles, leaning his head to one side and pointing a swirling finger at me. 'Oh, I'm going to, princess. But for now, I'm going to let him sweat. He can wonder whether he's going to get you back, whether he's going to get what *he* wants. You've been gone all night. He'll be frantic by now.' He sniggers, his eyes rising to the sky, his hands forming prayer. 'Then I win two times.'

He lunges towards me, grabbing my throat, digging his fingers and thumb into my flesh, hard. I try to breathe but I can't draw air. My legs kick, desperate for oxygen.

He releases me and my head droops forward as I gasp.

'Don't get up,' he says, laughing as he leaves me in the room alone.

26

I squeeze my eyes shut, telling myself repeatedly that I don't need to cry.

Why haven't you found me?

A sob leaves my chest as a tremor runs the length of my body.

'Dad, if you're there, please help me.'

Dawn descends outside, the sky now a lighter shade of grey. It's the only guide I have as to how long I've been here. My guess is twelve, maybe thirteen hours. I'm freezing. It's hard to tell which part is producing the most pain. My head throbs. My arms and back are ablaze. Even my fingertips and my toes are stinging. I try to rotate my wrists in the cuffs but there's no give and being chained to the table stops me from sitting upright.

When Nick grabbed my throat, I lost Stuart's coat and I'm back to my black skirt and cream blouse: the clothes I wore expecting a day in my office.

I need a way out. Gregory hasn't found me yet, which means there aren't enough clues. If there were, he'd have found them. He'd be here, with Jackson, saving me.

Nick wants money and Gregory will give it to him.

But when? At what cost? His life? I have to get to him first. I could confess to Trina. *Then what would happen? Would she let me go?*

My best chance, my only chance, is Stuart.

He feels alone. He never met his parents. I can empathise. My mother left.

I wait. Hoping he'll come. Willing him to come. If nothing else, I need a drink. My body is weak and if I weren't sitting, I don't think I'd be conscious. I need water.

I watch the sky turn lighter still, grey in the dull winter weather, but day. There's something about the new day that makes me hope, lets me find the faith I lost in the dark.

He'll come for me.

* * *

I brace myself as the metal door screeches against the floor and when Stuart appears, I raise my eyes to the ceiling and thank my dad for his help.

Stuart stalks towards me. 'Put your head back.'

I choke on the water, my body rejecting the cool sensation. He retrieves his coat from the floor and hangs it back around my shoulders. Then he takes a banana from the side pocket of his combat trousers and peels.

'Please let my hands go.' I wince as the words leave my throat.

He unlocks the cuffs and releases one hand so I can slump back in the chair. He offers the banana to me and I want it but my arms are numb. I open my mouth and he nods, snapping pieces and placing them on my tongue. It's funny, I've never noticed how sweet bananas are but now I feel like I can taste every fragment of sugar as my jaw moves slowly, chewing and swallowing like I've never had solid food. When I'm done, I'm able to lift my arm for water and I gulp down the rest of the bottle, placing the empty on the table.

Something's changed. He doesn't have venom or fight. It's just Stuart. Soft-eyed, dark-haired, young.

'My mother left me when I was a child,' I say. 'I was five. She took me to school one day and never came to pick me up. She walked out on my dad and me.'

He shuffles on the table's edge, moving to the side then back where it started. He folds his arms, then moves his hands to his lap. Finally, he brings his hands to either side of his hips and grips the lip of the table.

'Did she love you?'

'I think so. She said so.' I shrug. 'I ask myself that question a lot. If she loved me, would she really have left? If she loved me, why didn't she ever come back or try to contact me?'

I don't know if it's working. He focuses on an invisible spot on the concrete floor. I wait. Like Gregory would, I leave space for Stuart to fill the silence. Eventually, he does.

'At least you knew her. I'll never know where I really came from.'

'You were adopted?'

'I was in the system for years.' His face twists with a look that's full of disgust. 'A delinquent, they called me. Then I got foster parents. Time and again, new parents. Apparently, my mother gave me to a family she knew at first. I think they thought one day, she'd take me back. I don't know.' He exhales, still fixed on the same spot of concrete. 'She never did. She killed herself.'

'I'm sorry.'

He lets out a short puff that rocks his body, then lifts his head to look at me. His browns are wide. Beautiful. 'I'm not even from Zimbabwe.' He laughs again, though the sound is drenched in sadness.

'Where are you from?'

He looks to the window now as if he's wondering whether he wants to talk at all. 'She had money. She was middle-class. The family who had me at first, they say she killed herself because she was forced to give me up. They say she was too young and I would have brought shame on her and her parents.'

'I'm sorry.' I say it again because I don't know what else to say. Those two words have so little meaning.

He makes a noise somewhere between anger and pain, and rubs his hands over his face. 'See, the kicker is, my mother had a younger brother. He's alive.' He walks to the window and turns to face me, dropping his back against the wall and lifting one foot flat against the surface behind him. 'She gave me up but they never did anything to hurt him. They never made him want to kill himself. They went on with their lives. Playing happy families.' His square jaw tightens and the look on his face, those familiar eyes, makes my stomach sink. 'By the time I turned eighteen, I'd spent so many years hiding in my room, messing with computers, I was a tech whiz. I could hack anything, create software that no other kid of eighteen could create. I used that. I tracked down her family.'

I hold my breath now and I think I'm more terrified than I've been in the entirety of the last fifteen hours. 'I traced them all, my grandmother, my grandfather and my uncle.' He moves away from the wall and stands over me. 'My search brought me to England.'

A million disordered thoughts crash through my mind.

'My uncle is a billionaire. A tech billionaire. Imagine the coincidence. I watched him for weeks, never knowing whether to approach him, not knowing if I had the courage and if I did, how I'd do it.'

My eyes sting and this time, I don't think I'm strong enough to cool the fire.

'I put *Black Diamonds* on the market.' He laughs again and rubs a hand across his chin. Then he paces next to me. 'I thought, I thought if I made something of myself, that he'd be interested in me. But deep down, I knew, I knew they'd gotten rid of me once, they wouldn't want me now.'

'Stuart, who is your uncle?'

He stops but it's so clear. Those brown irises, magnetic, alluring. His dark, square features. His height.

'You know it's him,' he whispers.

His name floats from my lips like it's being carried on wind. 'Gregory.'

He doesn't react, as if he's known this moment would come, as if he's been waiting for it.

'You're Elsa's son.'

He nods once and his lips twist like he's fighting emotion.

I move my free hand to my mouth as silent tears roll down my face. Kevin Pearson raped his daughter and she bore his child. Gregory said she was sent away for a time but he never understood why. Now I do.

'Stuart, he doesn't know.'

'Bullshit!' He turns and fiercely punches the wall, cracking the plaster further, a strangled wail escaping him as he looks at his damaged hand.

I try to stand but my legs are lifeless. 'Stuart, you have to believe me. He doesn't know. I know about Elsa, about your mother. I know she killed herself and I—' I hang my head and my words are barely audible.

'I know why. She went away, Stuart. Gregory was only a boy and he didn't know why she left, never mind why she came back.'

He faces me, his eyes wet. I can feel his thoughts flying, as frantic as my own.

'Think about it. If he knew and didn't care about you, he would never have employed you and taken a chance on you. He loves Elsa. If he knew her son was out there, if he knew he had a nephew, he'd want to know you.'

His shoulders sag and his breath hitches.

'He tried to help her, Stuart, and one day, he can tell you about her. You could have a family. *Your* family. Gregory cares. He's the most loving man I know. I want you to know him, to see that about him.'

He slumps onto the table in front of me as a tear rolls down his cheek. I reach out cautiously and when he doesn't pull away, I wrap my hand around his. '*I* would like to get to know you, Stuart.'

He looks up to me now and I know I've gotten through to him.

'I don't know how this happened,' he whispers. 'I wanted to hurt him. I wanted to punish him for being the child they chose. I wanted to take from him the way they took from me.'

'But he didn't, Stuart. Please, believe me.'

'I do.' He squeezes my hand then wipes his face with his other. 'I don't know what to do. This wasn't part of the plan. He was supposed to just buy the game for the price Nick wanted.'

I nod, taking a deep breath, not yet able to put all the pieces together. 'You need to go to Gregory. You need to tell him where I am. You have to warn him about Nick and Trina. Trina has a gun. I don't know about Nick. You have to tell him.'

'He'll kill me as soon as he sees me, Scarlett. There's CCTV, the cleaner. He'll know what I've done to you.'

'Then you have to make him listen. You have to tell him everything.'

'Isn't this cosy!'

We snap our heads to the door to see Nick.

'I have someone on the phone who'd like to speak to you, princess.'

I take my hand away from Stuart's. He's afraid.

Nick leans towards me, twirling my hair around his index finger, then he holds the phone to my ear.

'Scarlett?'

'Gregory?' His voice is more than I can take. A violent sob bursts from my chest, then another and another. 'I love you!' I scream as Nick pulls the phone away.

'There's your evidence. Ten o'clock.' He hangs up the phone then angrily takes my chin in his fingers. 'Looks like your man's coming to get you.'

I cast my eyes to Stuart and try in that moment to tell him to go. I don't know whether he follows me or his own moment of enlightenment but he slips out of the room.

'I love you! Gregory, I love you!' Nick Henshaw mimics in a high voice before releasing my chin and bending forward to his knees, laughing from the depths of him. 'Ah, you kill me.'

Before he leaves, he cuffs my wrists in my lap and locks the door behind him.

* * *

'Aren't you a sight for sore eyes,' Trina says as she takes a seat at the table. 'Well, lady, time's up. For you. For him. Whatever. It's nine forty-five. Your boyfriend will be here soon and when he comes, what do you think is going to happen?'

'He'll give Nick the money.'

'Well, yes. I meant *after* that.'

I stare at her now, wanting to rip her fucking head off, knowing I don't have the strength but balling my fists in my lap nonetheless. I look at the door and contemplate whether I could make a run for it. She unholsters her handgun and rests it on her thigh. A silent warning.

'Do you think Nick is going to keep him alive, Scarlett? After everything that lying bastard has done, do you really think he'll be allowed to hand over the money and walk away?'

She's right. I know she's right and it's making me sick. My stomach is in knots and I'm praying, praying and hoping, that I really did get through to Stuart. That Gregory listened to him. That he comes prepared. Or doesn't come at all. That someone comes. Anyone else to deliver the money. Then I feel guilty because whoever comes is walking into a fatal transaction. I know it and all I can do is hope.

Trina picks up her handgun and turns it in front of her face, considering every edge and nodule. 'Nick's is a lot like this. Cleaner. Newer, perhaps, but similar.' One side of her lips turns up and she puts the gun back on her hip. 'It was a good plan, don't you think?' She shakes her head with a smirk. 'Nick wants to take credit but he knows it was me. You see, I trailed Gregory. And you in the process.' She holds up her hands as if in apology and bile rises in my throat. 'I knew things were off. I watched you both and you know something; it made me sick. Seeing your worry, him without a care in the world, going about his business.'

'It wasn't like that.'

'Oh it was. You were just too close to see. Then I looked deeper into his files, and lucky, lucky, he had a sibling. Sister killed herself. Daddy was locked up. Couldn't stand the thought of what Daddy had done to her. He's like him, you know, Gregory. Like father, like son.'

'Don't you dare liken him to that bastard. Don't you fucking dare!'

'Keep your hair on.' She laughs. 'So I kept digging and found out Daddy gave his daughter a baby. I banked that intel. Then I came to see you in Dubai.' She leans her head to one side with a fake sympathetic smile. 'I really did try to give you a way out. You threw it back in my face. I guess, in lots of ways, you're to blame for all this. You forced me to think up another plan. And as I'm doing that, what do you know, the illegitimate son pops up in London. It was beautiful really, the way it started coming together. Of course, Nick Henshaw was very willing to get one up on a man who stole from him.'

'That's bollocks.'

She shrugs. 'Is. Isn't. I don't care. It was Nick's idea

to take the game from Stuart and I have to admit, it was a neat idea. Take the game, cut Stuart in on the money. But it was me who knew about Stuart in the first place. I was the one who connected the dots and put them together. The problem was, I couldn't quite see how I was going to get what I needed. Nick could force Gregory into buying the game, give him a taste of his own filthy, rich, corrupt medicine, but how would I get my confession? I tried leaking to the tabloids but you, and his money, cut me off.' She laughs, slapping her hands together and grinning against the tips of her fingers. 'Then you brought it all together for me. You tied that game up in a court case. It was obvious then how we could all get what we want. And that's what you're going to do now, Scarlett, right now, you're going to give me what I want.'

'Why would I give you anything?'

'Because I can end this. This is the grand finale, Scarlett, you must know by now that I have a cunning end.'

'So what's your end?'

'You tell me the truth. You tell me about the bribes, confess the truth. When Gregory turns up, I arrest Nick. Make this whole thing look like him. Then you, me and Gregory go to the station. I win my case. I get my job back. I get the respect I deserve and your boyfriend gets the justice he deserves.'

I want to tell her I don't know anything. I want to keep my promise to Gregory, but she's offering his life. If I give her the bribes, he loses his freedom. If I give her me, she gets her arrest. She gets her grand finale and Gregory is free. Finally. The little boy from my dreams can move out of the shadows.

27

Relief. Excitement. Terror. The mix of emotions sends my adrenal glands into overdrive, making my body sweat. My pulse increases to the point that I can feel it throbbing in my head. The sound of tyres driving across uneven surface makes me want to fight, protect him.

'That's your man,' Trina says with a sardonic grin.

Gregory is here, coming to do what's necessary to get me out, risking his life. I don't know if Stuart got to him. I don't know if he knows what to expect. All I do know is that he's following Nick's instructions and there's a good chance he could pay for my life with his own.

'Time is running out, Scarlett. I can stop this. Put an end to it for all of us.'

I hear a car door open and close. Then another. I will not let him die.

'Do it. Please, Trina. I'm begging you. Stop it.'

'You know what you have to do, Scarlett. Just say the words.'

I lift my head to the window. I can't see anything, only concrete. My breathing becomes erratic and beads of sweat form on my brow.

'It was me. God damn it, Trina. There was no bribe. Gregory was protecting *me*. *I* killed his father. *I* killed Kevin Pearson.'

She stands quickly and takes her gun in her right hand. She clicks off the safety and points it right between my eyes. She squeezes her eyes shut as I sit, paralysed.

'Liar. You're a fucking liar!' She opens her eyes, her hand shaking, her finger braced on the trigger. With the base of her other hand she thumps her temple. 'You're a lying fucking bitch!' She slams the gun across my face so hard I spit blood to the concrete.

Then there's a bang. A bang so loud, it echoes in the room and vibrates deep in the drum of my ears. It's a shot and it didn't come from inside this room.

I fall from the chair to my knees. 'Gregory!' I scream his name over and over.

Trina charges from the room, leaving the door wide open, her gun braced in both hands. 'Fuck! Fuck!'

There are cars, shouting voices, sirens, commotion.

I have to go. I have to go to him.

I stagger to my feet, my legs buckling at first. With my bound hands, I pull myself up to stand and break free from the room.

The corridor is dark and damp. I use the wall to help me move, leaning into it with my shoulder.

Another shot.

Please, God, no.

The grey sky of outside is much brighter than the room I've been held in. I can hear voices, frantic voices, swearing, screaming, but I can't see. I have to squint but my legs keep moving forward until they reach something. I open my eyes to see feet on the ground. Time stands still as the feet slowly move. Gasps of air. Groans. I'm looking at the body of Katrina Martin.

Her hands are pushed tightly into her abdomen. Her face is grey and pained. Blood is pooling around her back, a sea of thick burgundy flowing out of her.

'Scarlett!'

'Scarlett!'

Voices shout. More than one. Non-distinct in the background as I watch Katrina Martin take her last breath. Her eyes widen. Her legs stop moving. One crimson-stained hand falls from her abdomen, landing palm up on the ground.

Squinting through one eye, I look up. There are cars, four, five black cars. DI Barnes lowers his gun. Other armed police start to move, making their way towards me. Jackson stands in front of the Mercedes, bent forward, his hands on his knees as if he's dragging air into his lungs. Two armed police move past him and I follow them to a man on the floor. His legs move but he looks barely alive, his face covered in blood. I grab my chest, reminding my heart to beat. The man is Nick Henshaw.

Then I see him, crawling to his feet by Nick's beaten body, his white shirt stained with smatters of blood, his face marked.

He's alive.

My legs give out under me as the world fades to a small, black tunnel.

28

GREGORY

I think I died three times. When she was taken. When Katrina Martin ran from that building with a loaded gun. When Scarlett fell to the ground.

She's been scanned, they've cleaned her up. The first thing they did in the ambulance was connect her to a drip and give her painkillers for the bruising and cuts around her face and head.

Now, she sleeps.

The pills they gave her took her under almost straight away. Her body was weak, her mind exhausted. She's been asleep for almost ten hours. Peaceful. Beautiful.

The city is dark beyond the windows of her private room in the hospital. The dim lights displaying the image of her in the glass panes. The hospital bed I've put her in.

I raise her delicate hand to my lips and more tears fall, as if there's an endless stream. I tell her again that I'm sorry.

I promised to protect her. I made that promise to myself in the split second it took to fall in love with her. When I opened the door to my boardroom and thirty years of waiting came to an end. In that moment, I knew there would never be another woman for me. I knew it then. I know it now.

I promised myself each time I fell deeper that I would never hurt her. The moment she stole my breath descending the staircase of Claridge's in the royal-blue gown I bought for her. Her hair was pinned back, her lips red, eyes alive. Her smile blew me away, like it does every time.

I promised myself when she stepped out of the car at the theatre. When she giggled with happiness because I'd bought tickets to the play she wanted to see. When my heart gave over to her the first time I held her naked body in my hands. Her flawless skin, smooth as velvet under my fingertips. I told her in the way I kissed her that I would always be hers.

Every conversation we've had. Each time she's made me laugh and pushed through another part of the walls I built around myself years ago. When we stood at the top of Primrose Hill, and, despite the cold, she wanted to stay in our moment. When she read to me *The Count of Monte Cristo*. When she recited Violetta's words to me at the opera. *Love me, Alfredo, love me as much as I love you.* I didn't love her as much as she thought she loved me. I loved her infinitely more. I do still.

I turn her engagement ring around her finger then hold her palm to my cheek. She looked mesmerising the night I asked her to marry me. To be mine, forever. Her hair blowing in the Caribbean breeze. Her hazel-green eyes lighting up as the waves of the ocean danced in her irises. She promised to be by my side for the rest of our lives.

I broke my promise.

I rub the tears from my eyes because I want to see her. Clearly. All of her.

I didn't just break my promise. I failed to protect her and I brought my darkness to her. I hurt her and I couldn't make it right. She's worth so much more. She's better than that. Better than me.

The thought of her waking is bittersweet. I want to see those eyes that captured my heart. I want to tell her that I love her. But it could be the last time. If she walks away, I won't blame her, and I won't chase her.

There's a soft knock on the door and I turn to see Amanda. 'Ed and I are going to get coffee. Do you want one?'

I shake my head because I can't speak. She turns her lips into a soft smile that I don't deserve, then gently, quietly closes the door behind her. It reminds me of the other faces behind the wall. I haven't spoken to my mother since she finally told me the truth. After nineteen years, she told me I have a nephew. Elsa's child. He came to me. He told me everything, told me where Scarlett was. But I'm not ready to look him in the eye. I'm not ready to talk to either of them and God knows how I'll cope with any of the things life throws at me if Scarlett leaves.

'I don't know how to live without you any more,' I whisper.

Time continues to crawl and I know, with each second, I could be moving closer to the end.

She eventually stirs. Her fingers twitch in my hands. Her shoulder shrugs.

'Scarlett.'

She leans her head to one side and slowly opens her eyes. They widen when they meet mine. Then she turns her head around the room and she winces as painful memories bring her up to date.

This is it. The moment she crushes me. And I can't

hear it. I don't want to make her say it. I'm terrified she will. I turn my lips into her palm then hold it against my cheek, closing my eyes, trying to box her touch against my skin. My tears roll heavier down my face and her own eyes glaze.

I stand and lean over her, stroking my thumb down the side of her face. Her skin is marked but still soft to touch.

'I'm so sorry,' I cry, breaking down as I press my lips to her forehead. 'I couldn't protect you. I failed you and I'm more sorry than I can tell you. I always will be.'

The rubber seam of the door to the room makes a soft noise as it opens. I close my eyes, holding my lips to her head, wanting one more second. Then I stand and release her hand. Her eyes are full of sadness and the sight rips my heart to shreds. She opens her mouth and for a moment, I feel hope in my stomach. But she doesn't speak.

'You're awake, Scarlett,' says the nurse who's been checking on her every hour. The nurse moves to the bedside and I take a step back, my eyes still focused on exquisite hazel-greens. 'Do you know where you are?'

Scarlett watches me as she struggles to respond to the nurse. 'Hospital.'

'That's right. Do you know who I am?'

'A nurse?' she croaks, still fixed on me, watching me take another step backwards.

'Yes, good. Now, I'm just going to ask you to do a few things for me and we'll get the doctor to come and take a look at you.'

I move my hand to my heart as it breaks in my chest and I mouth to her, 'I love you.'

'We've patched you up and you have a few stitches but your scans are all clear. You've got a concussion and you were dehydrated but otherwise yo—'

'Where are you going?'

Her voice freezes me on the spot and I wait for her to end us. End me.

'You don't have to go, baby,' she says. 'Stay. Please.'

The weight falls out of my legs and I feel like I could crash to my knees. She sucks in air quickly and a tear rolls from her clouded eyes. I want so much to wrap her up in my arms and tell her that everything will be okay. I go to her and take her hand.

'I love you.'

God, I love you too, baby. I love you so much.

'All the shit I've brought on you. Everything I've done to you and you still say that?'

She reaches up and wipes my wet cheek. 'You're the other half of me, Gregory. Whatever life throws at us, we'll get through it. Together.'

'I'm fucked up, Scarlett, and I *keep* fucking up.'

She nods and half-laughs, half-sobs. 'Yes, you are and you do. You're also the kindest, smartest, bravest, best man I've ever known. Will ever know.'

I hold her face and rest my forehead against hers. 'I love you to Pluto and back, Scarlett Heath.'

A half-smile creeps onto her lips and those eyes sparkle.

Then I kiss her, holding my lips to hers, floating under the softness of her skin. She kisses me back and wraps her arms around my neck, pulling me to her.

'We might have to put the wedding on hold a little while, unless you fancy standing at the altar with the Corpse Bride.'

I chuckle in her hold, my chest bursting.

This is exactly where I'm meant to be and I know, because with her by my side, I'm ten times the man I could otherwise be.

She is my everything. My reason.

'Aurora,' I whisper.

EPILOGUE
FIVE MONTHS LATER

'Scarlett, we're going to the farm for a weekend; what the hell is in these bags?'

I strap my feet into my sandals. 'The weather might change. I need clothes for every eventuality.'

'Baby, the only thing you need to prepare for is being naked. A lot.'

I stand from the stairs and tuck my shirt into my skinny jeans before slipping my arms around his waist. 'In that case, I should probably take the Mercy corset out of my bag.'

A low growl escapes his chest and he bites the tip of my nose. 'You win. The bags can stay.'

'I thought that might change your mind.'

'Let's go before I take you back up those stairs for a second breakfast.'

With my lips barely touching his, I move my hand to the crotch of his jeans, feeling him harden against me. He drops my bag to the floor and pushes me back against the door of the apartment. He kisses me with urgency, his hands pulling my long, dark hair.

'I'm going to enjoy fucking you this weekend.' His words are full of lust.

'I look forward to you doing so, Ryans.'

He rolls his hips against me with a wink that liquefies me on the spot. 'Let's go.'

His square jaw is set the whole time he's manoeuvring our bags into the small space in the DB9 but he doesn't say anything. I smile to myself as I sit in the car and he takes thirty seconds to cool off by the driver's side door. His counsellor has told him when he's frustrated, he ought to count to thirty, so I count now in my head and sure enough, when I reach thirty, he climbs into the car.

He pulls out of the Shard's basement and clicks the music to Oasis's 'Roll with It.' As we drive out of the city, far too fast, we both shout the lyrics and I move my hands, dancing, twisting.

The July sun beams down on us as we leave concrete for greenery and head up the driveway to the farm. We spend more and more time here now, our haven outside the city. Since the kidnapping, Gregory does just about anything he can to keep stress out of my life – except lighten my GJR workload, that is – despite the fact I tell him I'm fine. But this weekend is something of a celebration, too. Nick Henshaw has finally been sentenced and put where he belongs: behind bars.

As Gregory pulls up outside the house, I turn down the ridiculously loud music. Kian is by the car before I'm even out of the door. He nods to Gregory with a grin and catches the keys Gregory throws to him.

'It's about time!'

I shift my focus to the door of the farm where Amanda stands, handing baby Penny to Williams, who carefully takes hold of her head and lifts her onto his chest. He's still terrified of her.

'What are you doing here?' I ask.

'Ask him,' she says, looking at Gregory, who shrugs.

'A surprise,' he says.

Amanda shakes her head then yanks my hand, pulling me into the house, dragging me upstairs to the master bedroom.

'Surprise!' Julia and Lucas squeal in unison. They look as glamorous out of work as they do in Harrods.

'What on earth? What are you two doing here?'

Then I spot Sandy, holding up a large, cream clothes bag. Little men do jiggery in my abdomen.

'Is that what I think it is?'

She grins and Amanda draws the zip of the bag to the floor. 'Happy wedding day, bestie,' she says, pulling out a wedding dress. *My* wedding dress.

After the shooting, I was covered in cuts and bruises; I didn't want a wedding just weeks later like Lara had planned. And that gave us time, me time to tell Gregory that I didn't want a big wedding at all. I didn't want three hundred and fifty guests that didn't know us and didn't care whether we were in love or not.

I run my hand over the crystal-encrusted lace. Julia fans out the train so I can see the complete look: an intricate strapless dress with a small train.

I'd told him I'd plan but maybe next year. I didn't want Lara to create some masterpiece that just wasn't *us* and I wanted to be able to concentrate on my role at GJR for a while. We bickered just weeks ago because I hadn't made any progress. He told me he wanted the world to know I was his wife.

Lucas holds up a cathedral veil on the opposite side of the room. 'Let's get you ready.'

I bite down on my lip, feeling and thinking too many things to get a hold on any single one. 'I'm getting married?'

'You sure are,' Julia sings.

He wasn't joking. He threatened to take it out of my hands, so he could make me his as soon as possible. Part of me wanted it to be true but I didn't think he'd really do it.

'Holy shit.'

'Mouth, young lady,' Sandy snaps.

'Sorry. But holy shit!'

I should have known. When Gregory wants something, he gets it.

Julia, Lucas and Carrie – a beautician and stylist I've never met – work wonders. When they're satisfied with my complete look and leave to make their way downstairs, I'm left with Sandy and Amanda, now changed into dresses they picked themselves: Amanda in emerald green, Sandy in a deep shade of purple.

'You look beautiful,' I tell them.

'Let's get you in that dress,' Sandy says.

They help me navigate my way, pulling me into the tight elastic of the bodice and zipping me up, before clipping on a chiffon train and pushing the cathedral veil into my pinned-up curls.

'Gregory asked us to give you this.' Amanda opens a large, navy velour box to reveal a thick diamond choker. 'It's your something new.'

I laugh because *everything* is new.

'And, if you'd like to, I'd like you to wear this as your something borrowed and something blue.' Sandy unhooks a delicate sapphire bracelet that my dad and I gave her as a gift for her thirtieth birthday.

I hold out my wrist, not able to speak and unable to fasten the bracelet with my shaking fingers.

'Oh, and one more thing.' She moves to the bed and bends to pull out a bubble-wrapped parcel.

I sit onto the edge of the bed, sticking my tongue out to demonstrate how tight my dress is when I bend. I take off the bubble wrap and turn over a photo frame so the picture is face up. And when I see it, my eyes fill with tears.

'Oh, hell,' Amanda says, rushing to get a tissue and handing it to me.

It's the picture from my dad's bedroom, blown up. My father, Sandy and me on Brighton Pier. I shake my head as I dab the corners of my eyes, desperately trying not to cry.

'I love it, Sandy, thank you.'

'Let's get this show on the road before we all ruin our make-up,' Amanda demands. 'I hear there's a groom waiting outside.'

Suddenly, nerves build everywhere in my body: my stomach, my chest, my weak limbs. I nod and shake or do something with my head.

I'm about to become Mrs Scarlett Ryans.

I can't wait.

He's thought of everything. We move outside as the thirty or so guests, all family and friends we love, stand from white linen chairs either side of a white aisle laid out on the grass. A piano begins to play the first notes of Yiruma's 'It's Your Day.' I glance to the pianist, who smiles back at me. He hired the pianist from the charity gala who made me cry. Now she does the same thing again. My eyes fill as Amanda kisses me on the cheek then sets off down the aisle.

He's always said he wanted me to have the fairy tale.

He's giving it to me.

'Ready?' Sandy asks as she hooks her arm through mine.

'Ready.'

We walk the first section of the aisle behind one

half of the guests, then turn left and I see him, standing next to Williams and Jackson, his back to me. Williams turns to me then pats Gregory on the shoulder and whispers something in his ear. Gregory stands in that pose I love. His hands by his sides in his black, perfectly tailored suit. His legs parted, his shoulders tall and strong, his hips slightly forward. His hair is slicked back.

Blood pumps so hard in my veins that every single part of me might explode.

I want to see his face. I *need* to see him.

Sandy excitedly squeezes my hand and I look around our family and friends. Luke smiles at me. Lawrence dips his head. Lara wipes her eyes with a tissue and Stuart turns his lips in a half-smile that's so incredibly familiar. There's one person missing but I know he's looking in on us from his cloud and he'll be content because his little girl is the happiest she's ever been in her life.

Sandy takes my bouquet as I stand in front of the trellis archway and Amanda fans out my dress and veil on the floor. Then I take the final three steps alone. Towards the man I love. The man I couldn't have dreamt. He turns now, those mesmerising brown pools taking in every single inch of me. *His. All his.*

When our eyes connect, his chest rises with his breath and he presses his hands to his heart.

If it's possible, I fall just a little bit deeper.

* * *

MORE FROM LAURA CARTER

Another book from Laura Carter, is available to order now here:

https://mybook.to/LauraCBackAd

ACKNOWLEDGMENTS

To you, the reader, thank you for taking Scarlett and Gregory into your heart. Writing this, the final instalment in the *Billionaires of London* series, was bittersweet. I wanted to give Scarlett and Gregory the ending they deserve and a conclusion that you could really enjoy. But I was incredibly sad to write those final words, *THE END*. I hope this series will stay with you long after you've finished reading.

So many people have helped bring you Scarlett and Gregory's story. Every person I've worked with at Boldwood Books (and before that, Harlequin) from editorial to production has been incredible and invested in making a series we could all be proud of. But I have to single out Emily Y and Niamh, who have rooted for these billionaire books since the idea of them was floated.

A massive shout-out also to Gemma Lawrence and Ulverscroft for making an exceptional trilogy of audiobooks.

Now, to Tanera and Laura... We all know how much effort went in to bringing these dark romances back to market. You are an absolute force and I think we make a pretty great team. Thank you!

To all my friends and family who thought this series made so much sense and for reading every iteration of Gregory and Scarlett, I'm immensely grateful to you.

Finally, *finally*, I want to thank my husband. What a wild fifteen years it has been from the start of me writing these books to now. And I hope people still tease you about being my muse. You and our beautiful littlies are *my* everything and *my* reason.

Website: www.LauraCarterAuthor.com

Facebook: www.Facebook.com/LauraCarterAuthor

TikTok: @Laura.Carter.Author / @lauracarterdarkromance

Instagram: @LauraCarterAuthor

ABOUT THE AUTHOR

Laura Carter is a top 10 Amazon and internationally bestselling author of romance and romantic women's fiction. She lives with her family in Jersey, Channel Islands.

Download your exclusive bonus content from Laura Carter here:

Visit Laura's website: www.lauracarterauthor.com

Follow Laura on social media:

instagram.com/lauracarterauthor

tiktok.com/@laura.carter.author

facebook.com/lauracarterauthor

ALSO BY LAURA CARTER

Brits in Manhattan

The Law of Attraction

Two to Tango

Friends with Benefits

Always the Bridesmaid

Billionaires of London

Ruthless Love

Twisted Love

Tainted Love

Standalone Novels

Fake It 'til You Make It

Stuck in Paradise With You

Table for Three

Catch a Falling Star

In This Together

The Wild Card Series

A Rookie Mistake

Boldwood
EVER AFTER

x♡x♡

JOIN BOLDWOOD'S
**ROMANCE
COMMUNITY**
FOR SWEET AND
SPICY BOOK RECS
WITH ALL YOUR
FAVOURITE
TROPES!

SIGN UP TO OUR
NEWSLETTER

HTTPS://BIT.LY/BOLDWOODEVERAFTER

Boldwood

Boldwood Books is an award-winning fiction publishing company seeking out the best stories from around the world.

Find out more at www.boldwoodbooks.com

Join our reader community for brilliant books, competitions and offers!

Follow us
@BoldwoodBooks
@TheBoldBookClub

Sign up to our weekly deals newsletter

https://bit.ly/BoldwoodBNewsletter

www.ingramcontent.com/pod-product-compliance
Lightning Source LLC
Chambersburg PA
CBHW010658100726
47900CB00010B/2710